White Sands

Vol. 1

White Sands

A DIFFERENT KIND OF LOVE TRIANGLE

Adam Patterson

Jones Hurst Media Group

White Sands: A Different Kind of Love Triangle

Printed in the United States of America

First Printing, 2016

ISBN 978-0692580462

Jones Hurst Media Group

Big Stone Gap, VA 24219

DEDICATION

Sometimes you really can make lemonade out of life's lemons.

After living, loving and growing in the big city for twenty-five years, I was faced with one of life's biggest curve balls: the declining physical health of a loved one. My beloved Mother needed back surgery. It took seven long years for her to finally agree to the first of two. She recovered beautifully from both and bounced back like the spry, now seventy-six-year-old she is.

While Mother slowed down and I took on more and more of her duties–no easy task since I never had the desire to be a caretaker–to stop me from going insane she said, "Why don't you write that book you always talked about." And for that, Mother, I thank you.

This book is dedicated to my beloved mother, Flora M. Patterson, my father, Johnny Patterson (J.P.), family and friends for their support and encouragement. And a special thank you goes to my aunt, Elizabeth Collins.

CHAPTER 1

WHITE SANDS — SEA VIEW, GA

Dusty stared at the big wrought-iron gates as they slowly opened. He was going to work with his mom today. School was out for the summer, and he had been looking forward to combing the beach for crabs with the guys from the neighborhood. Even at the age of nine, he knew you had to get to the beach early, before the tourists poured into town.

But instead of hanging out with his friends, he was being forced to spend the day with some snooty rich kid he didn't even know. The rich kids from Sea View went to South Sea Academy, the private school.

"Why do *I* have to go?" he asked.

Caroline Marler took her eyes off the road, but only for an instant, to glare at her son.

"Dusty, we've discussed this. These are the people I work for. Besides, keepin' little Alex company for one day won't kill you. He's an only child just like you. And who knows? You might even make a new friend."

I have enough friends, he thought.

"Why couldn't he come crabbin' with me and the fellas?"

"Dustin Marler, his momma just died. Now you be nice, and I don't wanna hear another word about it."

"Yes, ma'am," he replied.

To Dusty's surprise, Alex wasn't stuck up. He was just a normal boy like him. He also had a giant flat screen TV, the latest video equipment, and every video game a little boy could ask for. There was also a pool and a pool house, all located right on the beach. It was a kid's paradise.

So the routine was established. Dusty would ride to work with his mother six days a week and hang out while she busied herself taking care of the big house. Soon he was begging his mother for permission to stay over on weekends so he and Alex could camp out on the beach. Caroline eventually discussed the issue with her employer, who was also Alex's grandmother, Margarette, and she readily agreed.

Margarette de Palma was from Sicily, and if there was ever a fish out of water, she was it. Caroline wondered many times how this widowed grand Italian dame ended up on a beach in South Georgia. She was somewhat reclusive, and her being in Sea View had never made sense to Caroline. Then after Sophia's death, Margarette spent most of her time alone in her bedroom painting portraits of her beloved daughter.

As a mother, Caroline could only imagine the emptiness Margarette must have felt losing a child. Caroline prayed she would never experience that grief. She also prayed she'd find a way to comfort her, but Mrs. de Palma was very private. So Caroline busied herself with taking care of the house and the boys.

As summer progressed, calling Dusty in from the beach became increasingly difficult, resulting in his splitting time between the two households. Caroline made it perfectly clear that if at any time he should become a nuisance, he would find himself back in his tiny bedroom across town before he could even *think* to apologize.

And Caroline had to admit, the idea of having her nights free sounded wonderful. She loved her son, he meant the world to her, but she was only thirty and by no means dead. The thought of a social life had always been something she held on to for the future. After the fiasco his father caused five years earlier, she wouldn't dare bring another man around her son; it had taken him years to get over Bud's death. And Margarette, who lived for Alex's happiness, treated Dusty as if he were another grandchild. Now, the prospect of dating had instant appeal, and she already had the perfect little black dress.

Dusty loved his mother, but Alex's bedroom suite was a little boy's dream. Grandmother de Palma only checked on them twice after Caroline left for the day: at seven to bring them homemade fruit tarts and at ten for lights out, before retiring herself for the night. After ten was when the party started; they had all the sugar and soda they could handle and plenty of late night television, which usually meant the two ended up in a snoring heap around two in the morning.

Dusty had a blast that summer and was not looking forward to its coming to an end. In fact, he prayed every night that it could somehow last forever. And then one faithful day, his prayers were answered and just in time.

Caroline emerged from the house one afternoon carrying a tray of cookies (her signature recipe) and a pitcher of sweet, lemon iced-tea.

"You boys are gonna start to prune if you don't get out of that water," she called.

She walked over to a patio table with a large umbrella. "Now come on over here," she called. "I've baked some of my famous oatmeal-raisin-coconut-pecan cookies."

Cooking in the South was about excess: more butter, more sugar, more ingredients.

"And I have sweet tea, of course," she said as she put the tray down. "Don't make me call you again."

9

"Yes, ma'am," the boys answered in unison.

They didn't mind getting out of the pool for Caroline's cookies. The three of them sat at the table shaded by the big umbrella and munched on the delicious cookies. The lemon tea was extra tart, and the boys made faces and giggled.

"Are you boys enjoying your summer?" Caroline asked.

They nodded in unison.

"It's nice to have a best friend, isn't it?" she asked.

"Yeah," they answered, again in unison.

"Well, summer's almost over and it'll be time to go back to school soon."

Alex spoke first this time. "I don't want to go back to school."

"Me neither," Dusty said.

"But you have to go to school," Caroline continued. "What if you went to school together?"

Margarette was glad to suggest the idea. After all, keeping the boys together had been her plan. And, just in case Caroline wasn't in total agreement, Margarette had poured it on thick, making sure to mention the fact that both boys had lost so much already in their young lives. All Margarette knew for sure was that her grandson was happy again because of Caroline's little boy, and she wanted to keep it that way.

"We don't go to the same school," Dusty said.

"Well, Mrs. de Palma has made some arrangements," Caroline began in a way she thought the boys would understand. In truth, it was more complicated than she could have imagined. "So, the two of you will get to go to school together, isn't that wonderful?"

They looked confused.

"I don't want to go to public school," Alex said.

"Well, you won't have to. Dusty's gonna go to South Sea Academy with you."

The boys high fived and chest bumped before ending up back in the pool. Caroline sipped her tea and smiled. All her hard work and unwavering faith was finally paying off. And she was getting another chance at life.

She'd never really loved Dusty's father. But when she found out she was pregnant, marrying Bud had been the only option. Caroline's father had not been happy about the situation, and he never forgave Bud for ruining his daughter's life. Big Pop had little, if anything, good to say about his son-in-law. But despite his better judgment, he begrudgingly loaned Bud a substantial amount of money for a business venture that promptly fell through. Then all hell broke loose. And instead of pulling himself up by the bootstraps, Bud put a gun to his head and took the easy way out.

Caroline had faced it all with hell-bent determination, vowing to never give up for the sake of her son. She cleaned other peoples' houses for five long years, along with the occasional odd job to make ends meet.

All the good positions in the homes of the upper-class residences of White Sands had long since been secured. But then a new home was built and a new family moved in.

Caroline knew that God had smiled on her when she landed the position in the new home. Sofia de Palma was a delicate swan of extraordinary grace and style, and her mother, Margarette, though a little standoffish in the beginning, was also always elegant and regal. Although Caroline hadn't spent much time around the rich, from the moment she began working for the de Palma household, it was clear to her that Sofia and her mother were of a different breed. The furnishings were definitely Old World and the art collection had to be worth a small fortune. Caroline wondered where the vault was hidden.

And her job didn't even seem like a job, but more a group effort to keep the house running. She helped in preparing simple, regular meals, with Sofia's assistance. Even Grandmother de Palma pitched in, making her authentic Italian sauces. There were always snacks to be made for little Alex, especially fruit tarts with French vanilla crème filling; and with a house that size, there was always light cleaning, regular bed changes and laundry to be done.

On her first day when she was given a tour of the house, she had looked to the heavens and caressed the silver cross she always wore around her neck. Yes, there was obviously a big pile of money somewhere. The number of windows facing the water alone required more than a stepladder and a Sunday afternoon. Fortunately, Caroline had been instructed to bring in additional help whenever she felt the need, at whatever rate she deemed adequate.

But life, funny thing that it is, always has a way of changing. Everyone had been so happy when Sofia discovered she was pregnant, especially Sofia. Gifts arrived from exotic shops in foreign lands, and the large walk-in closet adjacent to the master bedroom was turned into a nursery.

When Sofia and her unborn baby died suddenly, a light disappeared from the house. Caroline, too, had grieved over Sofia's death. But that single, tragic misstep at the top of the stairs had made a way for her child—and for that she was grateful.

She did not know why no one spoke of Alex's father, who turned out not only to be alive, but also the source of the money behind the de Palma household. There had always been secrecy surrounding him, and the rare trips Sofia took to New York before her death were always shrouded in mystery. Still, Caroline knew it was not her place to ask questions.

There was definitely a fly in the buttermilk, but as long as she was paid her very generous salary and her son's education was taken care of, that big ole' fly could drink itself drunk. The winds of change were finally blowing in her favor.

The boys started school in August and Dusty began his new life. He and Alex did everything together. They took the same classes, studied together and even shared the same clothes after shedding their uniforms. They were inseparable the entire first year, and although Dusty was a little more sociable, they remained pretty much to themselves. Before anyone knew it, summer had come and gone again, as did another year at the Academy.

Dusty took an interest in football, while Alex, not one for team activities, reluctantly joined the swim team. Both excelled and became key players in leading their respective teammates to victory throughout each season, making them both well-known and respected among their classmates.

He had basically moved in since the weekends spent camping on the beach. Once school started, what began as weekends slowly became Thursday through Monday, with Tuesday and Wednesday evenings spent at home with his mom. The arrangement seemed silly, those two days a week, but he gave them to her. With everything that he suddenly had, came the realization of everything he had never had. Caroline loved her son and only wanted the best for him.

Right before graduation from junior high, Dusty convinced Alex that they should ask permission to have a party to celebrate. So, together the boys talked Grandmother de Palma into letting them have a party. Caroline, of course, jumped at the chance to throw the first in a series of summer parties that became the talk of the community. She was a good cook and preparing the food herself allowed her to spring for live entertainment.

CHAPTER 2

1487 N. SHORE LANE — SEA VIEW, GA

The de Palma house quickly became the place to be. The laughter and youthful excitement of the party Caroline threw reminded Margarette that life was meant to be lived no matter what. So when Alex and Dusty asked if they could claim the pool house as their crash pad so they could have friends over whenever they wanted, Mrs. De Palma readily agreed.

The idea of a group of teenagers with raging hormones having all that alone time, however, unnerved Caroline. Alex had slipped that one by her, but Caroline made Margarette promise to come to her before making any more decisions concerning the boys. She realized, she could never replace Sophia, but there was an unspoken agreement that Caroline would be mother to both boys while Margarette played doting grandmother.

So during their meeting of the minds, Caroline sat quietly while Mrs. de Palma laid out the rules and regulations. The boys were to limit themselves to a select few of no more than ten kids during the week and a strict 10:30 curfew was nonnegotiable. On weekends, the curfew was more flexible and the number of friends could vary, but there were absolutely no coed sleep overs allowed. Alex and Dusty were also to sleep in the main house Monday through Thursday, but could "crash" in the pool house on weekends with a few of the fellas.

Alex knew Caroline was behind his grandmother's words and admired her for it. Whatever he was privy to, Dusty was privy to and Caroline was a fierce she-wolf when it came to her son. Still, he went for it suggesting a no adults allowed policy, which Caroline nipped immediately in the bud. She had no problem reminding them they were minors and while in her care would behave as such. She also warned both boys that if their GPAs dropped one-tenth of a point, she would pad lock the pool house so fast their heads would spin. The thought of his head spinning always made Alex laugh, but he knew that Caroline was serious. Everyone knew she didn't fool around when it came to education, so the boys generally behaved themselves during the week, but when Saturday came, all bets were off. During the week, however, they were less rambunctious and hung out with just the guys: Jimmy Ray Daniels, fifth-generation Georgia Bulldog, Reece Jackson, son of a high-profile Atlanta-based politician; and the girls: Julia Roenstein, whose mother had a brief career in local television, and Melinda Sue Johnston, whose father owned a string of auto dealerships along the southeastern coast.

Alcohol had become a big part of their weekend routine, thanks to Julia, whose mother bought booze by the case and was usually so toasted, she rarely missed any. It was also around this time that Jimmy Ray introduced them to his special brand of homegrown. Since agriculture was his family's business, growing good weed was a snap for Jimmy Ray. So the gang spent most weekends in the pool house playing video games, goofing off online, and of course getting high. There was also a lot of making out, mostly between Julia and Jimmy Ray. They dry humped constantly and on more than one occasion didn't stop until he climaxed in his

Dockers, which would send Julia into mock hysterics. She would scold him about ruining her clothes and land a few choice hits, usually hurting herself more than him. This gave him an excuse to sweet talk her and turn the tide by saying he couldn't help himself or that she had gotten him too worked up.

The whole business was somewhat strange, considering the fact that they were already having sex, but Jimmy Ray was a bit of an exhibitionist. He enjoyed everyone watching or pretending not to watch, in Melinda's case. He especially got a charge out of the comments from the guys, with whom he was in perpetual competition.

Alex was the prettiest, so pretty he could have been a girl, while Dusty's sun-bleached locks and rosy cheeks ranked him a close second. Reece was the black guy, but Jimmy Ray was the stud of the group. He was taller and his muscles were bigger, and he fucked more.

Hell, Dusty was still a virgin. He knew all about Julia and the hand jobs. He even knew that she snagged Alex's cherry a few months back, after they'd had a fight. He had been stubborn and waited too long to apologize, so she fucked Reece too, but he didn't care. He knew it didn't mean anything and that she was just acting out. Her past was no secret, thanks to her step-dad's high-profile trial—and besides, hearing stories about the other guys kind of turned him on. Jimmy Ray chalked it up to strategy. He figured that knowing what the other guys did would somehow improve his own skills.

Dusty was by now basically living full time at the de Palma House. He was genuinely happy for his mom; she had a life now and a boyfriend, but he was really happy that he was spending more time at Alex's, where there was little to no immediate supervision. The late-night routine had escalated to smoking pot and downing Red Bull, and on rare occasions, sneaking one of the cars out of the garage. *And* Alex's increasing interest in outrageous porn on the web. Nothing normal, but wild shit so they could laugh or get grossed out while they were aroused.

Δ

When junior high graduation rolled around, Mrs. de Palma asked Caroline to plan a huge party and to spare no expense. The event was planned for early evening at the pool house of course. White lights were strung up everywhere and there were even big round paper lanterns hung across the pool. There were food and beverage tables, an ice cream and dessert station, as well as a non-alcoholic bar serving frozen tropical fruit drinks.

Romeo Sloan, one of Atlanta's premiere disc jockeys, was hired at Alex's suggestion, instead of a band, making the evening a huge success. So much so, that the seed was planted in Caroline's brain to one day start a catering business of her own. Even Mrs. de Palma enjoyed the events, in her way, by bringing her easel out onto the upstairs balcony to paint.

The parties also began the next change in Dusty's life. He was going on fifteen and his hormones were kicking into overdrive. The girls, their curves developing more and more, left nothing to the imagination in their skimpy swimsuits, especially when wet. He spent a lot of time in the water, that summer, hiding his seemingly ever-present erection.

Melinda was the one who stirred up whatever it was that got Dusty stirred up. One of their favorite games involved the girls on the boy's shoulders while in the pool, and he always paired up with the pretty, blue-eyed blonde. It was no secret that they liked each other, and the group more or less viewed them as a couple. It was without a doubt the best summer of his life.

Eight to a dozen kids could be found hanging out at the de Palma pool on any given day during summer, and Dusty always looked forward to seeing Melinda in one of her many bikinis. But it was Julia who accidentally swam too close under water one day when he was trying to hide a boner. And it was Julia who walked in on him, again accidentally, while he was naked in the pool house bathroom changing into his swim trunks. He thanked God, he had not been erect–or even worse–masturbating, but he was mortified none the less.

She never told anyone, which was cool, but she did smile at him a lot more and started calling him big boy. He hoped she meant what he thought she did, but didn't dwell on it. He had seen other guys in the showers after gym, but never stared, and figured he was pretty normal, even though his classmates teased him for having baby fuzz down there.

However, things changed during that summer; the summer he turned fifteen. He grew four inches almost overnight, shooting up to six feet. It was totally unexpected. Since his voice had changed the summer before, he and his mother figured he had already gone through puberty. Everyone noticed the growth spurt, especially Caroline, who had to purchase a completely new wardrobe for her son, including shoes. Dusty was ecstatic, fearing he would always be short compared to his male classmates, who had all gone through puberty a year or more earlier. His mother explained during one of their bi-weekly dinners that she too had been a late bloomer, and that her breasts weren't fully developed until she was nearly seventeen.

"Oh, my God, you did not just say that. Mom, I don't want to hear about your...boobs developing. Gross."

"Well, excuse me. I remember a time when you talked to me about anything."

"Okay, Mom, let's talk. I've been meaning to have this conversation with you anyway."

Caroline eyed her son. He seemed so mature, so grown up. She thanked God for the umpteenth time for South Sea Academy, worth every penny she didn't have to pay.

"What is it sweetheart?" she asked.

"It's about you and Walter, and before you flip out, don't worry, I like Walter. He's not bad for an old guy," he teased.

Caroline protested. "I don't flip out and he's only forty-two."

"It's pretty obvious he sleeps over when I'm not here," Dusty said. "So, I guess he isn't really *that* old."

Her cheeks flushed, a trait from her Dutch heritage.

"Dustin Marler," she huffed. It was clear she was flustered, so he decided to make it quick.

"I just don't think it's fair that he has to go home two nights a week," Dusty continued. "I think it's time you two took your relationship to the next level and move in together... I can live with Alex full time..."

"Now, just a minute young man...."

It *was* time to take things to the next level, Caroline thought. Walter had been hinting at this very thing for months. But she couldn't seem eager.

"Mom, come on. It's perfect; I'll be leaving soon enough anyway. College is just around the corner."

"That's another three years," she complained.

"Spend them with Walter. You deserve it. Ever since I can remember it's been all about me. It's your time now. Besides, it's not like I'm going to Outer Mongolia. I'm just across town, I see you every day."

Caroline's mind raced back through every moment since she'd first held him in her arms. She'd raised him to be responsible and hardworking, worthy of respect—and that's exactly what he was turning out to be. And she had to admit it would be nice to focus on her relationship. It helped that Margarette had fallen in love with Dusty and referred to him as her other grandson.

"I guess it would be alright."

Dusty wanted to shout. Alex had been right: It was that easy.

"Seriously, Mom?"

"Yes, Sweetie, but only if Margarette agrees."

Of course Margarette would approve, Caroline thought, but the most important thing was she knew he would be safe.

Dusty had to admit, by all accounts, his Mom was pretty cool, even if she did try to talk to him about late blooming. During the first gym class of his sophomore year, however, it became clear what his mother's words truly meant.

"Holy shit Marler; you been eatin' Miracle Grow or what?"

It was Jimmy Ray as usual, mouthing off in the locker room shower. He was the self-appointed Unofficial Chief of Boner Patrol, and if you popped one he was bustin' you. Even though, in this case, there was no erection, what hung between Dusty's legs definitely deserved a shout out.

"Hey, Reece," called Jimmy Ray, "I thought you black guys were supposed to have the biggest ones."

All the guys laughed and Jimmy Ray hooted, "Yee-haw, one for the white boys!"

The guys laughed again and more than a few glanced Dusty's way. He had never been so embarrassed in his life. Like most guys, he had been masturbating on a regular basis for a couple of years now, and one day it just seemed bigger, but he hadn't realized how much bigger.

One night, after he and Alex finished homework assignments in the upstairs study, Dusty's curiosity got the best of him.

"Do you ever check other guys out in the showers at school?" He felt weird just asking the question.

20

Alex could not resist the chance to tease him. "You mean, look at their dicks?"

"No," Dusty replied, feeling the heat in his face. "Fuck off."

"Hey, I'm just giving you a hard time," Alex chuckled. "No pun intended."

"God, you're such an asshole."

"Relax," Alex said. "All guys wanna know how they measure up."

This comment made him feel a little better.

"And nobody's got one as big as yours," Alex laughed.

"What?"

"Your rep is solid."

Now Dusty *was* embarrassed. "Whatever," he said as he threw a pillow at Alex, hitting him in the face.

Alex threw the pillow back and went into his bathroom to retrieve the bottle of scotch he kept hidden there.

"Anyway, Julia confirmed it," he said, returning with two shot glasses and the liquor bottle. "Even bigger than Jodie Slagle."

Dusty's heart skipped a beat. "What?"

Alex poured them each a shot.

"Yeah, she was giving me a hand job in the bathroom during study period last week."

"No way," Dusty giggled nervously. Julia had also given him a hand job last week.

"She just started talking about you while she was yankin' my dick."

Dusty shook his head. "What the fuck?" *This was just too weird.*

They pounded the shots and Alex poured two more.

"You'd better not tell Melinda," Dusty said.

"Duh," Alex replied, throwing back the scotch.

"Apparently she's on a quest to wank all the upper classmen and we were the warm up."

"What?" Dusty asked.

21

"Yeah, Reece, Jimmy Ray and I all made the top ten at least. Another?"

He held up the bottle. Dusty didn't say anything. Alex poured anyway.

"She's not really gonna do it, you know," Alex said. He could read Dusty like a book. "But she did do Slagle, who we've all seen thanks to his accidentally leaked photo." He made quotation marks in the air.

"I can't believe she told you," Dusty said.

"I can't believe *you* didn't tell me."

"She said it was our secret. Melinda can never find out."

"Relax," Alex said and poured more shots. "On the bright side, you're the biggest dick on campus."

CHAPTER 3

1487 N. SHORE LANE, SEA VIEW, GA

By midsummer Dusty and Melinda, were indeed an item, and Jimmy Ray and Julia seemed to be on again. Alex, who thought it ridiculous to date exclusively, kept his options open. It was the weekend of Dusty's sixteenth birthday and they were hanging out in the de Palma pool. Caroline, with Margarette's approval, had arranged a small cookout for Friday night for friends and family, since the following night, the day of his actual birthday, there was a party for Dusty and his friends—no adults allowed.

The guest list for the barbeque included Melinda, her father, Frank Johnston, and his longtime girlfriend, Noreen Jacobs–whom Melinda despised–Jimmy Ray and his parents, Buck and Dee Dee Daniels, Reece and his parents, Atlanta mayoral candidate Grayland Jackson and his wife, socialite Naomi Winters-Jackson. The fact that Grayland and Naomi were in attendance pleased Caroline immensely. What displeased her, however, was the presence of Courtney Roenstein. God only knew what she was on at any given moment. Caroline's heart went out to Julia. How much could one girl endure? Dusty swore each time she brought it up that his friend was okay, but Caroline had her doubts. Did a child ever recover from such a thing? The tiny frown that furrowed her brow caught

Walter's attention as he removed the last slab of beef ribs from the grill.

"Now what's worrying that pretty little head of yours?" Walter asked from behind. He slipped an arm around her waist and she leaned back, welcoming the secure feeling she got whenever he was around.

"Oh, nothing," she lied. "I'm just thinking about how lucky I am to have you."

"Not as lucky as I am," he whispered against her ear, pushing his hips forward. She was his second chance.

"Oh, Walter, behave. There will be time for that later."

Walter grinned. Caroline Marler was, if nothing else, organized, and time for that later meant just that. And she was happy, at last, after all those lonely years. Her life, too, had changed dramatically since she had come to work at the de Palma house. She was beginning to build a reputation as an event planner and pondered the idea of starting a small catering business. And if she limited herself to small parties of no more than twenty to thirty guests, she felt certain she could still manage the house.

CHAPTER 4

THE NIGHT: SEA VIEW, GA

The "gang" spent the following afternoon lounging around the pool until it was time for the party at Julia's later on that night. They all agreed it was best to have the *kids' only* party there, knowing full well that Mrs. Roenstein would surely be passed out before ten. This would allow Dusty and Melinda to sneak out and spend their special night together at a nearby hotel. The plan went off without a hitch and he was well prepared, having prepacked a little bag of lubricants and condoms.

They arrived at the hotel in one of the cars they had borrowed from the garage.

Melinda waited in the car while he procured the key, telling the clerk the room was for an out-of-town aunt. Everything was perfect. In the room, she put on her new lingerie and he had made sure to spray cologne down there. The night was perfect until. . .

"Wait, no. It hurts."

He stopped pushing. "It's supposed to hurt the first time."

"No, I mean it *really* hurts."

They were silent on the drive back to Melinda's. When he rolled to a stop in front of the Johnston house, she finally spoke.

"Dusty, I . . ."

"It's okay; it's not your fault," he said, fearing it was him. *What was the old saying? Size isn't everything.*

She knew he was disappointed and it made her feel even worse. She attempted a smile.

He smiled back. "It's not like we can't try again, right?" He was hopeful.

She gave him a quick kiss on the cheek and jumped out of the car, vowing never again. He watched until she was safely inside before he pulled away from the curb. He reached into the glove box and pulled a joint from his stash bag. It was still burning when he got home so he sat in the drive way, thinking and smoking.

Δ

He could see the flickering light of Alex's flat screen in the upstairs corner window. He's home early, Dusty thought. Buzzing from the joint, he decided he needed something to drink, so he let himself in and went quietly up the staircase and down the long hallway that led to Alex's bedroom. He knocked and then tried the door. It was locked. He laughed, knocked again and jiggled the door knob. A moment later Alex opened the door, tying his bathrobe. Dusty pushed past him.

"Man, you took like, forever. I need a drink."

Alex went into his bathroom to retrieve the bottle he kept hidden.

Dusty called after him. "What were you doing any way?" he asked already knowing the answer.

He was thirteen the first time he walked in unannounced on Alex, who simply said, "Are you comin' in or not?" By fourteen he learned to always knock before entering.

Alex returned with the scotch and two shot glasses. "What do you think I was doin'?"

26

Dusty laughed again, enjoying his high. "You *are* the Master Masturbator."

Alex smirked and poured two shots.

"So, I thought you'd be out until morning." He handed his friend a glass. "How was the big night?"

Dusty did his shot and held out his glass for another.

"It sucked." He tossed back the second shot. "She said it hurt too much."

Alex climbed back into bed, propping himself against the headboard. He shrugged out of the robe and pulled one of the oversized goose-down pillows onto his lap.

"It always hurts the girl the first time," he said, draining his glass.

"Alex, don't you ever listen?" He held his glass out again. "I said the same thing."

Dusty emptied his glass and held it out for another.

"She said it was something different."

"Don't you think you should slow down?"

"I need to forget this night ever happened." Dusty pounded his fourth shot. "What if something is really wrong with her?"

"Well, we know *something* is wrong with her; we're just not sure what."

Alex drank from the bottle this time.

"Good grief, is everything a joke to you?" Dusty asked. "This is serious."

"Sorry. Damn—ease up. It'll be better the next time."

"Yeah, well... What if I'm too...?"

"Too big...?" Alex smirked. "Women give birth for fuck's sake."

Dusty was not amused. "No. She said something was wrong."

"Okay, okay. We'll Google it?"

Alex moved from behind the pillows and crossed the room to his computer. He was naked as was his habit lately. Being around him like this weirded Dusty out a little, but nothing surprised him when it came to Alex. Once he entered his room for the night, everything came off. *Weren't all teenaged guys pervs?* Alex just didn't hide it.

A lot of the guys on the swim team shaved their bodies; but Caroline, after finding a tub full of hair, had strongly urged regular waxing. So Alex's skin was incredibly smooth all over with a deep golden tan. And Dusty had to admit his friend was as pretty as a guy could be without being a girl—thus the weirdness.

"Okay," he said, planting his bare ass in front of the computer desk. "It says here your dick is just too big."

"Ha, ha. You're fucking hilarious."

"Would you relax? Most guys would love to have that problem."

He navigated to the proper website.

"Okay, here we go. Ask Dr. Oz at Oprah.com blah, blah, blah ... What causes painful intercourse for women?"

He glanced up at Dusty, who stared wide-eyed at the monitor.

"Okay we can disregard this and this—and this, too, because you have to actually have sex to get that. Maybe—no, too young... Okay, this might be it. Yes, minor problem, minor procedure..."

Alex turned to face his friend. "Looks like dyspareunia, which could be caused by vaginismus, interstitial cystitis or vulvodynia. Either way it's not good news."

Dusty looked panicked.

"What...?"

"Jesus, take another shot. She's not terminally ill. But she will have to see a doctor to figure things out."

Dusty shook his head. "Doctor...?"

"Yeah, and any procedure takes parental consent, since she's a minor. So, it's either get Frank's green light on banging his only daughter or wait two years."

"You're fucking crazy," Dusty blurted out.

"It's right here. Read it yourself." Alex jumped up and Dusty took his place in front of the desktop.

It was all there: the whole, ugly truth. The more he read, the worse he felt. He had already waited nearly two years for real sex with Melinda and now he might have to wait another two. *Two more years of lame ass hand jobs.* He didn't feel so good. Alex was standing somewhere behind him. He pointed at the screen.

"You'd better hope its vaginismus. It says here she can treat it herself with vaginal dilators. Hmmm, I guess they mean dildos."

He leaned in toward the monitor. Dusty turned his head to look at Alex and nearly fell back, chair and all.

"Jesus, what are you trying to do with that thing, poke my eye out?"

Alex looked down at his erection. "Fuck off, asshole. We're looking at va-jay-jays, what do you expect?" He snatched up the bottle of liquor and headed for the bathroom.

"Let's jerk off," he said over his shoulder.

He hit the light switch on his way, turning off the overhead. The alcohol had gone straight to Dusty's head. He flashed a sloppy grin and flopped down on Alex's bed. When he landed on the mattress he felt something underneath his thigh.

"What the fuck?" He reached beneath the sheet and pulled out a ring attached to a corded control. "Is this what I think it is?"

Alex returned from the bathroom with two red solo cups of water.

"If you think it's a vibrating cock ring," Alex replied, "then yes, it is what you think it is." Apparently he had missed that one when he stashed the other toys.

Dusty tried to tear his eyes away from his naked friend, but couldn't help looking at the way his erection bobbed about as he walked around the room. Guys were really funny looking with hard-ons, he thought.

"Where'd you get this?"

Alex handed Dusty one of the cups.

"Duh, the internet; a valid credit card number can get you *anything* you want."

Tonight was the night he would reveal his dirty little secrets to his best friend.

"I've got all kinds of stuff."

Not only was Dusty curious, but as usual, his night with Melinda had left him extremely horny. He was a moth to the flame.

"Like what?"

"Pocket pussies, ball stretchers, nipple clamps, oils, lubes ... vibrators."

Dusty gave his crotch an involuntary squeeze.

"Geez, you're a freak."

"I was just about to try my new acrylic Fleshlights when you interrupted me."

"Your what?"

They're like pocket pussies built into a flashlight shaped tube; easy to hold on to and long enough for deep dickin'. Haven't you ever seen one?"

Dusty shook his head. All this talk was really getting him worked up.

"Well damn, man," he croaked. "Get that shit out before your dick breaks off."

"You wanna try one?"

"Hell yeah—Melinda is killin' me."

Alex went to the bedside table. He tossed one to Dusty.

"Here. I'll use the ass one."

He went back into the bathroom again and returned with two towels.

"We'll sit on these, the lube gets messy."

Dusty sat back and leaned against the headboard. He examined the Fleshlight. It was clear and indeed shaped like a flashlight, except where the light would be there was a perfect replica of a vagina.

"Oh my God—this is crazy."

"Feel how soft it is," Alex encouraged. He was looking forward to where this was heading.

Dusty pushed a finger inside. He felt his dick stirring inside his trousers. "Oh, man—I gotta try this shit."

Before he could even think about leaving for his own room, Alex switched the DVD player back to play mode.

"If we're gonna do it, we're gonna do it right." he said. He lit a joint and passed one to Dusty who was staring wide-eyed at Jenna Jamison going down on some lucky bastard.

The boys watched mostly in silence, with the occasional *"Oh man, look at that shit"* from Dusty while he squeezed himself through his khakis. It wasn't long before the flick did the trick and Dusty was on his feet.

"Man, I can't take it. I gotta do something," he said, shoving his pants down and stepping out of his boxers.

"Damn," Alex said. "That thing is a monster."

Dusty dropped back on the bed, feeling self-conscious but then he thought, *what the hell.* He tried to shove his dick into the gadget.

"Hang on," Alex said. "You gotta lube it up first."

He grabbed the other flesh light and applied a generous amount of the gooey liquid into the opening. Dusty, his eyes darting from his own groin to Alex's, followed his friend's lead. He didn't know why he was looking and started to wonder what the hell he was doing when the moaning from the porno regained his attention. He turned back to the screen and started pumping the sex toy.

When it was over, the two lay silent for a long time. Suddenly Dusty began to chuckle. He pulled the sheet over his lap.

"I can't believe we just did that?" he said.

"It was good though, right?" Alex asked.

"Oh yeah..."

They fell quiet for a moment. Then Alex said, "I want to tell you something, but you have to swear not to tell anyone."

"Believe me, nobody will ever know anything about this night," Dusty replied, not at all sure how he felt about what had just happened.

"Ah, forget it ...You'll find out soon enough any way."

"Wow, Alex de Palma sounds serious."

"I'm not Alex de Palma."

"Okay, here we go..." Dusty said. "Let me guess ... you're a Russian spy."

"I'm not fuckin' around. You have to promise not to tell anyone."

The tone in Alex's voice made it clear he was serious.

"Okay, okay," Dusty said. "I'm sorry. What the hell?"

Alex tuned on the bedside lamp.

"Oh, God," Dusty groaned.

"Let's smoke first," Alex said.

"Are you fucking with me?"

"No, I really need to tell you something. You're my best friend."

Alex sat up and folded his legs Indian style. He reached in the nightstand drawer. Dusty's mind bounced back and forth between what he had just done and what he was about to hear. *What in the hell was going on?*

"Blunt?" Alex asked, holding up a cognac-flavored wrap.

"Since when do you smoke blunts?"

"Since Julia introduced me to them."

Dusty grinned. "Good ole Julia."

Alex broke up the weed while Dusty patiently waited. He learned long ago that you could not rush Alex *whoever he was*. They smoked in silence until Dusty couldn't stand it anymore.

"So, who are you, really?" he blurted out.

"My real last name is... Vandiveer."

"Vandiveer...?"

It sounded vaguely familiar, but he was so high.

"My father is Baron Vandiveer."

The bell went off in Dusty's head. *Oh shit,* he thought.

"No shit," was what he said.

"He wants me to come to New York in November for my birthday."

Dusty was stunned to say the least.

"Your father...?"

"I know. You thought he was dead."

"Everybody thought he was dead."

"No, he's very much alive and living in Manhattan."

Dusty turned to look at his best friend, who he had thought, shared everything with him. How could this be? He ran a hand through his blonde hair.

Dusty shook his head, trying to gather his thoughts. "I'm confused. Why didn't you tell me about your dad?"

Alex didn't answer right away. "It's kind of a long story."

"I think I need another drink," Dusty said.

Had Alex lied all this time?

"You know where the bottle is."

A challenge? No matter what his name was, Dusty knew his friend well. He tossed the sheet aside and walked naked into the bathroom. Alex kept his eyes on him the entire time.

"Why are you lookin' at me like that?"

"Like what?"

"I don't know, all goofy and shit."

"You're all goofy and shit."

Dusty flopped back down, covering himself and took a swig from the bottle of liquor. Alex flipped his ear.

"Cut it out."

"Jesus, you're so uptight all the time."

"No I'm not," Dusty complained.

"It's okay to look, you know."

He passed Dusty the blunt.

"I kinda like being looked at," Alex said. "Why do you think I walk around naked all the time?"

"I'm not gay or anything," Dusty said.

He hit the blunt, waiting for Alex to declare the same.

"I know. You're just curious."

"Shut up, I'm not curious!"

"You're a sixteen-year-old virgin with raging hormones. Anything remotely sexual gets you going."

Dusty raised his hands. "Okay, you're creepin' me out, let's talk about something else."

That something else was Alex's father and family secrets. Alex talked and Dusty listened to what seemed like the life of a stranger. When at last it was all out Alex felt as if a great weight had been lifted off his shoulders.

"What I don't understand, is why now?"

"Don't look at me," Dusty shrugged. "This is *way* too much for me."

They were both wasted, backs against the headboard.

"I don't know what to do," Alex slurred.

Dusty swung his legs over the side of the bed.

"You should go to New York. He is your father."

He stood up and everything immediately started spinning.

"What are you doing?" Alex wanted to know.

"It's like three in the morning. I'm going to bed." Dusty's knees gave way and he tumbled to the carpet.

Alex laughed. "Get back in bed you dumb fuck."

Dusty struggled to his feet and weaving, staggered the few feet back to the giant bed. He tumbled in face down and Alex covered him, caressing his back.

"I'm beginning to wonder about you, Alex."

It feels so good to lie down was the last thought Dusty had before darkness engulfed him.

"You're the only person who's never lied to me," Alex whispered on deaf ears. "I love you for that."

He leaned over and gently kissed Dusty on the cheek then rolled quickly onto his side and passed out.

CHAPTER 5

JOHNSTON RESIDENCE — SEA VIEW, GA

"So, how was the 'perfect night'?" Julia asked.

"OMG—you are so nosey," Melinda replied. "I'm not a virgin anymore—happy now?"

"Oh, whatever, I don't really care any way. I can talk about my own sex life. Jimmy Ray likes me to put my finger in his ass."

Melinda scoffed. "You are so disgusting."

"Excuse me princess. Don't hate because I know how to please my man."

"Yeah, well I know how to please mine, too," Melinda said, a little too defensively.

"Did you like it?" Julia asked.

"I guess. I'm sure it will get better."

"Oh, it's never any good at first. But after a while you learn..."

Melinda broke down suddenly. She couldn't stop the tears. She had to talk about it with someone. *What if she couldn't have sex, ever?*

"It was awful," she confessed.

Once the words were out, there was no taking them back.

Julia tried to comfort her. "Of course, it was awful."

"No, I mean it was horrible." The tears kept coming.

"Tell me everything," Julia said.

Melinda spilled all the details of how perfect he had been the whole night up until that excruciating pain.

"And it wasn't my hymen or anything. God, I lost that in third-grade gym. Ms. Gibbs pushed me to the floor when we were trying to do Chinese splits. It's got to be something else."

The tears kept coming. "And poor Dusty, He tried to be understanding, but I know he was hurt. I made him wait so long."

Damn, that's fucked up, Julia thought. She knew he was big–really big–and that could be rough on a virgin, but women gave birth for crying out loud. *What if it really was something else? What if Melinda was one of those girls who were underdeveloped?*

"Maybe you needed lube."

"He had some."

Julia was pacing now. She wanted to figure this out. "Yeah, yeah, okay. We'll check out Dr. Oz.Com or whatever, but first..." She stared at her friend, secretly enjoying her dismay.

"You do realize there are all kinds of things to do other than actual intercourse."

Melinda huffed. "I don't do blow jobs, Julia."

"Of course you don't," Julia said, rolling her eyes. "Anyway, until you figure out what the problem is, just let him put it between your thighs."

"My thighs...?"

"Your thighs," Julia said. "Look, I'll show you."

She stretched out on the bed and crossed her ankles.

"If you cross your feet like this and tense up your leg muscles, you can make it tight for him."

Melinda folded her arms. "What are you talking about?"

"Oh, yeah, and if you lay face down you can get to your clit."

"Julia!"

"Oh don't pretend you don't know what your clit is."

"Of course I know what it is. I just don't see why we have to talk about it."

Julia got up and opened Melinda's laptop. "You can be such a prude."

Melinda's mind was racing. She knew her friend was right. She would take Julia's advice.

"Do guys really need it?" she asked.

"All the fucking time," Julia replied.

She googled "painful intercourse for women" and it didn't take long for Melinda to realize she needed to see a doctor, but her gynecologist was a close friend of her father's.

"Julia, what kind of relationship do you have with your gyno?"

CHAPTER 6

WHO'S YOUR DADDY?—SEA VIEW, GA

Alex did go to New York for his birthday. In fact, Baron insisted his son stay the entire week. The necessary calls were placed to the academy and arrangements were made for the company jet to transport the heir to the Vandiveer fortune.

Margarette wore a lovely dress and one of her best hats for the drive to the small airstrip. She had prayed for this day to come, but now that it had, she was uncertain. She had grown to dislike Baron Vandiveer. If it had not been for him, Sofia would never have left Italy. If it were not for him, her daughter would still be alive.

Caroline drove everyone there in Walter's car; it was nicer than her minivan. Alex just stared out the window, wishing Dusty had been able to come with him, but Caroline did not approve of skipping school, unless it was a matter of life or death.

Alex was apprehensive to say the least, about the trip. Everything was going to change, how he wasn't exactly sure, but he didn't like it. This he *was* sure of. He had been on his own and in control of his own life far too long for his father to suddenly swoop in and try to be a *father.* Caroline and Walter seemed excited for him, but he knew his grandmother understood.

"Remember that I love you," Margarette said right before he boarded the private plane. She hugged him. "Don't let your father bully you."

CHAPTER 7

VANDIVEER CONSTRUCTION—NEW YORK, NY

When he landed in New York, there was a car waiting at LaGuardia with a body guard type riding shotgun.

"Welcome to the Big Apple, Mr. Vandiveer."

The flight had been short and uneventful, as was the ride into downtown Manhattan where he waited in the reception area of Vandiveer Construction for someone to tell him he could see his own father.

If the corner office was any indication of his father's success, Baron Vandiveer was, without a doubt, a very important man.

"Alex, my boy," boomed a voice from somewhere behind him. He turned to see his father standing by an elaborate, built-in bar.

He walked toward the big man, hand extended.

"Father..."

"Is that any way to greet your old man?" Baron replied, pulling his son in for a brief hug.

Alex thought a handshake was more than sufficient; considering he could surely count the number of times they had been in each other's presence in the last ten years with fingers to spare.

"How was your flight?" Baron asked.

Alex wasn't buying the Mr. Nice Guy act.

"It was a flight. Why am I here?"

"What kind of a question is that? You're my son. I have every right to see you."

"But why now," Alex challenged, "after all this time?"

Baron took a long look at his son before he spoke again.

"You're angry with me. I will give you that—but just know everything I have done is for your benefit."

"My benefit or *your* benefit...?"

"The fact that I am your father has never and will never change. And for that reason alone, I demand your respect. Are we clear?"

Alex was a master at game playing. His father would not win.

"Perfectly."

Baron took a deep breath and exhaled slowly.

"How about some lunch? Anything you want, just name it and I will have the chef prepare it," Baron said. "But please, nothing too extravagant. I only have a few hours. I tried to clear my schedule, but it was impossible."

Alex was not surprised. The door swung open and the woman from the outer office entered. "I'm sorry, Mr. Vandiveer, but Mr. Goldstein insisted..."

Leonard Goldstein pushed his way in. "Baron, we've got a problem."

"It's alright, Janice," Baron said.

The busty brunette turned on her heels. She knew she could not have physically stopped the attorney, but she would have loved the chance to try. She did not care for lawyers—especially that one.

"There's been another incident on the 59th Street project," Goldstein said.

"Leonard, have a drink with me. Whatever it is, I'm sure it can wait." Baron moved toward the bar. "You remember my son, Alex."

Goldstein turned to see a young man standing across the office. His expression softened the instant he saw him.

"You're little Alex?"

Alex did not return the smile for the sake of being polite. He was sure he had never met this man before.

"My God, I remember the day you were born." He extended his hand. "I'm your Uncle Leo, not by blood of course. Leonard Goldstein." They shook hands.

"Pleasure to meet you, sir," Alex reluctantly responded. He wanted to go home.

Baron handed Leonard a healthy pour in a crystal highball glass.

"Nothing for me, father?"

"The boy becomes a man." Leonard raised his glass in salute.

"You're drinking, are you?" Baron asked.

"I'm doing a lot of things you might never guess, *Dad*."

The sarcasm in Alex's voice did not escape his father's ears; still he admired the boy's spunk. There was a lot of lost time between them. He snatched up another glass and poured the amber liquor over ice. Alex took the drink offered him and tasted the familiar elixir. He welcomed it and wished Dusty had come with him.

Leonard stepped closer to Baron and tried to speak quietly.

"Baron, we must discuss the 59th Street project."

Baron was seldom resistant when it came to business, especially urgent business, but his stern tone said it all.

"Must I repeat myself Leo? We were just about to have some lunch. Join us. I insist."

You did not refuse any invitation from Baron Vandiveer. He walked back to his massive desk and pressed the intercom button on the state of the art phone system.

"Janice, Mr. Goldstein will be joining us for lunch. Please alert Luciano. Are the papers regarding my son's trust here yet?"

"They arrived this morning, sir."

"Excellent, could you bring them in please?"

"Right away, Mr. Vandiveer."

"Since you're here, Leo... I hope you don't mind."

Leonard shook his head, his mind elsewhere.

"Trust...?" Alex asked.

"In spite of what you think of me, dear boy, I have worked very hard to build a legacy that one day will be yours and hopefully passed on for generations. I was a nobody from nowhere once, but I fought. I fought hard and I won. No matter what you may believe, I loved your mother very much. You are our son and the future of the Vandiveer name. Isn't that right, Leonard...?"

Baron escorted them into the executive boardroom, where a young woman was busy adding a third place setting on a gigantic mahogany conference table.

"Your father is the picture of health," Leonard Goldstein said as they entered. With a chuckle he added. "Why, he'll most likely out live us all."

Janice entered as they were taking their seats. Another woman filled water glasses, while a man in a chef's uniform, presumably Luciano, stood at the ready.

"Janice, please hold all my calls for the next hour."

"Yes, Mr. Vandiveer," she said, placing a leather attaché on the table to Leonard's left.

Baron waved Luciano over. He ordered medium rare porterhouse steaks with pasta marinara sides then turned his attention to the business at hand.

"Shall we, Leo?"

"At once," Leonard said, opening the case Janice left.

Alex sat quietly as his financial future was laid out in front of him. Once again he found himself wondering just how rich his father was. He focused on his composure, prideful in his ability to remain cool, but inwardly he was definitely freaking out. The numbers were, in a word, staggering.

A trust fund in his name containing $2.5 million–of which he would have limited, though generous access–had already been established. On his eighteenth birthday, he would receive $5 million, at twenty-one, another $5 million, and $10 million on his twenty-fifth. It was not all cash: There were stocks, bonds, dividends, and shares in properties. But the point remained the same—the numbers were more than he could have imagined.

Papers were presented to him, which he signed, with a somewhat shaky hand.

"Your grandmother is getting older and misses her family," Baron said when Leonard closed the attaché case. "How would you feel about coming to live with me next summer, here in New York?"

"Your father has a beautiful rooftop mansion and the city is home to some of the finest schools in the country," Leonard stated.

"You expect me to leave my life," Alex asked, "just like that..?"

"Margarette has done more than could be expected," Baron said.

"Has Grandmother complained about me?"

Baron Vandiveer was not one to negotiate. He was also short on patience, but he restrained himself.

"I have not mentioned this to her as of yet. I thought we should discuss it first."

Alex wanted to cry. "You can't make me leave my friends."

Of course he could, Baron thought, but he realized he was in no position to push his son into anything. He remembered how rebellious he'd been at sixteen. "Perhaps, after your graduation then..."

Was his father offering an olive branch?

"I'll think about it," Alex lied.

The meal was served and Alex, not one for small talk, ate in relative silence while his father and Uncle Leo discussed substandard structural beams used in a building on 59th Street. They just can't help themselves, Alex thought.

After an agonizing forty-five minutes or so, Baron asked an odd question—odd to Alex anyway.

"What about my son?"

"There's the press conference," Leonard said.

"Press conference...?" Alex asked.

"It is time the world learns about my rightful heir." Baron stood indicating lunch was over. "Another drink old friend...?"

Leonard declined. He did not like Baron's position on the 59th Street Tower but would handle the situation himself and suffer the repercussions later, should there be any. They could not risk another floor collapse, and the company could not risk being linked to another class-action lawsuit, no matter how favorable the outcome of the last. In the end, as long as the reputation of the business didn't suffer, all would be forgiven. Leonard got back on board the prodigal son train.

"The press will meet us tomorrow at five in front of the Grand and we'll be live on all the local stations. That way the story will break just in time for the six o'clock news and within twenty-four hours the rest of civilized mankind will know the heir to the kingdom."

Leonard looked at Alex and smiled.

"You will be fresh meat for all the tabloids and entertainment news shows, young man. A funny thing how wealth is now somehow synonymous with celebrity," he said. "And it certainly doesn't hurt that you took after your mother in the looks department."

There was something about Uncle Leo that Alex didn't like, though he couldn't quite figure out what that something was.

"Your father is one of the richest men in the country. With that face, nothing will be beyond your grasp. Money plus beauty equals the best kind of privilege."

Leonard stood and left with the leather case. Baron stood as well.

"I have meetings the rest of the day. Janice has made arrangements for you to be taken to my home. I will be working late and most likely staying in the city tonight. Malcolm knows you're coming and will make sure you are made comfortable."

Am I being dismissed? Alex wondered. The stiff hug followed by the double shoulder grab removed any doubt.

"Please think about what I said about your coming to New York permanently," Baron said. "It's time you start to learn about your true legacy son. I've built an empire and though I'm strong, no man lives forever."

Alex stared at the lines and creases in his father's face and realized he didn't even know how old he was. But he was certain that Baron Vandiveer and Leonard Goldstein were thick as thieves.

"Call me before you leave town," Baron said smiling.

He released Alex and pressed a button on the conference table to summon Janice.

The same limo was waiting for him downstairs with the two goons that had driven him from the airport. The bigger goon was standing by the open rear door waiting to close it after Alex was secure inside. Just like at the airport, Alex thought.

Malcolm was expecting Alex at the house, which was indeed a mansion atop a skyscraper just as Uncle Leo had described. The big goon, whose name was Rocko, escorted Alex to the door and after a brief interchange with Malcolm left with a promise to return the next day to see Alex to the airport.

Alex had never taken an interest in knowing who his father was but his curiosity was finally winning over his disdain. That night after dinner, alone in one of the guest suites, he called Dusty.

"Yo, what's up?" Alex tried to sound matter-of-fact. The truth was he was scared to death. He wasn't sure he wanted the life his father seemed to be planning for him.

"Same shit, different day," Dusty said. He, too, was scared. He'd googled Alex's father and was stunned to find out just how wealthy the man was, and how wealthy his best friend was, or would be.

"How's New York?" he asked.

"It's okay. I went to my dad's office today."

"Yeah?"

"Yeah. He owns the whole building."

"Damn. He must be loaded," Dusty replied with feigned surprise.

"He gave me two-and-a-half million dollars for my birthday."

"What?! No fuckin' way!"

"Fuckin' way!" Alex yelled. The room was so cavernous, there was no chance anyone could possibly hear him. "He even owns the plane that brought me here."

"Fuck."

"He owns a construction company and a bunch of hotels and shit. I couldn't keep up. But who cares, right?"

"You're so lucky," Dusty said.

"No, *we're* so lucky," Alex said. "And rich! Do you realize how much money that is? And there's more to come." Alex could never imagine life without his friend. "Hey, listen, I'm going to be on TV tomorrow."

"No shit. What channel?"

"All of them. Baron's having a press conference. His lawyer, who calls himself my Uncle Leo, said it will air on all the major networks. Just pick one."

"My mom's hosting an engagement party tomorrow night for Frank and Noreen. We can all watch. This shit is crazy."

Alex laughed. "Melinda will shit a brick."

"Funny."

They talked for another thirty minutes or so. Mainly it was Alex who did the talking of all the future plans he had for the two of them. First thing on the agenda: a set of matching Kawasaki Ninja ZXRs.

CHAPTER 8

1487 N. SHORE LANE — SEA VIEW, GA

"Real Estate Tycoon, Baron Vandiveer stunned Wall Street and the rest of the financial world today, when he announced the arrival of a sixteen-year-old bouncing baby boy. Baron Alexander Vandiveer II was introduced at a press conference in front of the real estate mogul's flagship hotel, The Royal Grand. Only a few people in Vandiveer's innermost circle knew this son existed...."

The story continued, listing Baron's massive real estate holdings in New York, Chicago and Atlanta then cutting to interior shots of the lavish rooftop mansion in the sky and his downtown apartment.

As Dusty, Melinda, the rest of the gang, parents and respective partners watched, mouths agape, the entertainment reporter wrapped up with a voice over covering footage of photographers and journalists rushing Alex, while Baron and bodyguards shielded him.

"The heir to the sizeable Vandiveer fortune responded with a firm 'no comment.'"

The screen froze momentarily displaying a close frame of Alex throwing up a peace sign, and wearing a familiar smirk.

Caroline was the first to speak. "Well, I knew Alex's father was rich, but I had no idea..."

"Mom!" Dusty blurted out. "You knew Alex's father was alive?"

"Yes." She hesitated. "Margarette loves you like a grandson; it was only natural that we grew close...."

Grayland Jackson spoke up. "Baron Vandiveer has always been a power player with–let's just say–questionable ethics."

Reece stared at his father. "You knew too?"

"During the early nineties, he got mixed up with a group of developers, who also raised eyebrows in the political community; there was a building collapse and lives were lost. I was part of the legal team."

"What?" Reece asked.

"Oh, goodness," Caroline gasped.

"Vandiveer was found innocent of any wrongdoing. However, public opinion was divided and there were a lot of threats made against him—retaliation from said investors.

Nine people were killed because of that collapse and important people went to jail. I heard something about a wife and child in exile, but never dreamed..." He sipped his vodka cocktail. "Small world."

Of course he knew all about Alex. During his years as a high-powered Atlanta-based attorney, he had had a few dealings with Leo Goldstein and the Vandiveer camp. Grayland had in fact recommended Sea View as a relocation site.

"Well, this just keeps getting better and better," Noreen said, practically salivating.

"So, that's why they came here," Caroline thought out loud. She cleared her throat. "I knew Alex's father was some major high-roller, but..." she said, swirling a perfectly chilled sauvignon blanc in a large wine glass, "I never imagined this."

The conversation developed a life of its own. This was big news for the small town of Sea View, especially the White Sands community. Everything made sense, but somehow Dusty felt betrayed. He and Alex were like brothers, closer than brothers, best friends. And Alex had kept this secret from him.

CHAPTER 9

1487 N. SHORE LANE — SEA VIEW, GA

Another school year passed while Alex became increasingly accustomed to his newfound wealth and his popularity had entered the stratosphere. The checks came without fail, Baron's way of allowing his son to wade in the prosperous waters he made flow. It was also his way of testing Alex in the matters of money and the respect it required. Alex had risen to the challenge beautifully, though a few impulse buys did manage to raise an eyebrow or two.

One such purchase: two identical Kawasaki ATV-Quads for racing in the dunes, which neither Caroline nor Margarette were happy about. He tried to buy Dusty a car for his seventeenth birthday, but he had refused it. So they shared the Range Rover, with little to no problem. And since Caroline absolutely put her foot down when the subject of the Ninja motorcycles was brought up, the quads were the compromise that was reached. At least they'd be limited to the beach with the ATVs. Dusty loved his new life. But, as always, when least expected, things have a way of changing.

It was the end of junior year at the Academy and it had been a stellar year for the boys with each of them placing in the top five percent academically, thrilling Caroline to pieces. Alex wanted to rent a luxury yacht and sail to Miami for a week of fun in the sun on him to celebrate, but the gang was psyched about having the first big de Palma blowout of the summer. Caroline had a catered party scheduled; Margarette was in Italy spending time with a dying brother; and Frank and Noreen were on their honeymoon at the Niagara Falls. They would be unsupervised and by the time the other parents found out, it would be too late.

If only they had gone to Miami that weekend. If only they hadn't decided to throw the party at the pool house, unsupervised. *If only...*

Why had they all gotten so drunk and high? Why had Melinda decided on that night of all nights, when everyone was so wasted, to make her move?

Eventually she realized that her contempt for Alex was actually something else. Why did the good girl always want the bad boy, especially when she already had the best guy a girl could have?

And why, oh why, had Alex allowed things to go where things had gone? He was drunk and he was angry at her for betraying Dusty. Through his actions, however, he regrettably, did the same thing, but no one was thinking with a clear head. He shoved her against a palm tree and grabbed her thigh, lifting it so he could push a hand under her sarong when she started yelling and pushing him away. She saw Dusty an instant before he saw them, leaving no time for Alex to react to the onslaught of slaps.

"Let go of me," she yelled.

"You started it," Alex said right before Dusty punched him.

The blow knocked him off his feet and he reached for his aching jaw.

"It's not what it looks like," he managed to say.

Isn't that what they always said? Dusty pounced on Alex and landed a few more punches. He didn't know why he was so mad. Something didn't feel right, but he could not control himself.

"Dusty," Melinda screamed, "Stop it! Stop it!"

By now the others had gathered. He whirled around. "Are you defending him?" he asked.

Melinda did not dare speak for fear the truth would come out.

"Is what he said true? Did you want it?"

She wanted to answer him, to lie but she couldn't.

"Did you?!"

It was a drunken Jimmy Ray who answered. "Okay, everybody just calm the fuck down, alright. Dusty, man, everybody wants to bang Alex. Hell, I've even thought about it. I mean, he's so damned pretty."

A few snickers and giggles erupted. Jimmy Ray always tried cracking jokes to lighten the mood during serious situations. This time, however, it didn't fly. Dusty glared at them, the privileged kids of Sea View, with their designer lives. He was not like them. He would never be like them. He ran for the garage.

Alex struggled to stand, clutching at his side. *Cracked rib?* "Dusty! Wait!" He laughed at Melinda. "You're fucked." He chased after his friend. "Dusty, come back, I can explain."

Melinda tried to go after them, but Julia stopped her.

"Haven't you done enough damage for one night?"

If only they had gone to Miami. If only Melinda had not made her move. If only Alex had pushed her away.

The gang sat, ashen and sickened in the emergency room at Northside Hospital's Sea View clinic. Dusty was in surgery, his leg broken in three places, suffering from contusions, a dislocated shoulder and there was a potential threat to his spine. Football senior year was definitely out of the question. He had rolled one of the quads in the dunes trying to get away. He hadn't known why he was running, he just knew he was. When they found him he lay twisted and unconscious some twenty feet from the wrecked ATV.

Alex was the first to reach him, the others moments behind. For an instant they thought he might be dead. No one said it, but they all thought it.

"Call 911!!!"

CHAPTER 10

NORTH SIDE CLINIC — SEA VIEW, GA

After nearly an hour of silence, Alex spoke, his voice full of quiet rage.

"This is your fault. You did this to him."

"You tried to rape me, Alex."

"Call the police, then," he challenged, leaping from his seat. A mistake. Pain pierced his side and it was difficult to breathe. His eye was blackened in the scuffle and his lower lip split, but he didn't care. "Call 'em, bitch! I fuckin' dare you!" He was losing it. He could not live without Dusty.

Jimmy Ray stood in case things got ugly. Everyone looked at her. The girls knew, probably the boys, too.

She wanted to cry. "I'm going to talk to the nurse."

"Yeah, why don't you do that?" Julia said.

Of all the shit Melinda pulled this was by far the worst.

Δ

They all left eventually. Sobering up in an ER waiting room was not anyone's idea of a good time. Besides, from what they were hearing, Dusty wouldn't be conscious until morning anyway. They all left one by one, all but Caroline, Walter and Alex.

Alex spoke to Walter when at last he entered the waiting room. The older man's concern was Dusty's football career, as he put it. It seemed pretty ridiculous to Alex. He had all the money they would ever need. Why would Dusty torture himself with a life of broken limbs and head injuries? Alex's plan was to blow off college and go to Europe where they could study life; but football, according to Walter, was Dusty's chance to make something of himself. *But he was already something,* Alex thought. *Why couldn't they see that?*

He was still there when Dusty woke up. Caroline came into the waiting room to tell him. The rest was like a dream. Dusty was angry, really angry, at him. Everything was fucked up. Alex pleaded and promised, but to no avail. Dusty wanted no part of any of the plans Alex made.

So he left. He called his father and flew to New York. He would still go to Europe. Fuck senior year. Fuck college.

His father agreed with one stipulation. Alex was to go first to Sicily and spend time with his mother's family before making any further travel plans. Baron wasn't exactly thrilled about his son's decision to drop out of school, but how could he, in good conscious, allow his only son to pass on a life that most only dreamed of? Wasn't that why he had clawed his way to the top?

Everything was settled and within three days of landing in New York, Alex was preparing to leave the country indefinitely.

CHAPTER 11

THE ROYAL GRAND HOTEL — MANHATTAN

Ana Maria Santos stood stock still on the busy Manhattan sidewalk, not caring that she was interrupting the flow of human traffic. She stared at the gleaming marble façade of the Royal Grand Hotel and wondered what had led her here.

The picture, that's what. The one of her mother in the glamorous dress and the red lipstick, standing with the handsome stranger in front of this hotel. That's what had led her here.

The picture had been one of her mother's prized possessions and she had always spoken fondly of the time she had spent here. She always said she knew people at the hotel, important people.

Ana was hopeful. Maybe someone could help her. Maybe she could get a job as a maid or something. Maybe somebody would help her without trying to make a few bucks off of her.

Actually, a lot more than a few. She had made close to two hundred thousand for Sally. It all started after she turned twelve due to a sudden growth spurt that left her tall and willowy, her face more angular. Within a few short months her breasts swelled and the hips came. At thirteen, her virginity was auctioned to the highest bidder. And once in the game, Ana decided to win it. She watched and listened. All the girls talked tricks of the trade and she quickly learned the top girl not only earned more but worked less. Getting to the top had been child's play since most of the "competition" either drank too much or did too many drugs.

Within a year she reached her goal. Her beauty brought the highest pay and her skill, the VIP clientele.

Still, she hated every second of it. Most of the men were unaware of how young she really was and it struck her as funny how latex and riding crops made them not want to care.

From the beginning she decided to take charge whenever and wherever she could in the life she had been forced to lead.

She always knew she would leave Sally's one day, so the more money she made the better her chances. And after two long years of turning tricks, the day had finally come.

Ana pulled her cap down, trying to hide her face and stared at the gleaming entrance. She stared at it a little too long. By the time she realized her mistake, it was too late.

She hit the ground hard and her backpack was yanked from her shoulders. As she struggled to get to her feet, another figure raced past her in pursuit of the first. She ran too, yelling. That backpack held the five thousand dollars she had managed to keep from Sally and a few measly changes of clothing.

Δ

Alex wondered what he was doing and why he was doing it. He was supposed to be climbing into the back of a limo bound for JFK to board a flight for Italy. Yet, here he was chasing a mugger down West 57th toward Park Avenue— and he was so *not* the hero type.

Suddenly out of nowhere the guy stopped and turned. *Oh shit,* he thought. The Gucci loafers, a gift from his father, skidded, sending him right into the forceful punch being delivered to his gut. The pain was unbelievable. He doubled forward and crumbled to the pavement.

This, too, interrupted the flow on the busy Manhattan side walk, but only momentarily. He managed to get to his feet just to be assaulted by the girl he tried to help.

"He got away!" she shouted, swatting at him.

"Jesus, you're a feisty one," Alex gasped, throwing his hands up. "I'm sorry. I tried, okay?"

She stopped swinging. He was the only one who came to her aid. *Damn Sally and her goons.* She decided to count her blessings; it could have been a lot worse. The few girls who tried to leave Sally's were either brought back battered or never heard of again.

Leaving had been a risk, but staying any longer would have meant suicide. Sally could be a girl's worst nightmare if she wanted to. But still, Ana had to take the money and the chance, only now, both had just disappeared into the crowd.

She burst into tears. "It's just that...it's just..."

"It's just a book bag," he groaned.

"No," she wailed, "you don't understand. Everything I own is in that back pack. Now I have nothing and no one."

The picture was her proof and now it was gone.

"What do you mean you have no one?"

"I have no family, no friends, nothing." She was shaking now, sobbing.

Alex pulled her to his chest and hugged her with some difficulty, as the pain from the blow radiated through his gut. He laughed to himself. He did not know her, but something made him want to protect her. Maybe it was the banging body he detected beneath the baggy clothes. *Hmm*, he thought, *a real damsel in distress*. Was she worth saving?

"Shhh... It's okay now." He rubbed her back, trying to calm her. "Shhh. Everything is going to be alright."

Ana tried to calm herself; his arms felt so good around her. He looked and smelled like the rich men who once came to see her, but this one was young. And he knew nothing about her. She could just be a normal girl. A runaway perhaps.

For the first time in her life she felt safe. She also felt the stirring against her leg. She did not know him, but somehow knew he was telling the truth and that everything *would* be okay.

"Do you promise?" A smile was emerging between her sobs.

"Would I lie to you?"

He took a good look at her face and realized she was extremely pretty, beautiful in fact. His old life had ended, for now anyway, and he was about to start a new one. Why not with this amazing girl? She could be the sister he had lost— or something else.

"Looks like you could use a break." He grinned ear to ear and cradled her face in his hands. "Your life is about to change."

What had Uncle Leo said about pretty and privilege? He held her at arm's length and gave her the once over.

"Take off that silly hat, for Christ sake."

She was puzzled, but found him to be very charming and mysterious. She did as instructed, allowing her hair, a mass of cascading curls, to fall around her shoulders and down her back.

"Perfect," he smiled.

He grabbed her hand and led her back toward the hotel.

"You're going to need new clothes, new shoes, bags, luggage, of course; and then there's lip gloss and eyeliner and all that other shit you girls can't seem to live without."

She stopped. They were standing in front of the hotel.

"What are you saying...?"

"I'm about to rescue you." He smiled again. "I'm very rich and lately I've become very bored with myself."

"Rescue...?" She stared at him. She couldn't even finish the sentence, couldn't allow herself to think it.

"I was supposed to be on my way to the airport; not chasing some random mugger."

Could her mother actually have been right about something? *Good things happen at the Royal Grand*, she would say whenever she referred to the prized photo. She had given it to Ana the day she was murdered.

Was this really happening or was it some kind of hallucination? Was she actually laying sprawled on the sidewalk, the life force draining out of her, while people stepped over her body on their way to wherever it was they were going?

She felt like Alice falling down that rabbit hole when the doorman straightened and tipped his hat, calling the young man, *Mr.* Vandiveer. By the time they crossed the marble lobby, she knew she had entered Wonderland.

An ashen faced hotel manager was running toward them babbling about the police and hospitals. A limo driver, also in a panic, hurried toward them as well.

"Your father would never forgive me if anything happened to you, young sir," the driver said anxiously.

"What in God's name were you thinking?" the concierge scolded. "I was about to call the police."

"As you can see, Jorge, I'm fine and everything is again right with the world."

Alex motioned toward Ana. "There's been a slight change in plans...."

Ana did not miss the disapproving glance Jorge gave her. Neither did Alex.

"So, I'll need my father's suite."

"But sir, the Duchess will be arriving in a matter of hours."

"Then you'd better get moving. *I'm* staying in the penthouse. So you'll need to make other arrangements for her royal donkey face."

He turned to the chauffeur. "Have my things sent up."

The driver nodded and headed for the main entrance. Alex turned his attention back to a stunned Jorge.

"And I want someone sent over from Saks, Barneys and Bloomingdale's, immediately."

He eyed Andrea head to toe. "Size four...?"

She nodded.

"Complete wardrobes, accessories, everything."

He spoke the words so nonchalantly, as if his request were an everyday occurrence. *This just couldn't be happening,* Ana thought. She had to be bleeding on the sidewalk.

"And have lunch sent up. My usual times two with fruit tarts for dessert. And have a bath drawn and waiting."

The hotel manager did not like what he was hearing, but gave a tight smile and scrambled off. She watched in amazement, "my father's suite" and "Bloomingdales" still ringing in her ears.

"That was for the look he gave you," Alex said laughing. "Look at him run." His face hardened. "No one will ever look at you that way again."

Yes, he would protect her.

"Why are you doing this?"

He smiled a smile she would come to recognize as one of power. He inhaled deeply. "Because I can."

Δ

The Penthouse Suite was more than Ana could have ever imagined. Never in her wildest dreams did she expect to find herself surrounded by such opulence. All the furnishings were brown leather or beige suede; the wood shined and the glass sparkled. The garden tub was filling, as requested, and there were giant bouquets of fresh flowers everywhere. *How could this have all happened?* It was him.

"So, I'll leave you to your bath," he said. "Room service will be here soon."

She reached out to him.

"Don't go," she whispered.

She began to slowly undress him. It was obvious he wanted her, but there was no way she was fucking him. Not right away. Would he wait?

"You don't have to do this," he said.

"Do what?"

"Any of this..."

She tried to kiss him, but he pulled away.

He looked her square in the eye. "I never do anything I don't want to and from now on, neither will you."

What kind of boy turns down sex?

She unbuckled his belt, allowing his pants to fall to the floor.

"After all the trouble you went to, I thought you might need a hot bath more than me."

For a split second she thought of playing it shy, but only for a second; and although she was far from being a virgin, Ana realized she was nervous. He knew nothing of her past so the question was, how experienced should a girl of fifteen be?

She was so tired of all the games, but dared not open herself to emotion and feelings. It was much too soon for that. So she decided to go with her gut.

"Being naked with you does sound kinda nice ...," he said, looking down at the growing bulge in his boxer briefs, "as long as you don't mind this happening."

"I think *this* is kind of nice," she said, leading him to the waiting bath.

Δ

They sat on opposite ends of the huge tub, up to their chins in churning, scented water. She eyed him. He sat, head back with his eyes closed, allowing her to wonder.

"You're staring at me," he said, without opening his eyes. "You're wondering why I'm doing this. It's because I'm angry and I'm hurt and because I'm spoiled and selfish. If you promise never to leave me I will give you everything you've ever wanted."

"But you don't even know me..."

He opened his eyes. "Nothing that happened before we met downstairs on that sidewalk matters. My father is very, very rich. We can do whatever we want; *be* whoever we want."

He closed his eyes again and nodded, very proud of himself for making such a bold statement.

"This is like a dream...," she said softly.

"But it's no fun unless there's someone to share it with."

"You said you were supposed to be on your way to the airport. Where were you going?"

He opened his eyes. "Europe, Sicily to be exact."

"You missed your trip?"

"Oh, no. We're still going."

"We...?"

"Yes, *we*. I told you, I'm rescuing you." He leaned forward suddenly. "Shit. I just realized I don't even know your name."

She opened her mouth to speak, but stopped herself. He said nothing before they met mattered.

"Give me one," she said. "You're giving me a new life, why not a new name?"

"Alright, then," he smiled. Her beauty could not be denied. "Andrea."

He spoke the name without giving it much thought. It was to have been his sister's name.

"I can't believe this is happening to me." She wished she could tell the girls, but that life was over. "When are we coming back?"

"Whenever we want," he said with a sly grin.

She let out a little squeal and disappeared under the suds, just like Julia Roberts in *Pretty Woman.*

CHAPTER 12

PARIS

Andrea stared at her reflection. Her hair and makeup were flawlessly done. A lot had happened in the last year since she met Alex. They had flown to Europe as soon as she was able to get a passport, which was no easy task and quite costly since there was no record of her birth.

Thankfully, Uncle Leo had been able to pull a few strings. After calling in a couple of favors and making a few demands, presto-change-o, Ana Maria Santos ceased to exist and Andrea Sorcosi became legit.

She loved Italy and Italy loved her. The idea was planted that night in New York, when the sales clerks from the stores arrived with racks and racks of clothing *for her*, schlepped all the way to the penthouse. And the shoes! Cinderella never had it so good; and they had all asked what agency she was with.

Scrubbed clean, wrapped in the luxurious hotel robe and standing in the Vandiveer Suite with junior himself, the sales girls thought for sure she was a model. She had answered no; she also said no to actress and heiress. The memory of having total strangers fawn over her that first time was one she would never forget. It seemed a lifetime ago. She was used to it now, now that she was indeed, a model.

"Andrea, they're ready for you."

It was the production assistant. Andrea was about to be photographed for *French Vogue* again, this time for the cover. *Third time's a charm,* she thought.

Her career started almost immediately after arriving in Italy. She and Alex spent three months with his grandmother and Aunt Josephine (his mother's twin sister), her husband and four children. Although virtual strangers, they welcomed her with open arms. Clearly, they did not care much for his father, but Margarette seemed happier than Alex could remember.

Still, he grew restless and they moved on to Rome, where after only a week in a hotel, they decided they would settle there. A single phone call was made to Janice and in a matter of days they found themselves in a beautiful, fully furnished two-bedroom apartment with a marvelous view.

One of Alex's cousins had given them the name of a photographer, who started Andrea's portfolio and sent her on a few go-sees.

Everything happened so fast. Now she was posing for one of the most famous photographers in the fashion world, a man she called a friend, for the cover of *Vogue.*

She had already walked for many of the big names: Chanel, Louis Vuitton, and even the fabulous Donatella Versace. Her face had appeared in all the top fashion magazines, and there were rumors of a lucrative endorsement deal with Aaric C. Cosmetics, a brand-new, hot-as-a-firecracker U.S.-based company.

The European tabloids and society pages could not get enough of her. Her personal life with Alex frequently made headlines, because no one knew anything about them. They were very public yet remained very private.

It was the enormous amounts of cash that Alex both spent and flaunted that drew the attention of all the right–and all the wrong–people.

They were always in the company of Europe's hottest young celebrities from the music and movie industries. Soon they were practically stalked by the paparazzi when they were showing up at parties, hanging out at parties, and worse, leaving parties.

The attention fueled Andrea's already on-track career, especially after Alex landed a Dolce & Gabbana underwear ad campaign, just by being on one of her photo shoots.

The results were hot, but hotter still were the nudes of Alex leaked onto the Internet. Yes, the exotic model and her near-billion-dollar-heir boyfriend had just enough swagger and edge to keep the public hungry for more.

Who were these young Americans who appeared out of nowhere and have taken Europe by storm?

CHAPTER 13

JOHNSTON RESIDENCE — SEA VIEW, GA

"That's him, alright," Julia said, plopping down on the bed beside Melinda.

They stared at the full-page ad in the latest issue of *Vanity Fair*. It featured Alex sprawled on a piece of driftwood in a pair of white, designer briefs.

"Damn, the boy is fine."

"Oh shut up, Julia," Melinda snapped.

"What's the big deal? So he's modeling. Did you think he would run off and kill himself over you?"

Melinda had changed the attempted rape story to one where Alex professed his love for her and swore he would rather die than live without her. Julia had her doubts. After all, Melinda had already lied once.

"I wonder if Dusty has seen this."

Julia rolled her eyes. "Yeah, he's all about *Vanity Fair.*"

Melinda sighed.

"And what if he has? We all miss Alex. Things aren't the same without him."

"You mean you miss his money," Melinda huffed.

"We all have money. God you're such a bitch."

Not Vandiveer money, Melinda thought.

"What are you guys fighting about now?" Jimmy Ray asked, walking into the bedroom with Dusty.

"Nothing," Melinda lied, hugging Dusty.

He kissed the top of her head.

"I missed you," she cooed.

"Missed me?" Dusty asked. "We just went to drop your daddy's bird dogs off at the kennel. We've been gone for like an hour."

"Is anybody else hungry?" Jimmy Ray asked, buzzing from the joint he had just smoked.

They were meeting Reece and his new girlfriend, a former teen Miss Columbia, at the Crab House for dinner.

"How 'bout you, Julia...? You hungry...?" he asked while doing an obscene hand gesture.

"You wish," she quipped.

She had stopped sleeping with Jimmy Ray nearly six months ago. It was the longest break in the relationship since that first make-out session at Melinda's fourteenth birthday party. No one knew why. The truth was, Julia was banging a thirty-five-year-old married guy she had met at the local Home Depot—another experiment. She had gone there specifically to meet someone, but planned on dumping him soon. He bored her.

Δ

Reece and Santana were waiting at the table when they arrived. The sun was setting over the calm water on what was starting out as a perfect night.

Their server arrived as they were being seated. Everyone knew this was a choice table and anyone taking care of them was sure to get at least a one-hundred-dollar tip. Alex had set the precedent and it continued even in his absence.

The waiters and waitresses learned early on not to ask about him. It was a mystery to anyone on the outside as to why Alex left Sea View and even more of a mystery that none of his friends knew where he was.

"Hey you guys," Brandi, the always too happy, always too blonde waitress called.

She had been their server the last time they were there.

"What's up sugar?" Jimmy Ray replied, patting his knee.

Brandi took his queue and perched on the offered leg. She had already banged Jimmy Ray and now had her sights set on Dusty. She was aware of the rumors.

"Oh, my God, have you guys seen this?" She opened her check cover and presented the neatly folded page ripped from Vanity Fair.

"It's Alex, can you believe it?"

Julia, who had never particularly cared for Brandi, was beginning to have a change of heart.

Santana's eyes popped. "Oh my God, is that Alex?"

"They airbrushed his package," Julia said, without looking at the torn out page, watching Melinda instead. Oh how she loved to watch her squirm.

"Such a shame, he's got a nice piece."

Julia lit a cigarette and smiled. The proverbial cat had been let out of the bag. Maybe it wouldn't be such a lame night after all.

"Where did you get this?" Dusty asked.

CHAPTER 14

JOHNSTON RESIDENCE — SEA VIEW, GA

"They're coming. It says so right there on the cover."

"Julia, that's *Gossip Weekly*," Melinda rebuffed. "It's a tabloid. Besides, it says he's gonna be in New York, not Georgia."

"No. He's coming. I can feel it."

Melinda rolled her eyes. "Communing with the spirits again?"

"God, I don't know why I put up with you," Julia snapped.

"I don't see anyone else breakin' down your door."

"Oh, please. I have plenty of friends."

"Whatever?" said Melinda with another eye roll.

Julia huffed and placed a hand on her hip. "You're the one who hates everybody."

This statement seemed to please Melinda. "You're right, I do."

"So," Julia asked, changing the subject, "thought any more about attending Parsons next year?"

She was used to her BFF's *shit don't stink* attitude and couldn't imagine missing her.

Melinda did not respond. Instead she stared at the magazine cover, lost to the conversation. Reading her thoughts, Julia twisted the knife.

"So what if Alex does come back? This is his home, you know."

Jimmy Ray swaggered into Melinda's bedroom, grinning, stoned as usual.

"What if he does, what if he doesn't, what if he does, what if he doesn't? Damn. Is that all you bitches talk about?"

"Fuck off, Jimmy Ray," Julia quipped.

"That's not what you said last night."

She flashed a sultry grin.

"That was last night."

Melinda just looked at them. *God, were they sleeping together again?* She cringed at the thought. Jimmy Ray was so stupid. He flopped down spread-eagle on her bed. She could never imagine doing anything with him again, not that they had done that much.

Before she was with Dusty, he had talked her into giving him a hand job. She hadn't really wanted to, but he promised to warn her in time. What he did, however, was clamp his hand over hers so she couldn't stop and erupted all over, ruining her favorite sweater. Since it was her first time ever doing anything with a boy, she had no idea what to expect and certainly hadn't realized there could be so much. She still remembered the whining sounds he made when he did it. What on Earth did Julia see in him?

"And what about tonight...?" Jimmy Ray asked Julia.

"If you're lucky..."

He started thrusting his hips in the air chanting over and over, "I'm gonna get me some."

Julia laughed.

Melinda looked heavenward. *Why?* She asked herself, glancing at the magazine.

"Aren't we going to be late?" she asked with a sigh.

"We've got plenty of time," Jimmy Ray said. "Relax."

He pulled Julia down on top of him. She shrieked with delight and they started making out.

Melinda rolled her eyes again, trying to ignore them. God, she wished Dusty wouldn't work so much. And she was appalled that he worked on cars for a living. After he recovered, he insisted on earning his own way and got a job washing cars for her father at the local Cadillac dealership. The Escalade had become the top-selling luxury SUV in the surrounding upscale communities, so there was "plenty of room for an ambitious young go-getter," according to Frank Johnston. Once Dusty graduated, there would be a full-time position in the Service Center, should he be interested.

The horn sounding from the driveway meant he had arrived at last. She peeked out her bedroom window. God, she hated that old truck. She would have to talk to her daddy about giving him something more appropriate. She turned from the window.

"Don't make me turn the hose on you two."

Jimmy Ray jumped to his feet and saluted, his erection tenting the front of his khaki shorts.

"Good Lord, Jimmy Ray," Melinda complained.

Julia laughed again. "It's just a dick."

Melinda turned on her heels and headed for the front door. They raced after her down the hall, and Jimmy Ray pushed ahead taking the stairs three at a time.

"Dusty, Dusty, I missed you so much," he laughed, flinging the front door open. "Pookie Bear, you're home."

Dusty scooted passed Jimmy Ray's outstretched arms into the foyer.

"Oh, no you don't." he laughed. "Get that thing away from me."

It was the latest in Jimmy Ray's horny horseplay: rubbing or pushing his hard on against one of his unsuspecting pals. Whether they were playing around in the pool or standing in line at the Quickie Mart, it was all the same to Jimmy Ray.

"Ignore them," Melinda said, hugging him. "How was your day?" she asked.

"Long."

He smelled like motor oil.

"Are you working in the garage again? I thought you were going to try sales?"

Not this again, he thought.

"You need to take a quick shower."

"Wanna join me?"

"I said quick."

"I can be quick."

"Can I be quick, Julia?" Jimmy Ray chased her through the great room. Melinda's eyes followed them, ignoring Dusty's comment.

He kissed her cheek. "I'll be down in five."

While undressing in her bedroom, Dusty spied the *Gossip Weekly* magazine. He glanced at the cover. He saw Alex and his superhot girlfriend, Andrea what's her name. He looked so different. He guessed they all did, staring at his naked reflection.

Melinda hated for him to walk around nude, even when her father was out of town and there was no threat of getting caught. This made him feel a little naughty and his skin tingled. He opened the magazine to the article and eyed the pictures of his friend and the beautiful model. They were on board a yacht in the French Riviera, Alex in a Speedo and Andrea sunbathing topless, the black bar across her breasts, courtesy of the entertainment mag, left nothing to the imagination.

He felt another kind of a tingle and his hand moved to his groin. Even though sex for Melinda had become less painful over the last year, she still complained about discomfort; so what he got was slow, boring missionary.

He gave a little tug. He hoped, knowing it wouldn't happen, that Melinda would joined him, if not in the shower, at least in the bedroom for some alone time. He needed some attention. His penis was half way up when he heard her calling from downstairs.

"Are you in the shower yet?"

He hurried to the bathroom and started the shower. He looked again at his naked reflection and saw he was now at full mast. He closed his eyes and a hand around his cock. *This won't take long at all.* His mind drifted back to the nights with Alex, the booze and the gadgets. All the porn and lube and the security of no interruptions had made for some wild times as well as the best orgasms Dusty had ever had. *No, not long at all,* he thought, sighing quietly; releasing the tensions of the day.

Δ

They sat at their usual table at the Crab House, enjoying another beautiful sunset, another blow out for the gang, their last night together before going off to college. Reece, the intellectual of the group, was attending Georgia Tech; and Jimmy Ray, the University of Georgia, as freshmen. Santana, after a grueling summer and early graduation, would attend art school in Savannah.

Melinda would soon be working on her degree in fashion merchandising at the Parsons School of Design in New York. She had always dreamed of modeling, but at five-seven with a girl-next-door-look, catalog work was the most she could hope for. And she would rather die than do that.

Julia opted to stay in Sea View where she would attend community college and hopefully convince Dusty to enroll as well.

"Oh shit," Julia said, pretending to suddenly be frazzled. "I forgot. Dusty, can you take a look at something on my car?"

Melinda looked at him. "Well, don't just sit there, Dusty. Go help her."

Julia stood. "You'll be back before the appetizers get here."

Dusty got up to follow Julia, kissing Melinda's forehead as he left.

"No funny stuff," Jimmy Ray remarked.

Melinda smirked, "Yeah, right."

Julia just smiled. "You have nothing to worry about."

She had already fucked Dusty years ago. She caught him one night on his way to Alex's after another agonizing night of no sex with Melinda. It had been quick and awkward, but that's what first times were.

Julia passed him a packed bowl as soon as they were out of sight of the restaurant's deck. What Melinda didn't realize was that she had to pull him away so he could smoke a little weed from time to time.

After Alex left and the whole back injury thing, he had stopped partying altogether. The dismal reality of what his life had become, compared to what he dreamed it might be, was a large pill to swallow. Julia's fear was that he would become rigid and retreat within himself—and that wasn't good for anyone. They had already lost Alex.

It was difficult in the beginning but eventually Dusty started to loosen up again and "blow off a little steam," as Julia liked to put it.

"God, I appreciate this," he said, taking the bowl. "I've been so tense lately."

"Anything else I can help you with?"

He smiled at her, trying to hold in the smoke. He remembered their time together. How could he forget? She was his first *and* she kept his secret. Everyone assumed he and Melinda had both been virgins when they had finally done it.

"Took care of that before we left," he joked, with hand motions.

"Oh my God, Melinda would die."

"Then she should put out a little more."

Julia was cool, one of the guys. She wasn't as pretty, technically, as Melinda, but very confident in whom she was. And she definitely had her own style. She made most of her clothes. Although a little over the top, they worked for her—especially since she maintained her five foot eight, size four frame.

"They're dredging up a lot of earth from somewhere and dumping it in the bay," she said.

He blew smoke skyward and passed the bowl, "The bay?"

She hit it and passed it back. "Yes, the bay, the island?" The island was nothing more than a tiny sand barge that broke the surface of the water. "I think it's Alex."

"Get outta here," he said giggling. "You always think it's Alex."

The pot was beginning to work its magic. Julia always had the best stuff.

"He always said he would build a house in the middle of the bay," she said. "God knows he's got enough money to do anything he wants."

She hit the bowl again. "Oh, come on. We all know he'll come home one day. He's supposed to be in New York with that model in a few months to launch Nasty Mama's clothing line."

"How do you know this shit?" he asked laughing.

"It's all over *E!*. Don't you ever watch TV?"

"I don't watch *E!*."

She dug deep into her shoulder bag and produced a flask.

"Here, take a shot or two."

80

He readily accepted with a sly grin. Another secret they shared. Julia grinned too. She liked him. She had always liked him. Long before Melinda even noticed him, but as was par for the course, Melinda Sue always got what she wanted. *She was so damned pretty.*

"Let's head back," she said.

"Yeah, I'm really gonna be hungry now."

"I would slow down on the food, if I were you?"

"What is that supposed to mean?"

"It means it's time for you to take up running again." She was right and he knew it. Even after a complete recovery and an okay from the doctors, Dusty refrained from any physical activity, except at work. He was aware that he had put on a few pounds, but he was a dude.

"Hey, I'm a guy."

"Yeah, but *we* have to look at you with your shirt off."

Point taken.

Δ

Dusty went jogging along the beach bright and early the next morning. It felt good to run again. There was a slight rain falling and the beach was quiet. He was lost in thought and unaware of how long he had been running when he neared the isthmus that connected the main land to whatever was happening in the bay. A lot of earth had been shifted around. Whatever it was, it was going to be enormous.

CHAPTER 15

AGENZIA TRASTEVER — ROME, ITALY

Andrea stepped into the living area of the apartment she and Alex had shared for the past three years. They were going out tonight. He had rented the entire upper level of the Piper Room, the most famous club in Rome and arranged a lavish extravaganza to celebrate her eighteenth birthday.

Andrea was wearing a provocatively cut, strapless black leather bustier and a matching leather mermaid skirt with barely enough room to breathe. The hemline fell to the floor with a multitude of red edged leather fish scales that flared dramatically from mid-calf into a three-foot train. The ensemble had been given to her by Dolce himself during Fashion Week in Paris, where she walked a staggering twenty-six shows, tying the record of the amazing Tyra Banks.

"Really Alex, the floor…? That's a Tom Ford tuxedo."

He was sitting Indian style at the glass-topped coffee table doing enormous lines of cocaine and had been for a while. It was going to be a hell of a night. She wondered if she should be wearing something with straps.

"Have one, Duckie?"

He stood and helped her to kneel with some difficulty, onto the plush area rug, where she did half a line.

"One more," he urged.

Cocaine had become a part of their lives shortly after Andrea began her modeling career. It was readily available and easily obtainable, so why not? Everybody did it, it seemed. They were young, rich and very, very beautiful. It was expected of them.

Alex was fiercely loyal to her and his promise. He laid the world at her feet, giving her everything she had ever wanted. People now admired her and treated her with respect—all because of him. And in return she was the perfect girlfriend.

She learned to read his every mood and catered to his every whim. They made frequent trips to Sicily where she asked to be told everything about Sofia. Andrea was mesmerized by the stories and by Josephine herself. She was so lovely and elegant in her manner.

Andrea soaked up everything there was to learn from the thirty-nine-year-old beauty and educated herself about food, wine and social etiquette. Coming to Europe with Alex had allowed her to reinvent herself and rise like the mythological phoenix from the ashes.

The modeling world only reinforced her drive and ambition. She possessed the confidence of a woman ten years her senior and at eighteen, her exotic allure electrified whenever and wherever present. She extended a hand and he helped her up.

"My God, you are beautiful," he said, holding her close. "Do you love me?"

He had had too much. She would have to hide the rest and ration it out to him.

"Of course I do."

He kissed her. He did love her. She was a clever girl and she would do anything for him. They attended all the right parties, knew all the right people, and went to all the right places.

And now New York was calling. The music industry's latest mogul, Nasty Mama, a woman who was a cross between Missy Elliot and Jay Z, was looking to launch a new lifestyle line and wanted to use the two of them to "set it off"—runway, TV and print. Alex, always a fan of Nasty Mama, was thinking about it.

A trip back to the U.S. would surely lead to a trip back home. He had unfinished business there, but those thoughts were for another time. Tonight was about fun. He had tested her loyalty before. Tonight, he would test her again.

"Come along, my sweet. The car is waiting."

CHAPTER 16

PIPER ROME — ROME, ITALY

The club was packed with a line halfway down the block. Alex and Andrea strolled hand in hand right by everyone up to the front entrance where the velvet rope was lifted. They walked past the bouncers and headed for the VIP section. It was New Year's Eve and they were entering the Piper Room once again. Everyone knew them. Everyone wanted to be them or be *with* them. This made the selection process that much easier. They invited a dozen or so partiers into the area reserved for them and twenty-five other friends from the industry. Everyone was drinking and in full swing, but Alex, never one to mix business with pleasure, ignored the invited guests.

There were always the approved party crashers, all handpicked and all with potential. Andrea had grown used to the three-ways and it made no difference to her whether the third was male or female. She could separate what they did in bed with others from what they did in bed together. With others it was sport. She was glad, however, that there was only one other whenever the mood struck him; orgies were not her thing. And equally as glad that it was always a group effort and not up to her to perform dog and pony tricks. He never degraded her or made her feel used. Still, she secretly hoped for the day he grew tired of *entertaining*.

But as the wee hours of morning approached and Alex's mood darkened, it was obvious that day had not yet come. She prepared herself for the worst. She had stopped drinking hours earlier and slowed down with the cocaine, unlike Alex—and that was exactly what led them to the spot they were now in.

She had noticed him the moment they arrived. It wasn't so much the tan or sun-kissed locks, no doubt from time spent south of the equator, but more the alpha vibe Jean Paul exuded that grabbed Alex's attention. Soon they were engaged in bro-on-bro party games, testosterone-driven and to-the-death competitive, surrounded by countless satellite wannabes. It was obvious to Andrea before they even left the club that things could get out of hand and even more evident on the cab ride.

Jean Paul was all over her the second they climbed into the back of the yellow Fiat. His willingness, yet unruliness, had started early on. But Alex had insisted, in spite of her protests. Damn her luck. The guy was perfect— the right height, right build, and even the eyes were right. She knew Alex was too coked up for sex, but was secure in knowing he would be there. He was already waiting at the hotel. It was part of the game.

The paparazzi too, had become a part of it, as well as other celebs. They had been photographed leaving with another woman early on, so now the rule was to time their exit right after someone more famous was leaving. This way, they would not be followed.

Another rule was to pick a random hotel off the radar where no one would suspect The Beautiful would be caught dead—preferably one with no security cameras.

Jean Paul seemed a little agitated that another man was there, but seemed to forget once he was plowing away.

Andrea, feeling uncomfortable, asked for a breather, but Jean Paul would hear nothing of it.

"Shut up bitch," he hissed in his heavy French accent.

"Get off of me," she said, trying to free herself.

He slapped her hard across the face and forced her back down on the bed.

"We finish when I say," he spat.

"Funny, I don't see it that way," Alex said, placing a gun barrel firmly against the Frenchman's temple and cocking the hammer. It was an unmistakable sound. Andrea moved to the other side of the bed. She knew it wasn't loaded, but Jean Paul did not. The gun, however, seemed to sober him up a bit and the apologies started flowing.

Too little, too late... Alex kept the pistol aimed right at him.

"Get the strap on, my love," Alex said coldly.

She knew the night was going to be hell, but she did what she was told. Jean Paul was ordered to get on all fours. He protested when Andrea smeared the lube, but did not react when she entered him. The deranged look in the American's eye warned him that he could die tonight.

Any humiliation was better than death, especially the humiliation of enjoying what was happening to him. The bully was being bullied and it was turning him on. As much as he willed against it, the constant contact with his prostate was overwhelming, and soon he was moaning and pulling at himself, headed for release. When it came, it was like a tidal wave and he bucked wildly against the rubber appendage.

"I think he quite enjoyed that," Alex laughed, tossing the gun aside. "It's not even loaded. *I* need a shower. And don't bother searching for money, there isn't any."

Once they heard the water running, it was Andrea who started to apologize, but the sudden backhand to her cheek silenced her. She would have to have a serious talk with Alex.

Jean Paul darted for the bathroom, grabbing a heavy pewter candle stick on the way. He cried out as he raised his weapon to strike. This proved to be a crucial mistake, giving Alex time to react, the candle stick striking his shoulder instead of his intended skull. By the time Andrea reached the bathroom, it was over. Jean Paul was on the floor of the shower, a stream of blood flowing from his head down the drain.

CHAPTER 17

RITZ CENTRAL PARK — NEW YORK

"Holy shit, you guys. Look at this!"

Julia grabbed the remote and turned up the volume.

"Andrea Sorcosi, the latest superstar to cause shock waves in the fashion world was taken into custody by Italian authorities around 5 a.m. this morning after a night of partying. The couture model was questioned then released in connection with the death of French Ambassador Jean Luc Follier's only son, international playboy, Jean Paul.

The raven-haired beauty was spotted by photographers exiting the Piper Room with Jean Paul around 3:30 this morning, before apparently flagging a cab to an as of yet undisclosed location, where the lifeless body was discovered after a frantic 911 call from Ms. Sorcosi, herself.

Alex Vandiveer, son of near billionaire, Baron Vandiveer, was spotted entering the club earlier with Ms. Sorcosi, though he was not with the pair as they left the Piper Room, fueling rumors of a possible rift between the otherwise inseparable couple.

Ms. Sorcosi was visibly shaken as she slowly walked out of the Rome precinct, clutching at her side, wearing dark glasses and appearing to have bruises on her arms and face, a face hailed as one of the most beautiful of all time.

Authorities tell us Alex Vandiveer will be called in later today for voluntary questioning. So far no charges have been brought in what seems to be a case of self-defense.

We will be watching this story closely and reporting to you live. This is Eva Moretti, European correspondent for Entertainment Tonight, *signing off."*

In New York to bring in 2010 with a bang, the gang was in various stages of waking or sobering up. The guys were rummaging for food.

"Oh my, God," Melinda said. "She killed someone?"

"Who killed someone?" Jimmy Ray wanted to know, helping himself to cold crab dip.

"Andrea Sorcosi killed some French guy named Jean Paul Follier."

"Who...?"

"Probably one of their soap operas, bro," Reece said.

"No," Melinda jumped to her feet. "Alex's girlfriend."

"It was self-defense," Julia replied.

"Quiet," Dusty said, moving toward the TV.

"Could you ever actually kill someone?" Santana asked.

"Oh, God, never," Melinda gasped.

"I mean, if your life depended on it?"

"I could kill," Julia confessed.

Melinda scoffed. "Yeah, what wouldn't you do?"

It was times like this that made Julia want to tell Melinda that she had fucked Dusty first.

"Hell, I know I could choke a muthafucka out," Jimmy Ray boasted. "I'll break a bitch down!" he shouted, eyeing Reece and taking a karate stance.

"Don't even think about it," Reece warned.

"Shit," Dusty said when the segment ended. "There's got to be something on another station."

Melinda grabbed the remote. Surely this would break those two up. She knew exactly which channel to choose.

"There," Dusty said.

They all gathered around, watching in silence while an Italian entertainment channel broadcast the story, complete with plenty of coverage of Andrea on the runway and just as much of her with authorities. There was also plenty of coverage on Alex, her billion-dollar-heir boyfriend.

CHAPTER 18

POLICE HEADQUARTERS — ROME, ITALY

The Italian authorities spent hours questioning Alex. Even though they suspected there was more to the story, they released him with no charges filed. Although there was no problem putting Alex in the room, there was no way to prove he was present at the time of the actual crime.

Andrea's exam and rape kit, along with evidence collected at the scene, all lined up with her story. The toxicology screens and coroner's reports also supported her claims of kinky sex and drug use; listing the presence of ecstasy, cocaine, oxycodone, Viagra and marijuana in the deceased's bloodstream.

A horrified Ambassador Follier, though distraught, thought it best to keep such tawdry details from leaking to the press. He had the records immediately sealed, hoping to avoid any scandal or public ridicule. His family was one of the oldest and most prestigious, known throughout Western Europe, and he would not allow even this tragedy to tarnish the Follier name.

He had warned Jean Paul repeatedly about his outrageous life style, but he refused to listen. And now it was too late.

The investigation was closed after only a few weeks, thanks to the presence of Baron Vandiveer's high-powered U.S. attorneys. Alex had put in a call to "Uncle Leo" and promised a huge cash incentive if his father was kept out of the loop.

Within days of having their passports returned, the two boarded a private jet bound for Paris. Neither spoke of Jean Paul until they were buckled in, preparing for takeoff. He glanced lovingly at her, still wearing her Chanel sunshades.

Δ

She had started wearing the big ones to cover her bruised cheek, compliments of Jean Paul. The bruised ribs were courtesy of Alex. She had forced him to rough her up to aid in the self-defense story. He gave her three brutish punches in all and cried the whole time.

But she was tough. She'd had to be tough for herself her whole life and now she was being tough for Alex. There was nothing she wouldn't do for him.

The self-defense story had also been her idea. It was the only way, since Baron had also warned Alex about *his* lifestyle choices. When he first started appearing in the European tabloids, leaving nightclubs, high and obviously drunk, his father had sworn he would resume control of his trust, if he became an embarrassment in any way and force him to settle in New York. Alex did not want to live with his father.

Andrea turned to look at him and winced. Her ribs were still sore, but the bruises on her arms had faded and her face no longer showed any signs of the black eye he had given her.

"I will never forget what you've done for me," he whispered.

She remained silent. It had been her idea to tell the police that she was alone with Jean Paul that night. Alex had been pretty shaken by the horrific turn of events, but she had instantly leapt into action. It took him a long agonizing moment to actually hit her the first time, but it was over now.

She had evened the score. He had saved her, and now she had saved him. There was no reason to doubt him. He had never lied to her.

They flew to Paris and checked into the Pierre Hotel right off the rue Saint Martin. Gaultier was staying there as well. He was showing nearby at 325 Paris-3e and was a friend of the Euro-American couple, as he referred to them.

Andrea had walked many times for him and was doing so again the last week of January as a personal favor. Alex, though less than thrilled about it, was also committed to Gaultier and four other shows in as many days. He was not dealing well with Jean Paul's death.

Andrea tried to make him understand it had been an accident, but he felt responsible. If only Alex had thrown Jean Paul out instead of teaching him a lesson.

She kept as close an eye on him as was possible during the shows. Hanging out behind the scenes in order to keep tabs on Alex was not a problem with the designers; however, Fiona was not so understanding of Andrea's decision to take an unexpected, undetermined leave of absence. The conversation had begun with, *but you were cleared darling* and ended with *remember you're under contract.*

The agency was also less than thrilled with the loss of income, but Fiona conceded, leaving the door open for her return. There was no one hotter at the moment than Andrea Sorcosi, and her fire was a fire that would burn for decades.

She was pleased that Alex had only agreed to do a few shows. He, too, was a hot commodity, fulfilling beautifully the role of billionaire bad boy. His ever-increasing presence in the gossip mags fueled his public persona and popularity.

The Yves Saint Laurent show went off without a hitch, with designer Stefano Pilati gifting him a crocodile coat and matching shoes as a special thank you. When he was good he was the best, but when he was bad, he was the worst.

He did his thing for Gaultier, walking like the star he was becoming, and even granted interviews to the press and entertainment reporters from local and international television stations. But things took a downward turn on Friday night after the Givenchy show when he insisted on going out. So out they went and out they stayed, barely arriving in time for Viktor & Rolf's 10 a.m. showing the following morning and enraging designer Renzo Rosso, who was still new to the label. Alex's death warmed over look did nothing for the modern, light-hearted whimsy of the line featuring bowler hats and pipe motifs.

Designer Kazuyuki Kumagai, on the other hand, was thrilled when he turned up green around the gills for the debut of her fall collection. His rode hard look was perfect for the edgy, gothic, washed-out leathers.

CHAPTER 19

SOMEWHERE OVER THE ATLANTIC

Andrea Sorcosi was at the top of her game. She and Alex were seated in first class on their way to the U.S. and New York's Fashion Week. Early February meant it would be cold and grey in the city. And there were the memories, so many bad memories of her mother and her days at Sally's. And, of course, there were *the men.*

Alex was dosed and she was drifting toward slumber when suddenly she was there. She could feel the warm water of the lavender bath, smell the aroma therapy candles mixed with stale cigarette smoke and cheap perfume.

Returning to New York would indeed be bittersweet. Her mother, Maria Santos, had been a prostitute who worked in a brothel on the lower East Side for a woman named Sally McCullen and she, too, had been top girl—until she broke the cardinal rule of falling in love with a client.

Andrea could hear Sally's voice like it was yesterday: *"Fallin' in love with a man who could never be with a girl like her."*

Sally told Andrea the story many times when she came to her room, bringing special oils for the bath, to "prepare her" for her own clients. She always talked to

Andrea like she was one of the girls, chewing her gum—*"to disguise the liquor smell,"* she would say. Sally knew full well that any daughter of Maria Santos had the potential to become a real money maker.

Δ

He came to see Maria up to four times a week, and she was my top girl. Who was I to argue; it was good for business, some hot shot lawyer. You know the type. Works in the city and runs off to Connecticut on the weekends to be with the family. Then he married the daughter of a partner. Married his self, right up the ladder, he did. Then he stopped comin' 'round so much.

Sadly, Maria also had another love, cocaine. I tried to warn her about the stuff, but she said it helped her. God, she loved that man so much. She was hurt you know. He loved her, too. We all knew it.

But it would have ruined his climb to the top if anyone found out. Girls like us... The oldest profession in the world, but the world doesn't see it that way.

It almost killed her when he went on his honeymoon, a month long stay in Europe. She couldn't handle it after a while. Then the crack came and I couldn't handle that.

When he got back, things were different. He got a big promotion and couldn't see her as often; she got hooked. I hated to see her go, but there was nothing I could do. Crack is bad for business, honey. You were born, thank God, before the crack years. That's why you're so perfect, just like she was.

Ana you were just a baby when she left. We begged her to leave you here. Hell, with all us girls, there was someone with you twenty-four-seven. And we loved you so much. You were that bright light in the darkness, you know. You gave us hope, but Maria wouldn't have it.

We kept in touch, here and there. She told me when he started coming around again. But his wife was a smart girl and men always get careless. Like I said, Maria and I kept in touch.

Thank God, she called me that day. She said her ship was finally comin' in. When I didn't hear from her again, I started to worry. Called her for three days, then decided to take action. Good thing I had that extra door key or you might not be here...

Δ

Andrea's eyes opened. Her heart was beating fast and a trickle of sweat was running down her side. She had been dreaming, but was safe now, with Alex by her side. She had been too young at the time to form actual memories of the man Sally talked about, but she did remember the other men and the crack pipe.

Slowly, the men in the nice suits were replaced by day laborers, and Maria never smiled again. Then one day, one of the suits came back and killed Maria Santos.

Ana was hiding in the coat closet just like always; but this time was special because her mother had said so. She was wearing her shiny pink princess dress, which was a little small, but she still liked it. There was a tiny crack in the door jam and Ana saw everything—everything through the eyes of a nine-year-old girl.

When he pounced on her mother, Ana thought he was in a hurry. They hadn't even bothered to go into the bedroom and he still had his coat on. It ended as abruptly as it had started. But when he got up, her mother had not.

He left quickly and Ana waited. She was always supposed to wait until her mother unlocked the door. So, she sat there in that closet waiting, until finally the front door opened and in walked a giant man and the woman with red hair: Tony and Sally.

She waited for three whole days, but her mother never got up. Sally heard the faint tapping on the door, and Ana fainted as soon as she was freed.

Sally took the girl before placing an anonymous call to the police, vowing to never allow the state to get a hold of her best girl's kid.

But no one knew that that little girl was the fashion world's newest sensation. Ana Maria Santos was dead, now. Andrea Sorcosi was on top of the world.

Δ

She glanced lovingly at Alex. He was sleeping soundly. The three zanies and vodka stinger had done the trick. She had a feeling they would not be returning to Italy any time soon and wondered how long they might stay in New York.

Nasty Mama, in true gangster style, was thrilled with the trashy tabloid and media coverage of Jean Paul's death and was planning an insane launch party to introduce A&A Jeans for Women during New York's Fall Fashion Week. And the slogan, thought up by Mama herself–*I'd kill for a pair of A&A Jeans*–was as tasteless as it was deliciously salacious.

Alex was uneasy about it, but Andrea knew the industry well enough to know that it would guarantee enormous sales. She also knew the type who could afford three hundred dollar jeans.

She also wondered when he was planning his return home. He had been away for three years, running from a painful past. The fact that they were both abandoned as children was the strongest link in their relationship—stronger even than the Jean Paul fiasco.

Loyalty was everything in their world, a world that so far, only had room for two. But eventually he would go back home; he was rooted there. And since Alex spoke so often of his long lost best friend and the plans he had for him, she also knew he would become a part of their lives. The only question was when?

Surely he was over that ridiculous nonsense with that ridiculous girl by now. So, where did that leave her? She pushed the thoughts from her head. Alex *did* love her and she loved him, but he loved Dusty, too. And three never worked.

At any rate, there was plenty of time to make those decisions, she thought as they climbed into the back of the waiting limousine, courtesy of Baron Vandiveer. Andrea was less than thrilled about coming face to face with Alex's father, but she would cross that bridge, too, when she got to it.

In the meantime, their schedules were packed full with Mercedes Benz Week. She had finally given into Fiona's threats and gone back to work, booking shows with Herrera, Von Furstenberg, Hervé, Mendel, Narciso and Badgley Mischka. They both landed the Calvin Klein Collections, and Alex was walking for Nicholas K and Victorinox as well.

Obviously, they did not need the money, but Andrea enjoyed the adrenaline rush of it all. She was playing the role of a lifetime, and half the fashion world worshipped her on the runways. Europe had embraced her exotic look, and now she was about to explode onto the New York scene, being hailed the new woman of color. Her looks transcended race and everyone wanted her, so she could pick and choose.

There were also meetings lined up with Ralph Lauren to discuss a new perfume and Michael Kors was interested in Andrea being the face of his new accessories line. There was also a chance at the ever-coveted Victoria Secret contract. Not since the heyday of Kimora Lee had a multiracial girl been in such high demand.

Andrea breathed a sigh of contentment as the limo cruised down Astoria Boulevard toward 31st Street. Crossing the Queensboro Bridge into Manhattan in a chauffeur-driven limousine was a far cry from the day she took the subway to 57th Street. A melancholy smile curled the corners of her mouth from the memory of her with that backpack full of stolen money and that faded black and white photograph, searching for God knows what.

And indeed, God knew. He led her straight to Alex. Nothing but divine intervention could have brought her so far in such a short amount of time.

She glanced at Alex. He was snoring softly, his eyes shielded by twelve hundred dollar sunglasses. She laughed at the thought of that girl with the five thousand in stolen cash. That girl, who had suffered at the hands of so many, would suffer no more. Andrea Sorcosi was in control now, and no one could ever hurt Ana Maria again.

CHAPTER 20

PRINCE & THOMPSON — SOHO, NY

Melinda stared at her reflection in the mirror. She was preparing for bed in her room in the New York apartment she shared with roommate Audrey. Smiling, she lay down the sterling silver, ivory inlaid brush after her usual one hundred strokes.

She took pride in the fact that she was a natural blonde and her eyes were the bluest of blues. She and Dusty made the perfect couple, just like Barbie and Ken, as everybody said. And he was the sweetest, most caring guy she had ever met.

So why was it that she thought about and even dreamed about Alex Vandiveer? How could she hate him so much and want him so badly? Why did everything have to be so hard all the time? Her daddy gave her everything she ever wanted, but somehow it wasn't enough. She knew she was beautiful, but in an ordinary way, and she did have the perfect boyfriend, but...

She slid into bed. *But...* she thought—*but what?* Melinda forced her mind to happier thoughts. She had to admit she got a lot of attention from the men in New York due to her southern charm, and there were going to be parties all weekend to keep her occupied and boost her ego. *But...there it was again,* she sighed. *It was Alex. It had always been Alex.*

In the beginning, she thought that by going out with Dusty she could get closer to him and maybe even make him want her. Then, when they found out he had all that money, it was too much. And now, not only was he in New York for fashion week, he was becoming famous thanks to the A&A Jeans deal.

The launch party was one of the hottest tickets in town. Thanks to Nasty Mama's outrageous budget, the event was guaranteed to be unforgettable, packed full of A-listers from both music and film. And the ad campaigns were everywhere from bus stops to electronic billboards in Time Square.

Marg Brener, a photographer known for her black-and-white nudes entitled "Women from Around the World," was brought on board and produced, as was expected, spectacular results. Andrea was featured wearing the jeans topless with Alex nude and wrapped seductively around her.

Not since Posh and Becks had a couple made such a splash before even crossing the pond. The buzz surrounding Andrea was only heightened by her involvement in the mysterious death of French Ambassador Follier's son.

The whole thing was like some media blitz homecoming and even worse, Melinda feared she would run into them at some point.

Thanks to her position at *Glamour* she managed to score tickets to the Calvin Klein shows and made sure she would not be alone, just in case. Julia and Santana were flying in for a week of shopping, fashion and girl time. There was no way she was missing CK, but she would definitely need a little support if there was any chance of bumping into Alex and this Andrea person.

She shivered beneath the heavy comforter; it was freezing in New York. Why couldn't Dusty take some time off and come keep her warm she wondered. Who cared if he had just been up for New Year's Eve? All that money was just lying there, untouched. To this day she could not understand why he never cashed the checks that Baron sent. Damn, she was so close to the Vandiveer pie.

Δ

Fashion week was a blur and wildly exciting. Andrea was well received and created quite an uproar behind the scenes with photographers and reporters. New York embraced the young couple and they had no problem getting into any of the parties or nightclubs.

Alex partied hard. Almost too hard, loving yet hating the attention and, once again, did not fare well with the designers. His haggard appearance was by no means appreciated, but the press ate it up. The tabloids loved him and he always delivered, teetering, but somehow managing not to go over the edge. Everyone assumed it was his not-so-model girlfriend that kept him somewhat, in line. No one knew who she was, a mystery that also worked in her favor. True, no one knew where she had come from, but it was obvious to all where she was going. And it all seemed like a dream.

She was the girl with the old soul. That's what they called her. By all accounts, she and her wealthy boyfriend were very happy. But the question was there, on the tip of everyone's tongue: *Where was Alex when his girlfriend was brutally attacked?*

Celebrities–and the wannabes–love a good scandal, and they were all there: the starlets, Hollywood heavy hitters, rock stars, aging supermodels, and television's latest crop of hot young studs—not to mention the regulars: Rhianna, Katy, Justin and the William Rast crew, Nicole, Blake and the Twins.

The A&A Jeans bash was indeed, off the chain and, of course, they were all there, too. She saw them and they saw her. Some of the faces and names were different, but the scene was definitely the same. Hundreds of the rich and famous, the beautiful people, all huddled together under a giant tent, smiling and preening for one another.

Δ

Unfortunately for Melinda, second assistants were rarely on any lists, so none of the parties were accessible. Their seats for the Calvin Klein Men's Collection were less than fantastic; they had been nowhere near front row, but at least they were still in attendance. Amazing, but neither up close, nor personal, where Melinda was sure she saw Andrea seated front and center between Rosario and Mila.

Julia and Santana were, however, sufficiently impressed, especially since their passes allowed them behind-the-scenes access after the show. Alex, ghastly pale, but definitely recognizable as he prowled the catwalk, seemed to vanish as soon as the show was over.

It was Julia's idea to go searching for him, and she frantically pushed her way through the crowd, only to realize they were too late—disappointing, but not surprising.

Julia, forever diligent, casually asked until at last someone had the dish. Apparently the couple of the moment were slumming it up in the Hamptons.

Afterwards, the three girls headed to a bar in SoHo where all the students of the arts hung out.

Here, they were able to stand out as the girls back from the Calvin Klein Show—and yes, they would be attending the Women's Collection two nights later.

They were crowded into a large booth with several stagehands and set designers from the theatre district on the upper level of Lani Kai, a Hawaiian themed fusion bar located on Thompson Street near Melinda's loft apartment. For reasons unbeknownst to her, everybody was flipping out over Julia's homemade top, especially the gay boys. In her opinion, there were too many ruffles around the neck and ties and bows and more ties around the waist. Too much, Melinda thought, but she was used to Julia's over-the-top outfits.

When the topic finally turned back to the Calvin Klein show, she was able to once again become the center of attention, usually her favorite place to be, but not this time.

"Yeah," Julia was saying. "And seeing Alex on that runway brought back so many memories."

"VanDee…! Shut the fuck up! "Broadway Jarrod, from Brooklyn, always over reacted.

"We grew up together, didn't Melinda tell you?" Of course she didn't, Julia thought.

"Melinda knows VanDee, my one and only, and she didn't tell me." A meticulously plucked eyebrow shot upward and he glared at her. "How *very* southern of you…"

"How am I supposed to keep track of who you're in love with from week to week?" Melinda asked, making a feeble attempt at defending herself.

"I'm the vice president of his fan club!" he shot back.

A fan site materialized after the nude photos from the D&G underwear shoot appeared on the Internet.

"Tell me everything," Jarrod insisted.

"Yes, Melinda," Julia said. "Tell everything."

"There's nothing to tell. We went to school together like she said."

Julia rolled her eyes, dramatically. Broadway Jarrod liked this one.

"We *grew* up together, for cryin' out loud," Julia said. "We hung out together—all our fuckin' lives!"

"And you never told me this?" Jarrod asked. You know he is to be my husband one day. You are not a friend."

The rest of the group was looking their way now. Jarrod was good at attracting attention.

"Just what did you think I was going to do?" Melinda wanted to know.

"Give him my digits!"

Everyone laughed.

"Well, you never know," Jarrod countered with a head toss. "I could be his type."

"Get real!"

"You know, Jarrod," Santana piped in, "he's with one of the most beautiful women in the world."

"Have you ever seen Jarrod in a dress?" one of the guys asked.

More laughs.

"Well?" Jarrod asked, ignoring them and focusing on Melinda.

"We grew up together. He moved away. End of story."

"You drove him away," Santana said.

They were all grown up now. It felt good not to hold back. They were no longer in high school where Melinda reigned supreme. Seeing Alex tonight had been jarring.

"Oooohh, dirt...!" Jarrod gasped. He lived for this shit. "Spill it."

"There's no dirt," said Melinda. "He just moved away."

Julia fueled the fire.

"Yeah, after a fight with your *boyfriend*, his *best friend;* a fight you caused."

"Can we drop this? We were just kids."

Julia scoffed. "I need a bump. Anybody got any coke?"

"Mary does," Jarrod said gesturing toward the girl sitting beside him. "Let's go girl."

There was no way he was passing up a chance for dish on little Ms. Perfect. They hung out, but he knew she judged him. Everything came so easy to girls like her: pretty, blonde Barbie Doll girls with big, baby blues. It made him want to vomit. He gave a little smirk and another head toss leading the way toward the bathrooms.

CHAPTER 21

THE CRAB HOUSE — SEA VIEW, GA

Dusty followed Julia and the hostess to their usual table. There was no longer a need for the large patio table, now that everyone was gone.

It was Dusty's Saturday off from the dealership, so they decided to make a day of it. After enjoying a lovely breakfast with mimosas followed by a couple of bowls of weed and more Mimosas at Julia's, they moved on to the Crab House for lunch and Margaritas.

He was doing well at MelFrank and Julia, despite her usual *"I couldn't give a fuck"* attitude was acing all her classes. His mother and Walter had eventually moved back into her house, but Dusty remained in the big house alone. He closed off all the rooms except for his bedroom and the kitchen, making it easier to manage. He also dismissed the help. Things were a little overwhelming at times; his life had changed so drastically, now that Alex was gone.

The checks still came for household wages and expenses, and checks for him, which he never used. He felt he should earn his own way. It had been different when Alex bought him stuff, but without him, Dusty didn't feel right about spending Baron's money.

He was already buzzing from the earlier mimosas and was grateful when the appetizer arrived. The server also brought their second round of margaritas.

He and Julia had grown into a comfortable routine and genuinely enjoyed each other's company. He was aware that she once had a crush on him but by the time he had figured it out, he and Melinda were together.

"God, we had so much fun in New York."

"Yeah, it was great," Dusty replied, not really listening.

Julia just rolled her eyes and continued with her story. Of the group, she was the one who talked about him the most.

"I wish we could have seen Alex. You know he's still in New York. They're shooting the commercials for A&A Jeans."

"How do you know this stuff?" Dusty asked, dipping a pita chip into the spicy spinach artichoke dip.

She shrugged. "I love the celebs, what can I tell you? I especially love the ones that are our friends." She searched for her cigarette case.

"You know you can't smoke in here," Dusty said.

"One puff..."

"No puffs."

She closed her purse. *Note to self,* she thought, *look into e-cigs.*

"Remember how shy he was as a kid?" Julia asked.

Dusty remembered another side of Alex, a side no one else knew existed. Everyone thought that because Alex was quiet, he was shy or weird—but the truth was, he was just listening. There had been many long, nightly conversations between the two boys growing up.

"...and he was so cute," Julia continued. "...although he never really talked to anyone, well except you, and then boom—turns into Mr. Party at sixteen. God, I miss those days."

Dusty nodded, wishing he had made different choices, but the past was the past.

"And it wasn't just the money and the trips and the boat and all that other shit. It was him, you know? Hell, we loved him *before* all that shit."

"Yeah, I really miss him too."

"He looked so good on that runway. And Andrea Sorcosi..." Julia wagged her hand about. "Hot, hot, hot..."

She signaled the waitress for another cocktail.

"Yeah?" he asked munching on the dip.

"I think he's coming home."

Dusty smiled, "Here we go again."

"Look," she said. "He went to Europe—we know that. My guess is Sicily. That's where his mother's family is."

She looked out over the horizon and shook her head, suddenly lost in a memory.

"God, that's all Margarette used to talk about," she said. "I'll never forget the tea party we had, when she babysat for me that weekend. She used the most exquisite china from Rome. It was so beautiful. Anyway, I'm guessing they'll want to stay away from Europe for a while."

"What makes you say that?" Dusty asked.

"The whole Jean Paul what's-his-name thing; I mean God only knows what really happened that night. Wouldn't you want to distance yourself from something like that?"

She made sense, but then again, Julia always made sense.

"Know what I remember most about that tea party?" Dusty asked, changing the subject. "Your Cindy Brady curls."

She couldn't help laughing. "Shut up, I hated those friggin' pig tails. Jesus, I was ten. My mother is such a psycho."

"She is kinda nuts."

"It's all those fuckin' pills she pops," Julia quipped.

They laughed that uncomfortable laugh friends share when there's really nothing funny.

Courtney Roenstein was notorious for her antics at public and private events alike. She was always the talk of Sea View's social scene, but they both knew why Courtney popped those pills.

She couldn't deal with the fact that her second husband, the successful therapist and author, molested her only daughter; or that she stayed with him anyway. Courtney also had a hard time dealing with the fact that Julia had been the one strong enough to put him behind bars.

The whole sordid mess was all very scandalous. Abe Roenstein had authored three best-sellers on the subject of good parenting. The media had a field day with twelve-year-old Julia stuck right in the middle. She sent her step-father to jail and her mother ended up with the money. The lawyers got their share but the royalties from book sales and income from a family trust meant there was plenty left.

Julia stopped laughing. "How's *your* mother?" she asked.

"She and Walter seem to be very happy."

"That's nice."

"Yeah, she deserves it," Dusty said. "My dad really scarred her and... well, that whole thing is just fucked up."

"What is it with fucked-up daddy things?" Julia pushed her chair back and stood. "Excuse me, I need a line."

She headed for the ladies' room. He wouldn't say she did a lot of coke, but she did have her fun with it.

After their long lunch they called a cab and headed over to South Isle. The gates were locked now, but they could see the significant progress made on the grounds.

They made their way, with some difficulty, to the back of the property where they discovered two sets of stairs leading up to a sweeping deck and more locked gates. It was all quite impressive.

They sat out on the beach, smoking weed and drinking from a flask.

"He's coming home," Julia said. "I can feel it"

Dusty didn't say anything. What was there to say? *Wasn't it his fault that Alex was gone?*

"Jeez Louise." She sighed, lit a cigarette and blew smoke into the air. "I don't even know why I bother sometimes. Anyway, he's coming back and everything will be right with the world again. It's in the cards."

"The cards...?"

"Yes, astrology, it's my new thing."

Good ole' Julia, always something new, always something to talk about. He *did* enjoy her company. He wished Melinda was a little more like her, then immediately felt guilty.

Melinda was just spoiled. When her parents divorced, it was decided that her little brother would live with their mother and Melinda would stay with their father. She had always been daddy's little girl and on the high-maintenance side, whereas Julia was kicked back and easy going; and she had been his first. Dusty smiled at the memory. She ambushed him on the beach after he'd endured another sexless night with Melinda. He had not been able to argue with her *or* the bulge in his pants.

"I don't even want to know what you're grinning about," Julia said waving a dismissive hand.

Her words pulled him out of his trance.

"So what's the answer?"

"What was the question?" he asked.

She rolled her eyes and blew more smoke.

"Are you going to New York for Melinda's birthday?"

It was quickly approaching.

"Sure, I'm going," he said.

"Well you don't have to sound so excited about it." She grinned and leaned forward. "Is there trouble in paradise?" she teased.

Nothing would thrill Julia more, but not because she wanted him for herself. What happened between them was ancient history as far as she was concerned. She just felt he deserved more.

"Don't be silly," Dusty said. "Melinda and I are fine, just fine."

That, he had to admit was the problem. Everything was fine. Fine, but not as in dandy, fine as in boring.

"Tsk, tsk..."

She stared at him, grateful that they had remained close friends. He was so kind and good, everything she was not, but their secret tied them together.

Julia sighed and sat back. "I was so hoping for something, anything, no matter how small to go wrong for little Ms. Perfect."

"You don't really mean that," he said.

She blew smoke into the air. "Of course I do."

There was a fall coming. The cards said so.

CHAPTER 22

SOHO, NEW YORK

Frank Johnston booked half a dozen hotel rooms and secured a ballroom for Melinda's twenty-first birthday bash. Everyone, including Dusty, flew in for the weekend and the partying ensued. There were theatre tickets for Thursday night, dinner reservations for Friday night and a full scale event planned for Saturday night to culminate the festivities. Melinda's official birthday was April 1st, but never to be the fool, she always celebrated on the Saturday closest to the official day.

Noreen was, as always, by her man's side. She and Frank arrived on Wednesday night to take care of any last minute details, Noreen's idea, while Walter and Caroline, acting as unofficial chaperons, landed Thursday morning.

The Daniels arrived later that afternoon, along with Naomi Jackson, minus her husband. Courtney Roenstein, to everyone's relief, would not be in attendance.

Their kids were all grown up now. Still it was hard letting go. Frank never imagined a time when he wouldn't worry about his little girl, but truth be known, he was proud to see that she had managed to turn the stubborn willfulness of her youth into a fierce, persistent independence. Surviving New York was proof that she was going to be alright while carving her own way.

After dinner on Friday night, the gang headed over to Mercury Lounge on Houston Street for dancing and more drinking before ending up at Madame X. In the dimly lit crimson bordello parlor, they reminisced about summers past growing up in Sea View and Alex, much to Melinda's chagrin.

Saturday was a different story entirely. With Broadway Jarrod's help, they managed to score Bucfifdeybak, the latest Indy sensation, to play for the *Melinda Takes Manhattan* themed party. Melinda had been allowed a hundred invitation-only guests, still more food had to be purchased last minute.

Between her position at the magazine, school and people she had met on the club scene over the past three years, there must have been closer to two hundred crammed into the ballroom by the time the band started to play.

Frank, thanks to Noreen's stern urging, had been smart enough to have the bar switch to cash once the band went on, so he gladly agreed to the additional food cost. Still, hotel security showed up at twelve forty-five to shut the party down. None of the guests seemed to mind, because New York was the city that never slept.

The crew from Sea View along with a couple dozen others, including Broadway Jarrod, proceeded over to Niagara on Avenue A to finish off a spectacular evening.

This was the night Melinda first noticed Martin, slouched over the bar running game on an uptown cougar. Dusty was busy playing bar games with Reece and Jimmy Ray, while Julia and Santana whooped it up on the dance floor with Jarrod and his minions.

Even though Melinda wasn't nearly as smashed as the others, she had had enough to bravely waltz up to the bar and order a drink and his digits. She would have never asked any guy for his phone number before, especially one she was interested in. She also didn't know what she would do, or even if she would do anything with his number, but took it just the same. Melinda Sue Johnston was experiencing a lot of firsts since coming to New York. At last, she was growing up.

The weekend, by all accounts, was a blast and everyone made it to the airport on time for Sunday flights. Melinda said her good-byes to Dusty at the hotel, begging off the trip to the airport claiming she needed her rest to get ready for her early call on Monday. The truth was she was meeting Martin for a late lunch.

CHAPTER 23

SOUTH ISLE — SEA VIEW, GA

Dusty was actually enjoying his morning run. Julia's comments about his expanding midsection eight months prior were just a faded memory now that he was once again in peak physical condition. Before the accident, exercising had been as second nature to him as breathing. He looked good, felt great and was more confident than ever.

Youth made bouncing back to his former glory child's play. His forty-eight-inch chest and twenty-two inch guns complemented his ripped abs and thirty-inch waist. He got stared at everywhere he went and had to admit, he secretly loved the attention.

Summer had come and gone again, but this time, with no Melinda. She had been promoted at *Glamour,* so time off was impossible, forcing him into bouts of celibacy. The running, sometimes twice a day, was great stress relief.

He realized he had truly missed exercising and was grateful for Julia's jab, but was beginning to wonder how long it would be before he could share the benefits of all his hard work with someone.

South Isle, as it was named, had undergone a meticulously planned overhaul, becoming a tropical paradise.

Early on, the curious residents of Sea View thought a number of luxury homes would be built there, but then two years in, only a single foundation was laid.

Dusty usually turned around at the isthmus, the half-way point in his routine, but his progress over the last few months had been, in a word, astonishing. So today, he crossed the land bridge and continued right through the electric gates, which had been left wide open for the construction crew and their big trucks, unnoticed by the men working. They grew accustomed to sightseeing strangers wandering around the property. Not only was the house spectacular in scale and design, but there also seemed to be a lot of mystery surrounding the project.

Brendan Howard Construction, known for its signature dream homes, had been hired by an unnamed multimillionaire, who requested total anonymity. And in a small, tight knit community, mystery meant intrigue; but as long as the gawkers kept their distance from the main house, they were overlooked.

Dusty waved as a Ford F350 passed by. Julia was right. Something big was about to happen if the house, a colossal white-sand colored Mediterranean style mansion, was any indication. It had an elaborate fountain in the middle of a circular drive, a pool out back, a six-car garage, enormous windows and seven balconies.

The design of the house was simple, but brilliant; two massive wings shooting in opposite directions, from a gigantic circular section topped by a tremendous stained-glass dome that housed the foyer, a sweeping freestanding staircase and great room.

He peered through one of the many windows at the back of the house to see furniture being placed at the instruction of a very thin woman with blood red lips and black finger nails. He marveled at what had to be twenty-five-foot ceilings.

As he jogged back to the main land, he wondered if Julia might be right about something else. Was Alex planning his return?

Δ

March came and it was back to Europe and more shows for Andrea. She walked for Louis Vuitton, Gareth Pugh, Lagerfeld, Armani, Gucci, and Dior, to name a few.

Alex, unfortunately, still on a seemingly downward spiral, took an undetermined leave of absence from the modeling world. He did though remain present at Andrea's side, causing him to cross paths with some of the designers he flaked on. And he met their animosity with straight up defiance.

Alex did not now, nor would he ever, need them. He was the son of Baron Vandiveer and that granted him access to any and all things he wanted, and he was not afraid to prove that point to anyone who dared cross him. This new stance piqued the interest of the tabloid press.

CHAPTER 24

NEW YORK — VALHALLA

Back in New York, things were heating up. The A&A Jeans campaign was so successful that Nasty Mama decided to introduce a men's line, featuring Andrea nude and Alex wearing only the jeans— basically mirroring the women's campaign. So, playtime in the Hamptons ended for the young models.

Their joined-at-the-hip presence in New York also grabbed the attention of Alex's father who had Janice summon them.

Andrea stared at the giant leather globe spinning slowly on its brass and redwood stand. They were standing in the library of Baron's Upper East Side rooftop manor, Valhalla. Baron Vandiveer was indeed arrogant enough to name his home in reference to the gods. Baron, of course, knew they were there but kept them waiting, purposely.

He was hosting a small dinner party to celebrate the twenty-fifth wedding anniversary of Leonard and Gloria Goldstein. He also thought this would be the perfect opportunity to meet face-to-face with the girl who had captured his son's attention so completely. He knew nothing of her except that Alex met her in New York and they traveled to Europe, where they began a life together.

It was not a father's business who his son fucked, as long as it was a woman, but he needed to settle a nagging feeling he had about her. She seemed familiar somehow in photographs he had seen of her. He was not at all interested in that world, but when she started appearing in the tabloids and fashion magazines with his son, Janice had innocently brought them to his attention.

The pictures in the fashion magazines triggered no response, but the more casual, tabloid shots set off alarms. He was sure they had never met—how could they have? Still, his gut warned him.

Δ

"So where is this town again?" Andrea asked.

Alex walked over to the globe and stopped it on the North American side.

"Right here," he pointed, "on the coast of Georgia."

"I didn't know Georgia had any beaches."

He had never revealed much about his childhood— only that his mother died when he was little and that his grandmother raised him. He rarely referred to his old friends, with the exception of Dusty. Andrea listened attentively to everything Alex said about Dusty, and she wanted to know more.

The transformation of South Isle was nearly complete, yet Alex had shown no interested in returning home.

"The beaches are beautiful, but it's basically a small town with smaller minded people."

"Don't say that. I'm sure it's very nice."

She often longed for a sense of normalcy—the picket fence, kids, a dog, an SUV in the driveway. But there was plenty of time for that; she was still young. Besides, she didn't see Alex settling down any time soon.

"Alex!"

The booming voice startled her for many reasons. It was Baron. Although Alex had never introduced them, she and Baron had a history. She quickly pushed the memory from her mind. This moment was long overdue.

She turned to greet him, wearing her best cover girl smile, and wondered if he would recognize her. No, not yet anyway, thanks to good hair and makeup.

"For the love of Christ, boy, what are you wearing?"

"Good to see you too, Father," Alex responded.

Baron smiled at Andrea, his hand extended. She had seen his face countless times through the media of course, but she also knew him from the days he came to see her mother.

Why had he constantly haunted her life? And why had he been so important to her mother? *Did she really want to know the answers?*

"And you must be Andrea."

"Pleased to meet you, sir," she replied sweetly.

Still nothing…

He held her at arm's length, searching her exquisite face for his own answers.

"She's breathtaking, my boy, absolutely beautiful."

"Thank you, father…"

The tone in Alex's voice was one of disdain. Andrea gave him a calm reassuring look, reminding him she was there for him. She was glad she had insisted he remain sober leading up to the evening and only allowed him a little coke.

"The guests are arriving, sir."

They turned to see a member of the household staff. Baron offered his arm to Andrea.

"My dear," he said full of Old World charm. Then, without even glancing toward his son, he ordered Alex to go put on a *decent* dinner jacket.

The manservant waited by the carved double doors, pulling them closed behind them. Guests were not allowed to wander freely throughout the twenty thousand square feet. The formal living room, ballroom, and rooftop solarium offered more than enough space for the one hundred and twenty-five guests who were expected. There were already approximately sixty people gathered enjoying passed hors d'oeuvres and cocktails, while a string quartet played on the landing leading to the second floor.

The evening was tastefully boring. The guests, with the exception of Alex and Andrea, were mainly corporate types, their spouses and or significant others.

As usual, most of the men *and* a few women were sneaking glances or blatantly staring at her. She did not mind because she understood what her looks stirred in them. It gave her great power and a sense of control. No man would ever use her again.

Her hair was down in loose waves with a side part, her eyes brushed with charcoal and smoky grey; her lips deep red in a sophisticated matte finish. She was wearing a short, black Max Azria cocktail dress, long-sleeved with a plunging neckline and thigh-high Channel boots. She was also wearing more than half a million dollars in jewelry, thanks to a three hundred and fifty thousand dollar Neil Lane diamond and sapphire snake bracelet around her wrist, a gift from Alex on her eighteenth birthday. Tonight she would play the role of doting girlfriend.

There were round tables set for ten throughout the expanse of the ballroom along with a rectangular head table for the firm's senior partners and Baron. An army of young men and women dressed in black and white scurried about to make sure everyone *was taken care of.*

They managed to make it through the first two courses before Alex became restless. He simply pushed his chair back and stood. Andrea stood also and they made their exit to his father's dismay. She saw Baron's disapproving glance and was thankful they had not been seated at his table. She smiled sweetly and Baron's gut tightened.

Before Alex made it to the terrace, he lit a cigarette. She followed him to the edge of the rooftop garden, so beautiful, enclosed in glass and wrapped in the glowing lights of Manhattan.

She was silent as she watched him blow smoke into the climate-controlled air. There were prize winning orchids housed on that terrace, including a hybrid named after his mother. His father would be furious that he was smoking in his greenhouse. This made Alex smile, but only for an instant.

"He never loved her," he said at last.

"You don't know that," Andrea replied.

"She was a trophy, a prize winner, like these orchids."

"He's your father, Alex. And he loves you."

"Really...? Is that why I grew up in Sea View while he lived in New York?" He was disgusted.

"Sweetheart, you have got to calm down. We're only here for a few more days and then we can go anywhere you want."

She reached into her clutch and pulled out a silver bullet, packed with cocaine. She gave it to him.

"Anywhere...?"

She reached in again. "Anywhere. Now, take these. With the wine you've had, they should help you relax. But don't drink much more or you'll end up shit-faced."

"Okay, my love," He smiled. "You're always there for me."

"And I always will be."

They returned just as the entrees were being served. Neither ate. The soup and salad they had already consumed was more than enough for any model. Alex, against Andrea's advice, continued to drink, unfazed and or unimpressed by the extremely rare pinot noir. She however, drank only water for two reasons. She didn't feel the need to drink while doing drugs, and who needed the empty calories.

She glanced at Alex. The Xanax would kick in soon, calming him, but until then who knew. He looked a bit like a vampire, gulping the dark red liquid from the crystal goblet. Ordinarily this would amuse her, but she was not the only one watching. His father was also keeping an eye on him, mainly because of her presence at his side. But she still could not be sure he knew exactly who she was.

Baron leaned toward his old friend.

"Lenny, that's some piece with my son, huh?"

"Oh yeah, she's a beauty all right."

"She looks familiar somehow, like I should know her."

"What? You can remember all the broads you banged?"

Leonard spoke in jest but hit the proverbial nail right on the head. Baron wanted to forget this one, but there she was with his son. He had only suspected when Janice had shown him the tabloid photos, but now that she was here in the flesh, he was sure. It was the biggest regret of his life.

As if reading his mind, Leo said, "I don't mind saying, that's one I would like to tag and forget."

"Jesus, Lenny. She's young enough to be your granddaughter."

"Watch your fucking tongue. I'm not that damned old."

"Could you for once keep quiet and give me a minute? Do you remember a pro named Maria Santos?"

"Santos? Doesn't ring any bells..."

The truth was the name Maria Santos did more than ring bells. It set off alarms. He most definitely wanted to forget Maria Santos. They both knew her well and they both knew *damned* well that Leo was full of shit, avoiding the subject.

"What's the big deal anyway?" Leo asked. "So, she reminds you of someone you knew a long time ago."

That she did. Maria Santos had been an exotic beauty, until she ruined herself with drugs. Baron saw her a few times after she left Sally's, enough times to realize what she was up to.

As far as hookers went, she had been a peach, but he could never have afforded to get involved. Then, some five years later, he received a phone call from Maria out of the blue. She had obviously been high on something and tried to extort money from him. Something about a daughter, his daughter, but to his knowledge there was no kid.

Baron was very abrupt with Maria that day and very clear. He told her that if she ever tried to contact him again, he would have her killed. But then someone beat him to the punch.

The chances of that girl and this girl being the same was a long shot at best; and the chances of her being his daughter, an even longer one. Though he refused to believe Maria's outlandish story when she phoned that day, life had taught him that nothing could be ruled out as impossible.

Now who's being the crazy old man, he asked himself.

He continued to watch the pair and grew more uneasy. The long dark hair, the large dark eyes... Could there have been a child? To make matters worse, he was growing increasingly certain that she was the girl from the auction that night at Sally's. He prayed to God that he was wrong, but Baron Vandiveer feared his demons had at last come home to roost.

After dinner, the black-and-white army quickly cleared away everything, including the tables and chairs to make room for dancing. The guests were instructed to return to the music room for after dinner drinks and coffee bar.

Again, they escaped to the terrace. Alex was not much of a dancer, especially with the turn in his mood. He fired up another cigarette. Andrea remained silent as he smoked. *Fathers and sons,* she thought. She watched him while he stood as far away from the house as possible.

He turned and looked at her. She knew the look. It was closing in, the darkness. That's what he called it. Everything stopped when it came.

"I want to go home," he said.

"We are going, my sweet. I spoke with Camilla today, everything is on schedule. We should be in by Christmas."

"I want to be there for my birthday."

He was turning twenty-one on the twentieth of November. She would have to push the walk through up by nearly five weeks, expensive, but doable.

"I'll call Camilla first thing in the morning."

He hugged her.

"You take such good care of me."

CHAPTER 25

ROENSTEIN RESIDENCE — SEA VIEW, GA

"It's been really quiet over there today," Julia said.

"I swear, you're obsessed with that island," Dusty replied. "You've been watching for like, two years."

"It's been nonstop 24/7 for the last few weeks and then suddenly, nothing."

"And...?"

She was on the second level deck of her parent's home peering through her little brother's telescope. She straightened for a moment and stared at him, frustration showing on her face.

"Aren't you the least bit curious? Someone bought our island and built a palace on it."

"I wouldn't call it a palace, exactly."

She adjusted the telescope. "Well, it's the biggest thing Sea View has ever seen."

The breeze from the ocean ran its fingers through her hair and rustled the fabric of her dress. It was a perfect November night and Dusty had come over to keep her company.

She wanted to stay home in case her brother called from boarding school. He had been lucky enough to live his life removed from the truth about their family. He was too young during the trial and home-schooled until he was old enough to be sent away. He had escaped.

Her mother was at Club Med again—that was the story anyway. She was really in rehab, one of those places that combined getting clean with spa treatments and gourmet meals.

The sun had long since set, but the island was still well lit. Julia went back to her spying.

"Would you like another margarita?" Dusty asked, buzzed already.

"Whoa. What do we have here?" She looked at Dusty. He did not react. "A limo..."

Still no reaction.

"Dusty, look..."

He got up, looked through the telescope and shrugged. "Okay, it's a limo."

The car stopped briefly at the front entrance. It remained there just long enough for a female with dark hair to emerge and slip through the massive front door.

"Oh, never mind," Julia complained. "I swear you have no sense of intrigue."

He turned away from the telescope. "You mean I'm not nosey."

He did not mention the woman, knowing it would only irritate her that she had missed a piece of the puzzle. She pushed him away and peered through the lens again.

"Someone has to identify the bodies. Shit, they pulled around back. That monstrosity of a house is blocking my view. We should go over there."

"And do what, exactly? Announce our drunk asses as the Neighborhood Welcoming Drunk Asses." He laughed at his own joke.

Julia rolled her eyes. "Oh shut up. I'll have that drink now."

He nodded his head but didn't move. There was a cool breeze blowing in from the ocean stirring the air on what turned out to be an otherwise warm night. It was not unusual for Sea View to experience warmer temperatures even in late November. *The night is just perfect,* he thought his head back and eyes closed.

"You used to be fun, Dustin Marler. Remember? Fun?"

She rattled on and on as she always did. He didn't mind though and she didn't mind if he zoned out from time to time. Her way of dealing with things was to always be busy, always talking, always moving—to keep the demons at bay.

He loved her like a sister and was her best friend. He drifted in and out while she talked and couldn't be sure how much time passed. It was such a beautiful night.

"Okay, okay," she said at last. "I've bored another to slumber. Get up, I'm going to bed. You wanna stay over?"

She did not mean it in a sexual way. He was her only true friend and she intended to keep it that way. Claiming his virginity had been a kick, but that was as far as it went. He struggled to his feet.

"No, I'm good. It's a great night for a walk."

"Suit yourself."

She gave him a quick kiss on the cheek before disappearing into the house and Dusty made his way to the back stairs, leading down to the beach. The wind had picked up a bit. If he had to guess, he would say it was nearing midnight.

Δ

Andrea closed the massive door and leaned against it. Alex's request that the house be ready for his birthday had been no easy task, but it had been done. The thirty-five-thousand square feet had been made key-ready with days to spare. She always made sure she pleased him.

She wandered through the foyer, past the grand staircase and into the great room, which was the central focus of the back of the house. A series of French doors and windows stretching to the thirty-foot atrium ceiling allowed a flawless view of the Atlantic. The stained glass dome was a stroke of genius on the architect's part.

She surveyed the beautifully furnished living space. The sunken pit facing the fireplace, had seating for twenty, which included a custom built-in distressed leather sectional that looked extremely inviting and was sure to be a focal point once they began entertaining.

After meeting legendary socialite Roxie Roma during Fashion Week Paris 2009, and spending time at her South Hampton beach estate, it was decided that interior designer to the stars, Camilla Rivera, was the only person for the job. Andrea would have to send Roxie a personal thank you—a diamond tennis bracelet, perhaps.

Alex was still in New York "taking care of some loose ends," according to his father. This would give her a chance to stock the place with food, drinks and other necessities that he could not live without.

But first things first; she checked the top of the line security system's monitor located behind the bar. Almost every room in the house had one and with the touch of a finger she was able to view the front and rear gates, surrounding grounds, pool and carriage houses as well as any entrance or exit in the main house.

Camilla had been thorough during the walk through, explaining in great detail the cutting-edge technology. She knew her shit and was definitely worth every dollar of her overblown rates.

The left wing, or north wing, was made up of a large modern kitchen, butler's pantry, breakfast room, formal dining room, living room, and a library. There were also four bathrooms and, most importantly, a sprawling three-bedroom apartment, on the upper floor.

In the south wing of the house there was a gaming room, media room, eight second-level bedrooms and what was referred to as the ballroom. The space was equipped, however, like a nightclub, complete with a full service bar, D.J. booth, cocktail tables and banquettes. Adjacent and to the rear of this part of the mansion was a glass solarium filled with rare and exotic plants from around the world. The solarium also housed a forty by sixty-foot swimming pool and was where the indoor and outdoor pools connected.

Satisfied that the perimeter was secure and that everything was on lock down, she slipped off her Jimmy Choo pumps and shed the fitted, Calvin Klein sheath. A swim was definitely in order. After unhooking her bra and tossing it she dove into the crystal clear water.

The temperature of the pool, just as she expected, was perfect, as things in Alex's world tended to be. She always felt most at peace cocooned beneath the surface of any body of water, cut off from the world above. How had she come to be so lucky? *God protects the innocent,* she heard her mother's voice say, and *good little girls.* She was neither.

CHAPTER 26

ALTOBELI'S RESTAURANT — NEW YORK

Alex sat across from his father toying with his dessert spoon. They had just finished dinner at Baron's favorite New York eatery, an Italian place that was too busy, too noisy and too successful. The establishment's good fortune was thanks to the seemingly endless talents of a gifted piano player named Randy Barnes and an eclectic band of vocalists who circled him like the sun.

Alex's plan was to be home by now, but his father had insisted he stay in New York. Reluctantly he agreed, certain he would be threatened with the loss of his trust fund yet again, if he did not obey. The conversation throughout dinner was a miserable fail, and now Baron was listening to the final set while Alex waited.

Finally, after the platinum blonde bombshell with the little boy haircut and super sultry voice delivered her rendition of "Black Coffee," the head bartender was called to close out the show.

"I'd like to thank each and every one of you for coming out tonight. For those of you, who don't know, I'm Kathe Kelner and I would also like to dedicate the last song of the evening to our favorite Saturday night table hog, Baron Vandiveer."

Baron gave an almost unperceivable nod, while Alex raised his glass to the dark haired songbird. It took grapefruit-sized balls to make such a comment. Whenever he was in the mood for Italian—which was often—Baron went to Altobeli's, and he was always seated at eight and never left before midnight. Because of the restaurant's ever-growing popularity, there was always a wait for tables, and the stares from hungry customers made him feel superior. He did, after all, own the building.

The bombshell sashayed over to their table.

"Hello, Baron," she said in a throaty whisper.

"My dear, Ms. Rushing..."

Baron gestured and she slid into the booth beside him.

"Allow me to introduce you to my son, Alex."

"Call me Amy," she purred.

The way she extended her hand prompted Alex to kiss it.

"Pleasure," he said.

"Yes," she replied.

She was practically in his father's lap—a new girlfriend perhaps? She definitely fit the bill: beautiful, self-assured and seductive. He eyed Baron. Everything about him was big—big frame, big voice and the ever-present, big ego.

Alex flagged the waiter and pointed to his cocktail.

"Is it too late to get another?"

He knew, of course, that it was not; his father was a very powerful man.

"Do you have to drink so much?" Baron asked.

"Is that why we're here, to discuss my drinking? I thought I'd save Alcoholics Anonymous for when my career hits the skids. Gotta love a comeback, right Ames?"

She smiled and squint her eyes. She was definitely flirting.

"Career?" his father questioned. "Prancing and posing like a bunch of fairies."

He scooped up his wine glass and gulped the high-dollar shiraz. Alex laughed.

"With all due respect, Baron," Amy dared, "modeling can be very lucrative, not to mention the possible segue into television or even movies. Hollywood loves a pretty face."

Baron was infuriated. How dare she!

Through clenched teeth he said, "I do not recall asking for an opinion."

Amy Rushing, a cool one indeed, raised a perfectly arched eyebrow and excused herself, but not before slipping Alex her card.

"Gentlemen..." she cooed.

She nodded her good-bye and sauntered over to another table. She was very popular it seemed.

Alex turned his attention back to his father.

"Is that what you've been waiting four hours to ask me?" It was right out of a straight-to-DVD flick and he couldn't help laughing. "You think I'm gay?"

His drink arrived and he winked at the waiter. Baron glared at his son. *But surely this wasn't it either. There had to be something else, some other reason his father had taken a sudden interest in his life.*

Alex smirked. "I'm not gay father, if that's what you're asking. I bang the shit out of Andrea on the regular and have countless hours of video to prove it."

Baron stiffened in his seat. "Don't be vulgar," he said.

Alex did not respond.

"But since you brought her up," his father continued, "what do you know about this girl?"

Ahh, so that was it: Andrea... But why the hell did his old man care? Was it the family fortune?

"I met her in New York. You know the story."

"But who are her people?"

"Her people...? What does that even mean—her people?"

"Her background... Where did she come from?"

Alex finished his scotch, savoring the moment. His father wanted something, but what?

"You're serious?" He was getting to him and he rather enjoyed it.

"Yes, of course I'm serious," Baron barked. "My God, she killed someone."

No, Father, I killed the asshole.

"It was self-defense. Why so much concern all of a sudden?"

Baron sat back, eyeing his son.

"I'm not so much concerned as curious. Is it so unusual for a father to be interested in who his son dates?"

Alex laughed again. "A father...?"

No one laughed at Baron Vandiveer. There was a time when he would have stormed out, but this was his only son. Times changed, people changed, and yes, even power hunger moguls could change. Was it too late?

"Son, please." He attempted a softer approach. "Give an old man a break."

Alex slumped back in his chair. *Was his father trying? Did he deserve a chance?*

"Okay, first of all we are not dating. We've been living together for almost three years. I love her and she loves me."

"Have you discussed marriage?"

"Jesus Christ, I'm just turning twenty-one. No, we haven't discussed marriage. What is it, the money...?"

It was obvious to Baron that he was getting nowhere with his son. He decided to change tactics.

"Why not stay with me or at least at the Park Avenue apartment until Andrea returns to New York?"

"She's not returning; I'm leaving."

"You know, son, I really don't understand you."

Alex rolled his eyes, still Baron pressed on.

"Why are you so determined to throw your life away?"

"Throw my life away? You don't know anything about me."

"Then, stay here in New York so I can *get* to know you."

Yeah, well maybe I don't want to get to know you, Alex thought, but the words dared not pass his lips.

"I've gotta take a leak."

Once in the men's room he pulled out a bullet and did a couple of bumps. His cell phone vibrated just as he was putting his stash away. A topless picture came into view with a text from Andrea.

The house is beautiful and I miss you desperately; having a midnight swim; wishing you were here.

CHAPTER 27

SEA VIEW, GA

Dusty walked aimlessly down the beach. He didn't really feel like going home. *Home?* He laughed out loud. *What home?* He lived in his best friend's house. A friend he hadn't seen or heard from in years. A friend who had made sure he was taken care of. God, he regretted that night. Why had he acted so *stupid?*

He looked up and saw the bridge to South Isle. What the hell? Even though he would never admit it to Julia, he was curious about whoever it was who purchased the small island. *It was Alex's island.*

The main gate was closed, so he took the path around back just as he and Julia had done before. And just like before the back gates were also locked, but unlike before the backyard was lit.

Drunken curiosity got the best of him and he yelled out, "Hello! Hello!"

The wind was kicking up again, but he was sure he heard a woman's voice: "Hello. Is someone there?"

"It's Dusty," he called back, not sure what he expected. "Dustin Marler," he shouted. "I live just up the beach."

What was he doing? It was late. He thought he should just go, but then he heard it, a clicking sound. The gate had been unlocked. He pulled at it and it opened.

He headed up the stairs and stopped dead in his tracks. The house at night was quite an impressive sight. Then, he saw her.

After buzzing him in, she had ample time to dive back into the pool before he made it from the gate to the terrace. Now, she was bottomless as well. He just stood there, swaying slightly. It was obvious to her that he had been drinking and a mischievous grin curled the corners of her mouth. She hadn't even had to go looking. Dusty had come to her.

"I won't bite," she called from the deep end of the lighted pool.

As he got closer to her he realized she was totally naked. Dusty felt his face go red. She was truly beautiful.

"I'm Andrea Sorcosi."

It *was* her. Julia read all the fashion and celebrity mags and had been following Andrea since they first spotted her with Alex on *Entertainment Tonight.* Had it just been drunken curiosity that brought him here? Or had the brief glimpse through the telescope been enough for his subconscious mind to grab onto?

She extended her hand. He bent down to take it and introduced himself. Her magnificent breasts were visible through the glowing, crystal water.

"I'm sorry I can't get out," she said smiling. "I have no towel, but you're more than welcome to join me. It's heated."

She pushed off and glided with ease through the water. The pool itself was inviting enough, but the fact that a gorgeous, nude model occupied it was too much. He glanced around quickly, not sure why and stripped out of his clothes. Down to his boxers, he walked to the edge.

She giggled. "No clothes allowed."

He stood frozen, not sure what to do.

"Shut the lights off if it makes you more comfortable. The box is over there."

She pointed then disappeared beneath the surface again. He hurried to the control panel, found the switch, slipped out of his underwear and dove in. The warm water caressed his naked body.

When he reached the other side where Andrea was waiting, the small talk began as they each avoided the proverbial elephant. Sometime during the conversation, he wondered how long a guy could maintain an erection before it snapped off. He was grateful for the semi darkness.

"It's such a beautiful night," he said, trying desperately not to let his eyes wander from her face.

"Isn't it?" she agreed.

"You know, we always wondered what would become of this island. Alex always swore he'd buy it."

"And now he has," she stated.

Dusty smiled to himself.

"He said he'd install a draw bridge to keep the world out, but this is much more than any of us could have imagined."

"Well, you know Alex."

"I thought I did."

Andrea watched him quietly. He was still hurting. She understood pain and loneliness, but heartbreak was her specialty.

"What's he like now?" Dusty asked. "I mean ... it's been three years."

What was she to tell him? What could she tell him?

"Why don't we go inside? I'll give you a tour of the house and we'll talk."

Dusty watched as she swam toward the glass wall near the far corner of the house.

"There should be towels in the pool house," Andrea said before swimming under, resurfacing in the solarium, far enough away that she was just a silhouette. Still, he waited until she disappeared inside the house itself before getting out of the pool.

Had she known? She must have. He looked at his rearing cock and, as many guys in such a position do, began a conversation with it.

"What are you doing?" he asked in a harsh whisper. "This is not the time."

"But, she's so fuckin' hot!"

"Shut up! Nothing can happen."

He quickly entered the pool house. The lights were still on from the earlier walk through and the water had sobered him up enough to take notice of the amazing contemporary decor.

He randomly chose a bedroom and found a bathroom. He thought about masturbating, giving his cock a few tugs, but thought again after catching sight of his reflection.

"What are you, thirteen?" he said aloud. "Get a hold of yourself."

He dried off then grabbed one of the thick terry robes that hung on the back of the bathroom door. He stared at his reflection once more and noticed the monogramed V on the chest pocket. Alex was coming home at last. Had he forgiven him? He must have since he was coming back.

Dusty took a deep breath, exhaling slowly. His erection was fading, time to head for the house.

He found her in the great room, a fire going in an enormous fireplace, and marveled at the unobstructed view of the ocean. All the doors were open, and white shears billowing in the night breeze. He stood for a moment, taking it all in. She was curled up on the biggest sectional sofa he had ever seen gazing at the fireplace, her skin washed in the golden light of the fire. He wondered again what the hell he was hoping for. She looked up and smiled.

"Oh, good," she said. You found the robes."

"Yeah..." He grinned, feeling a little self-conscious.

"Come, sit with me." She patted the sofa cushion beside her.
"I could use a drink."

She got up and headed to his left. "The bar's over here. What would you like?"

"Oh, you don't have to make it."

"You are my guest and you shall be treated accordingly."

She smiled again and his dick twitched. Behave he told himself.

The built in bar was of course, well stocked. His eyes roamed, landing on a bottle of some twenty-five-year-old scotch he had never heard of. How many scotches had he and Alex shared? The taste had repulsed him in the beginning; but wasn't he only fifteen the first time he had tried it? There had been a lot of firsts with Alex. Against his better judgment, he decided to have one, pointing at the bottle.

"I'll take that scotch... with soda."

Her back was to him as she made the drink.

"You're not having one?" he asked.

"I'm not a big drinker."

He could not help but take the opportunity to have a good look at her body and it wasn't that difficult. She was wearing some type of stretch pants or leggings or something with a white wife beater and the smallest of cashmere sweaters. She handed him his cocktail and grabbed a bottle of water for herself, before returning to the fire. Again his eyes roamed over her body.

"So, you don't drink?" he asked.

"My beauty is my business."

He gulped at the scotch and tightened the belt on his robe. He was still nude beneath the plush fabric. His clothing was lying right outside near the pool, but he didn't want to get dressed. He was enjoying being almost naked around her. He wanted to flash her, to show off his big dick. *What was he thinking?* This was Alex's girl. She curled up on the sectional sofa.

"Now come, sit with me. Or do I make you too nervous?"

She, too, was aware of the fact that he was nude beneath the robe.

"I wouldn't say nervous, exactly."

She had said it in such a matter-of-fact way that he laughed, somewhat relieved. It brought him quickly back to reality, defusing the sexual tension instantly. He walked to where she sat, waiting for him.

"It's okay," she teased. "I understand what I do to men. Hell, even some gay men take a second look—and don't get me started on the lesbians."

They both laughed and he realized she wasn't bragging about her undeniable beauty; she was kind of poking fun at it.

"I mean, please, I love gay guys but I don't sleep with them—well almost never."

She laughed and it was magic. *Who was this girl?*

"Besides, as soon as they get anywhere near Alex, any thoughts of me fly right out the window."

"Alex was always..." He searched for the right word. "Magnetic."

"Oh my God, you have no idea. It all started with the underwear ads. He's very popular in Europe you know, but when we got to New York, everything went wild. The paparazzi are crazed. It's quite maddening."

She was mesmerizing. Whether she was playing with her ponytail, or toying with her water bottle, he took it all in.

"The masses are celebrity-crazed." he said. "A couple is like a two for one."

He was merely repeating what he had heard Julia say on the subject, not really paying attention, but instead watching her mouth as she spoke. The accent was slightly mysterious, neither American nor European, but the voice was like music. *Man, she's beautiful*, he thought.

"A two for one, eh...?"

She knew she could have him, if she wanted, but it wasn't time yet.

"Oh, yeah. Just look at Brad and Angelina." He didn't know why he said that.

She found him utterly adorable.

"So you're a celeb watcher?" She was teasing him.

"My, ah, girlfriend is always buying those magazines. *Shit! Why hadn't he said Julia—my friend Julia? Too late now.*

He finished his drink and got up to make another. He tried to sound casual.

"That's how we found out Alex was modeling and that he'd met you."

"Was it hard," she asked, "to read about your friend in a magazine? From what Alex says, you guys were close."

"We were..."

"You know what's really weird," she said sensing his mood swing. "Alex is famous for being Alex. I mean an underwear ad and a commercial... We're just models."

Models immersed in wealth and scandal.

"And we're the ones getting approached. I mean Denton Smith practically tripped over himself getting to us..."

He cut her off unable to contain his excitement.

"*The* Denton Smith...?"

"The one and only," she said. "Any way, Alex and I ran into him in a *shoes only club* in New York."

Dusty laughed. "Shoes only...?"

"Yeah, you know a strip club." She laughed too. "Any way, he was drinking, we were drinking and the next thing you know, we were making out in a VIP room."

"Making out?"

"Yes, making out, what are you, eight?" she teased. "We were just kissing."

"You were *all* kissing?"

"Yes, kissing. I'm young and I like to kiss boys. Anyway, at some point Denton turned to Alex and jammed his tongue down his throat."

She twirled her pony tail.

"And, well," she hesitated, "Alex gets crazy sometimes."

"Wait, Denton Smithson from Alpha-Monk?"

"How drunk are you....?"

"Alex and Denton Smithson...? He made out with Denton Smithson?"

How many times am I going to repeat the singer's name? he asked himself, suddenly feeling out of it.

"Oh relax. Guys make girls do it all the time. It was no big deal. Besides, Alex kisses everybody.

"Wow," was all Dusty could manage.

He wanted to say more but could not wrap his head around what he was hearing.

She finished her water and looked at him smiling. His mind was reeling. She could see it. Andrea stretched and faked a yawn.

"Goodness, it's getting late."

Again, he was brought back to reality. His head was spinning a little and his eye lids were growing heavy. He figured he was just drunk again and placed his glass down on a nearby table. The robe fell open, exposing his torso. Shit, he almost forgot he wasn't wearing any clothes. He pulled the tie belt and noticed his hand felt heavy and sluggish.

She smiled. The Ambien she slipped him was taking effect.

"And I was going to give you a tour of the house."

She stood and stretched again, causing her tank to rise, exposing the creamy smooth skin of her flat stomach.

"Oh well," she shrugged. "You can see it tomorrow. It's time for bed."

Andrea reached for his hand and led him upstairs to the apartment. He was silent as she guided him through the darkness until they arrived at a set of double doors that opened to a master suite. He was so tired.

"Andrea, I..."

She squeezed his hand.

"Don't worry I'm not going to jump you. I just don't like to sleep alone, something from my childhood."

He could not refuse her. They walked, hand in hand, into the room. There was an enormous canopied bed to one side of the room, a sitting area on the other, centered on yet another giant fireplace, and lots of windows.

He followed her into the biggest bathroom he had ever seen. She released his hand and opened one of the two mirrored medicine cabinets embedded in a mirrored wall above the vanity.

Dusty watched through hooded red eyes as she removed two new, clear toothbrushes and a silver tube of toothpaste. He thanked her and they brushed their teeth in silence, rinsed, then both gargled with mouthwash. She smiled at him and he smiled back. *Why was he so tired?*

"Grab a bottle of water," she said. "It will help with the hang over."

She pointed to the far end of the vanity. There, in perfect rows, were tall, slender, label-less bottles with silver caps, smaller versions of the one she had downstairs.

"You were pretty loaded when you got here."

Of course, he thought, all that tequila he had at Julia's.

"I like your hair like that," she said.

"Oh, thanks," he replied eyeing his reflection.

His hair was, by nature, more than wavy, but not quite curly, which equaled unruly.

"It wasn't like that when you got here." She grinned and tousled his hair. "I like this look better."

147

He could feel his cheeks flush, suddenly embarrassed by his near nakedness.

"Is there something I can sleep in?"

She made a face in the mirror.

"How can you wear clothes to bed? The fabrics get so twisted. It's more comfortable nude, don't you agree?"

He looked at her. Was she serious?

"Now, go on, while I floss. It's a giant bed. You won't even know I'm there."

What was happening here? Naked in the pool was one thing, but a bed?

He turned and headed back to the bedroom. God, he was so tired. He pulled back the silk duvet and with an eye on the doorway to the bathroom, threw off the robe and slipped beneath the covers. Andrea entered the room, bottled water in hand.

"Do you love those sheets or what?" she asked.

"Are you kidding? This bed is like Heaven."

"Three thousand thread count, Egyptian cotton. Alex won't sleep on anything less," she replied.

"What's he like now?"

She swirled a finger in the air, motioning for him to turn away while she undressed. Modesty had never been her thing, but she thought it played well.

"I'm sure he's just like you remember him."

He waited until he felt movement beneath the covers before he faced her again. She went on about Alex but he was not listening. *Was this really happening? Was he, Dustin Marler, about to share a bed with this amazing girl?*

The stirring between his legs started again. He rolled onto his side more, still facing her and tried to position himself discreetly. She was so beautiful. With Melinda away, he could only imagine the mess he was going to make the next time he had a minute alone. He tried to focus on her voice, but he was drifting. *Too much alcohol...*

"... a little taller maybe. And it's plain to see from his magazine spreads that he spends time working on his body."

An audible exhale, followed by deeper breathing, signaled her he had fallen asleep. He looked almost angelic. For the first time tonight the furrowed brow was gone. She studied his face. He was so handsome. All-American, beefcake—or was it beefsteak?

She whispered his name, just to make sure, then slid closer to him, snaking her arm beneath the covers. She found it. It was hard to miss. She delicately wrapped her fingers around the girth, or rather, tried to. He was bigger than she expected. Andrea gave a few little squeezes, causing a rapid throbbing, as it softened in her grip.

The poor guy struggled with that monster the whole evening, but now, it too was succumbing to sleep. She released him, rolled onto her side, then reached back and grabbed his hand. She pulled his arm tightly around her torso. Dusty moaned softly, pulling her to him and pushed his hips against her backside.

"Hurry home, Alex," she whispered, then closed her eyes and waited for sleep.

CHAPTER 28

SOUTH ISLE — SEA VIEW, GA

Insistent throbbing in both his heads slowly forced Dusty into consciousness. He had a pounding head ache and an urgent need to urinate. His eyes opened.

He groaned, then sat up too quickly.

"Shit!"

A hand instinctively went to the top of his head, which he was sure would pop off at any second.

Where was he? Oh yeah, Alex's. *Alex was coming home.* He threw the covers back, then quickly covered himself again. *Where were his clothes?* Double shit! It was slowly coming back. What was going on? He needed to think, but later, right now, he needed to get to the john.

Where was Andrea? More flashes from the previous night filled his head: Julia, the telescope and wondering aimlessly down the beach. How did he end up here? He pulled the covers back, still naked; he remembered the pool. His eyes fell to the floor by the bed. *Hadn't there been a robe?*

"Hello?" he croaked.

Fuck it. He pushed the covers aside and walked around the big bed toward the bathroom. The carpet felt nice beneath his bare feet. *...three-thousand thread count...*

nothing but the best for Alex... Andrea, the pool, the fire—it was all coming back now.

He urinated, with difficulty, and then returned to the vanity. He spied the water and grabbed one, chugging it, then grabbed another. His head hurt and he needed a shower. He turned on the tap and as the water heated up, wondered what time it was. Fuck, what day was it? He was on call at five. That's why he had even been drinking in the first place.

He stepped under the spray. Julia would never believe this. Could he tell her? Should he tell her? He certainly wouldn't be telling Melinda—that was for damned sure.

His mind wandered back to the night before. Damn, he was horny. He also felt a little guilty. His mind flickered. Did he do something last night? No. They just slept in the same bed. Still, something was there—but what? A dream?

He shook his head trying to jar his memory. Andrea danced through his mind. Some dream. He wondered where she was. Man, she was beautiful. And she smelled so good. How could he know that? He tried, but nothing came to him. *Hurry home, Alex.*

CHAPTER 29

ROENSTEIN RESIDENCE — SEA VIEW, GA

Julia had been awake for hours. She rarely slept, anyway. She stood in the kitchen of her parent's empty house. She would never consider this her home. This was *his* house, the one he had shared with her mother. But she had memories of her home; blurry though they were, they were still there. Memories of the little house she lived in until she was five. The one she had shared with her real daddy, before her mother divorced him and they moved into this house.

Funny, she always hated this house and now she was the only one in it. Her therapist suggested she move out, but why should she? That would mean a job and bills. Everything here was free. They owed her that much and she made sure she was expensive.

"Alone again for the holidays," she sighed.

She poured herself another cup of Chock Full 'O Nuts, her favorite coffee (pun intended), added a healthy dash of Bailey's Irish Cream and headed for the back deck.

She knew she was a whack job. Hell, she was obsessed, crazed even. She peered through her brother's telescope, waiting for something, anything to tell her what was going on over there, for no other reason than sheer boredom. She lit a cigarette and pulled her sweater closed.

"I wonder what Dusty's doing?" she asked out loud.

She inhaled on the cigarette again and grabbed her cell phone. *Put it down.*

"No," she told herself, "leave the poor boy alone for once."

She took another drag, stared at the tiny white tobacco filled cancer stick and grimaced, exhaling the smoke. *Nasty habit*, she thought.

"Yes, a very nasty habit," she said in her mother's voice. "Fuck you, Mother."

CHAPTER 30

SOUTH ISLE — SEA VIEW, GA

Dusty dried off and wrapped the towel around his waist. He looked at his reflection and decided to let his hair dry naturally. Melinda, who would be home soon for Thanksgiving, hated it when he didn't use a blow dryer.

Returning to the bedroom, he looked around for Alex's closet. Judging by the amount of sun beaming through the floor to ceiling windows, he guessed it to be somewhere around noon.

Above the fireplace on the far wall was an extremely artsy black and white portrait of Andrea on a bed wearing only stiletto heels and multiple strands of black pearls. He stared at the picture for a moment, feeling that familiar tingle.

"Get dressed," he said out loud.

He found a walk-in closet filled with designer clothes and shook his head. *Alex.* He scanned the racks of slacks and shirts. There were built in cabinets, drawers, and a lot of black. Black suits, black shirts and pants, black shoes, black hoodies.

After a quick but thorough search, he found some boxer briefs, dark jeans, which were a little tight for his liking, and a long-sleeved dark grey pullover, also a little tight, but he enjoyed showing off his muscles.

Dressed, he walked barefoot from the bedroom, across the sitting room and through the doorway he thought they had come through the night before. On the other side was a much larger formal living area filled with expensive leather furnishings and another large fire place, above which hung another nude of Andrea.

For a second he was confused, like he was somewhere else. He walked to the windows. Yes, same view. She was there, by the pool, gathering up his things. His heart quickened. He turned and hurried from the room, found the right door and stopped.

Had he missed this the night before? He was in a gallery of some sort leading to a sweeping loft that over looked a marble foyer. On the curved walls hung a series of black and white photographs of both Alex and Andrea in various stages of bondage and nudity.

Dusty stared at his friend, gagged in one, wearing a choke collar in another and positioned on wide-spread knees in yet another with his hands tied behind his back. He took a closer look at one not wanting to believe, but unable to un-see the nipple clamps connected by a chain that ran to a spiked cock ring.

The images were a little disturbing, but there was a definite twinkle in Alex's eye. *Was he the same Alex?* Time would tell.

Shaking his head, he continued down the stairs, taking them two at a time, knowing she would be there waiting for him. He was smiling and a little out of breath when he reached the great room. She looked up and smiled as well.

"Afternoon, sleepy head," she said. "I brought your things in."

She crossed the room coming toward him. The silk dress, or was it a shirt, she wore swirled about her as she moved. She had paired it with leggings and too many necklaces. Andrea laid his shorts and t-shirt over the back of a chair. He reached for his sandals. As he took them she leaned in and kissed his cheek.

"Thanks," he said, feeling the heat in his face.

Was he thanking her for the shoes or the kiss?

"I was beginning to think you'd sleep all day. I've already been for a run. Tomorrow then...?"

"What..., ah..., yeah, sure," he stammered. *Tomorrow...?*

"What are your plans today? Are you working?"

"I'm on call at five. What time is it now?"

She eyed him. "Almost one... *What* are you wearing?"

"I grabbed a few things from Alex's closet. You don't think he'll mind, do you?"

"I thought so. I packed those clothes. Well, I didn't actually pack them, but I tagged the ones for his assistant to pack. Your closet is on the other side of the apartment."

"My closet?" he asked

"Yes, *your* closet. Come, I'll show you."

They headed back for the stairs.

"We knew you'd be here and since I do most of the shopping..."

She did not finish her sentence, but turned instead to see if he was staring at her ass. He was. She smiled and he blushed. *God, he's fine*, she thought.

Andrea refocused, taking care not to trip on the staircase and continued to speak.

"Anyway, Alex was certain you'd be a tragedy in khakis and golf shirts."

"Should I be offended?"

"He was also sure that you'd be in excellent shape."

He followed her upstairs, through the curved gallery and back into the private living quarters. She veered right once they were inside.

"The Blue Room is yours," she said opening a door.

The room was decorated in shades of blue with white trim and was almost identical in design to the alabaster room he had shared with Andrea the night before.

"The closet is there. Just to make certain, I bought everything in three different sizes."

The only difference in this closet and Alex's was the presence of color.

"What the hell?"

"You should find everything you need," she said sweeping past him.

Wow. He ran a hand through his hair in amazement. "Why would you do this?"

"Like I said before, Alex wants you here ... with us."

He looked around, speechless.

"Over here, we have your shoes, sizes ten, eleven and twelve. You'll find a snapshot on the end of each box so you'll know what's what. Simple, right...? Over here, you'll find your belts and neckties. Here is your accessories station: watches, cufflinks, and jewelry. Through that door there, is your everyday wear; through that door, suits and formal wear."

"I don't know what to say exactly."

She pressed a finger to his lips. "Then don't say anything."

She left him to get dressed. There was indeed three of everything. He thought he had walked into another world when he passed through that gate last night—now he was certain of it. Alex was coming for him. Everything would be all right again. He quickly changed and returned downstairs, calling for her in the cavernous great room.

"In here."

He turned left, headed through an archway, took another left and found her in the breakfast room off the main kitchen, a silver-capped water bottle in hand.

"Oh, you look so handsome. I love your hair." She tousled it the way a mother would an adolescent child's. "That green shirt looks great on you." She looked down. "Where are your shoes?"

He looked down, too, at his favorite sandals, curling his toes. He rocked back and forth.

"Baby steps," he said.

He made her laugh.

"Are you hungry? We can eat as soon as we get to town." She glanced toward the security monitors in the kitchen. "The car should be here any... Oh yes, there it is now."

She went to the monitor and pressed an intercom switch. "Meet us around back, please," she said entering a code to open the main gate.

"The car...?" he asked.

"Yes, the car. We're going shopping."

"Shopping? What could you possibly need?"

He loved watching her, talking to her, just being with her. She reached for her Kate Spade bag and a lamb's wool Hermès wrap.

"You obviously haven't checked the garage. We'll need transportation, now won't we? Not to mention a driver."

"You don't drive yourself?"

"Only if I have to," she admitted. "Besides, my car only seats two, and I know for a fact Veronique and her brood will be here for the holidays."

"Veronique and her brood...?"

He was so cute, repeating her words.

"Yes, darling, yes... How will they get here from the airport?"

He was totally lost now. "What are you talking about?"

"We are social, we go places, we do things, and we throw parties." She looped her arm through his. "And in case you haven't noticed, there's nothing here but a beautiful beach. So we will have to bring the *scene* to us."

She led him through the state-of-the-art kitchen, past the latest in stainless steel appliances, toward the back entrance.

"Now, first things first—where should we have lunch?"

This was crazy. The house, the clothes, the car...

"Hello?" she said. "Are you even listening to me? God, Alex does that shit to me all the time. You two could be brothers, except for the fact that you're nothing alike. Polar opposites, really; he's so dark and mysterious, while you..." she thought for a moment, *"you* are like sunshine. Like Robert Redford in that old movie. What was the name of it? They played that song about the rain."

"Butch Cassidy," he said.

"....and you're the Sundance Kid. Yes, that's it."

They laughed. Was it merely a coincidence?

"Alex used to call me that."

"Really...? I didn't know."

It was a lie. Of course she knew. She knew everything when it came to Alex and Dusty. A shiny black limo was waiting outside.

"No matter," she said. "Now where can we get lobster salad?"

CHAPTER 31

ROENSTEIN RESIDENCE—SEA VIEW, GA

Julia was still on her parent's deck. She had smoked way too many cigarettes already and was definitely feeling the effects of the Bailey's and coffee. She looked through the telescope again. She saw the car pull around back earlier and now it was returning, but tinted windows prevented her from seeing inside. It moved through the electric gates and onto the land bridge connecting the small island to shore.

There was no way for her to know that Dusty was a passenger or that her life, too, as she knew it, was about to be changed forever. Should she follow? No, she had been drinking. She was always drinking, lately. She needed another cigarette. She was slipping. She could feel it. God, she didn't want to. She looked to the heavens. The sky was so beautiful.

Just this once, okay God...? Just this once.

CHAPTER 32

THE INN — SEA VIEW, GA

The car took Dusty and Andrea to The Inn, one of the three resort hotels in Sea View. She drew a lot of attention with her bigger than life persona. The outfit, the enormous handbag, the designer shades. Everyone stared at them as they made their way across the lobby toward the restaurant, yet she seemed oblivious to it all.

But not Brittney James, the hotel's assistant concierge. She had been hired because of her talent for knowing everything about everybody, who was anybody, once they passed through the lobby doors of the Inn. She recognized Andrea immediately and moved quickly to head them off.

The hostess beamed, giving them the once over, her smile fading when she got to Dusty's feet.

"Good afternoon," Andrea said, flashing her perfect smile.

The girl looked from Dusty to Andrea. The smile was back, but she seemed nervous. Ms. James arrived just in time.

"Ms. Sorcosi," Brittney said, extending her hand. "Welcome to the Inn."

Andrea turned, spying the young woman's name tag.

"Thank you, Brittney. My friend here tells me this place has the best lobster salad in town. We'd like a table for two, please."

"I'm sorry; we can't seat you in the dining room," the hostess said, "not in sandals, sir. Hotel policy..."

She instantly regretted the statement. Brittany's glare promised she would be sorry later.

"Are you denying me lobster salad?"

"No, of course not, Ms. Sorcosi."

"Then what...?" Andrea asked.

The tone of her voice surprised Dusty. It also excited him.

A tall man in an impressive suit approached them.

"Is there a problem, here, Ms. James?"

"Mr. Randall?"

Sinclair Randall was the George Hamilton of South Georgia. Forever young and forever tanned, he was a notorious womanizer, with a keen eye for beauty, and always on the prowl for new conquests.

He recognized Andrea instantly from last month's *GQ* cover: body paint and well-placed rubies.

"Ms. Sorcosi," he nodded, "Sinclair Randall at your service."

"Sir, I was just about to explain the hotel's policy concerning shoes in the dining room..."

"That will be all, Ms. James." Brittany smiled tightly and turned on her heels. *Pompous ass*, she thought.

Δ

"Alex taught me that trick early on," Andrea said to Dusty. "I mean, I'm still a kid and perfect strangers will kiss my ass. I have to say I do love the drama of it all."

She smiled and winked at him.

"It's the money," she whispered.

Her chin was resting on her hands, elbows on the table, platinum and diamonds about her wrists. They were seated in a circular booth for six in the Ocean Room, the hotel's formal dining room normally only open for dinner. It was called the Ocean Room because of glass openings in the walls that made visible a giant saltwater tank. The aquarium, featured throughout the hotel was a contributing factor in the revival of the once tiny beach community.

Sinclair had opened the dining room and arranged for a server from the café. So many times in situations such as this, the person in charge would serve, but not Sinclair. He was always in charge.

"Even as a child, there was always drama," she continued. "I mean, I witnessed my own mother's murder when I was nine, for god sakes."

Dusty was visibly stunned.

"Strangled," she said. "And I was taken away, kidnapped really, when I think about it. But that's for another time. How exactly do you fill your days with Melinda off at school?"

It took a moment to respond. He made a conscious effort not to pry.

"Well, let's see. There's my job at the dealership. I'm there five days a week for three weeks a month, then six days the fourth. Julia and I spend Thursday nights hanging out and there's the occasional dinner with mom and her new husband."

"Your mother has a new husband?"

"They've been married a few months now."

"Oh," she said. "That's so nice."

He smiled. "Yeah, I'm really happy for her. And she just wrote her first cookbook. Walter, that's her husband, talked her into it."

Dusty was distracted by her beauty and it jumbled his thoughts.

"Anyway," he said, "she started her own catering business, which is still thriving; then Walter got her to write this cookbook on desserts, which in turn led to opening a bakery."

"Wow, that's fantastic. Just goes to show it's never too late to follow a dream."

Yeah, mind blowing he thought. He must sound like a complete idiot.

"She always said she was a late bloomer."

"Forty *is* the new twenty," Andrea said.

He nodded.

"So," she went on, "what about your father?"

Dusty dropped his head. "Suicide..."

She touched his hand.

"Oh, I'm sorry. How did he do it?"

It was an extremely personal question, she knew, but that was the point. She had opened up to him, now it was his turn. It was important if she was going to draw him in.

"He shot himself in the head."

Her hand tightened on his. "He must have really wanted to die," she said.

Dusty was silent while Andrea continued in a flat, quiet tone.

"I'm not sure if my mother wanted to die, but I'm not sure she wanted to live either. She just, gave up, you know."

"Yeah...," his voice was barely audible.

"Do you miss him?"

"I never knew him. I was barely two when it happened." He laughed. "It was all over money."

He had overheard the story many times, enough to put the pieces together anyway.

"Apparently there was some business venture. My father borrowed the money from my mom's parents and things fell through. Big Pop never let him forget it, so one day he just shot himself."

Andrea let out an audible gasp. "Oh my God, that's terrible."

A waiter hurried over.

"Is everything alright?" He eyed the beefy blonde suspiciously.

Right as rain, Andrea thought. She smiled, knowing Sinclair was standing by, waiting anxiously to impress. "I'll have the lobster salad."

Dusty ordered a bacon cheese burger with a side of spicy horseradish coleslaw, onion rings, and a stuffed portabella appetizer to start.

"And sparkling water—at least two liters," she added then changed her mind. "You know what, forget the lobster salad. Do you have any Ahi?"

The waiter nodded.

"Seared, please ... maybe over some field greens, with a yummy vinaigrette."

The waiter nodded.

"Of course." He smiled and left the dining room.

Andrea smiled, too, at Dusty. "You're hungry, huh?"

He smiled back. "I like to eat."

"You have such a beautiful smile," she said. "Really nice teeth..."

"Thanks."

Was she flirting with him, he wondered. She certainly unnerved him.

"I like your hair like that, too. It wasn't like that when you came over last night."

The hair again.

"I, ah, usually blow dry. Melinda doesn't like it this way."

She did that head thing that people do when they're not sure they heard what was just said.

"You're kidding, right."

"No..." he chuckled, praying he was not blushing.

Sinclair had the waiter deliver a complimentary bottle of champagne while he called all of his contacts trying to find out why

Andrea Sorcosi was in Sea View. He scored when he dialed realtor Charletta Perkins. Charletta closed the South Island deal.

A house, especially one of this magnitude, could mean a lot of high dollar repeat business for the hotel. *Wasn't that Vandiveer kid from Sea View?* They must have friends, chic couture friends. He quivered at the thought.

Andrea thanked the waiter for pouring the champagne, never taking her eyes off Dusty.

"Now, where were we...? Oh, yes, the hair..."

He couldn't believe she would be interested in him, let alone his hair. She took a sip from her glass, waiting.

"Aren't there little things that you do, or don't do, to make Alex happy?" he asked.

"When you put it that way, I suppose you're right. I can't really imagine denying him anything; he saved my life. Hell, he *gave* me my life."

"Gave you ....?"

"I was no one, nothing, someone else's property." Her eyes widened. She would not cry. "Then I escaped," she continued. "And he saved me. There was a bad guy and everything; it was so romantic. Alex was my knight in shining armor. He still is."

"Sounds like something out of one of those chick flicks," he chuckled.

"Chick flick...?" She eyed him, smiling mischievously.

He was finally starting to feel comfortable with her. He finished his champagne and refilled their flutes.

"Well, I can assure you," she said, "it was all very real and *very* scary."

Dusty was enjoying being with her in their private dining room. He couldn't remember the last time he had done anything cool, the kind of cool where money is required, not so much for what it buys, but what it means. He enjoyed his Thursdays with Julia, but they were nothing like this, nothing like Andrea.

"So, how did you and Melinda meet?" she asked.

Melinda again... *Oh, that's right I have a girlfriend,* he thought. *And Andrea has a boyfriend.*

"We all went to school together, a small private school, here in town. And, I don't know, we just sort of ended up together."

"Don't tell me she was the first girl you ever had sex with."

He felt his face go red. "Nooooo..."

She loved toying with him. He was so cute.

"Oh look, the food's here," he said grateful for the save.

After they were served, she moved the conversation on.

"So tell me about, Julia."

CHAPTER 33

ROENSTEIN RESIDENCE — SEA VIEW, GA

Julia was sitting at the island in the kitchen. She managed to eat some fresh berries and cream. It was the only thing she could get down no matter what her mood. She scanned the granite countertop. Bailey's, check; car keys, no thanks; cigarettes, why not?

She stared at her phone and wondered why Dusty wasn't answering her calls. He hadn't answered last night when she called to make sure he got home alright and both calls this morning went straight to voicemail. Had enough time passed to call again?

It was almost two... She knew he didn't have to work until five, if at all. Maybe it had finally happened. *Everyone left her eventually.* She reached for the bottle of Bailey's. It was empty. She laughed.

"All gone," she sighed.

She picked up her glass coffee mug and smashed it against the granite. She grabbed a piece of the broken glass, pulled up her long skirt and sliced into her upper thigh. As she watched the bright red blood start to ooze and felt the first sting of pain, a rush of air escaped her lips. She could breathe again, if only for a moment. But it helped her to focus. She was slipping and she knew it.

CHAPTER 34

THE INN — SEA VIEW, GA

"So, I know everybody asks you this, but the whole modeling thing...do you love it?"

Andrea looked up as if in deep thought, then landed her gaze on him.

"That's a hard one. How do I answer...? It can be ... very exciting, very glamorous *and* very rewarding, but it can also be very boring, at times irritating, and almost always exhausting."

"All the travel you mean?"

"And the location shoots. I mean furs in summer and bikinis in winter, flying from here to there and back again. Sometimes you've barely got time to get into makeup before the shoot. And you can't eat anything!"

He had noticed she more or less just pushed her food around with her fork. She may have taken three bites, max. *So, she ate the baby field grass*, that didn't count.

"However, if you can establish yourself as a brand, like I've been fortunate enough to do, the money can be outrageous. But the thing I love most about modeling is that the industry could care less about your background. It's a place where girls like me, if they work really, really hard, can make something of themselves—become a somebody." She looked down, her long, thick eyelashes fluttering, and pushed her plate away. The damsel in distress routine always worked. It was classic though a little sad, but sometimes it could be sweet. She looked up and flashed the smile that had already graced countless European covers.

"Let's be really bad and order dessert."

He smiled back. He liked her. "Why not two?"

They laughed and she signaled to the waiter who had not left the room. He hurried over and began clearing the table, his head cocked so he would not miss anything the beautiful couple had to say.

"We're going to be naughty," she whispered, her eyes on Dusty. "We want the biggest, richest, most chocolaty dessert you have and cheesecake."

The waiter pushed for the up sale. They *were* riding in a limo.

"Might I suggest a dessert liqueur?"

The champagne was gone and they were feeling the effects.

"Marvelous," Andrea said, her eyes locked on Dusty.

"Could I suggest ...?" the waiter started.

She looked at the server for the first time. He stopped speaking.

"Tell Sinclair to send the best," she said smiling before turning her attention back to Dusty.

The waiter gave a nod. "Of course, Ms. Sorcosi."

He walked away wondering what the A&A Jeans girl was doing having lunch with the guy who serviced his Chevy Colbolt.

"I'm feeling a little buzzed," she said.

"I know what you mean."

"See, it pays to have a driver."

He laughed. "You must live a great life."

This time she laughed. "You could say that."

The waiter arrived with dessert and two frosted glasses of a rare, aged blood oranaecello. When he was gone, Andrea grabbed a fork and took the point off the chocolate cake.

"You're part of that life now, Dusty." She opened her mouth, slid the fork inside and closed her lips around it. "Mmmmmm..."

She put the fork down. He knew it would be her only bite. And of course, he had heard what she said about being part of Alex's life. Once again he chose to ignore it.

"How can you eat so little?"

"It's not that little, really. I graze."

"You graze?" he asked.

"Yes, I graze," she said, her eyes lighting up. "I eat whatever I want, whenever I want, but only a bite or two. And I drink water all day, every day."

He thought back. There was always water around, behind the bar, in the bedroom, the bathroom, the kitchen, even the car.

"That way I can drink alcohol, occasionally, and have that random bite of cheesecake. Teeny, tiny little bites. Alex's Aunt Josephine taught me that."

"Seriously?" he asked.

"Seriously," she said.

She was mesmerizing.

"And of course I exercise," she confessed.

Her hair fell in her face. She looked at him and smiled.

"I thought about having a bite of your burger, but decided on the champagne instead."

She was sucking him in and he couldn't stop it. "You're assuming I would have given you a bite."

"Dusty, you know you could never deny me anything."

She batted those incredible lashes again and tossed her mane of hair. He had fallen completely under her spell in less than twenty-four hours. She was like no one he had ever known.

Their waiter returned and Andrea paid the check, leaving a two-hundred-dollar tip for him and five hundred for Sinclair. She asked where she could find the ladies' room, excusing herself to freshen up. Dusty was standing by the entrance when she returned.

"Okay. What's the name of the place you work, again?"

"MelFrank Motors," he said.

"MelFrank," she repeated. "Don't you work on commission or something?"

"I work in the service department."

He had tried sales. It lasted two weeks.

"Not that it really matters anyway. You'll have to quit when Alex gets here."

"Quit?"

"He's not going to allow you to work."

"Allow me?"

"Unless you want to act or model... or, become a rock star. Something cool like that. Ever thought about it?"

"You can't just decide one day to become a star."

"Of course you can, darling." She looped her arm through his and slipped on her Chanel shades. "Let's find the car."

It was right where they left it, out front with the driver.

"It's only two," she said glancing at her diamond encrusted wrist watch. "Can they tell you now if you have to work?"

"Have you ever had a real job?" he asked.

"No," she said with a giggle.

The hotel parking attendant held the door as they slid into the back of the waiting limo.

Dusty leaned forward once inside.

"MelFrank Motors, please."

The driver nodded and they were off.

"So, you're gonna get yourself a Cadillac?" he said, teasing Andrea.

"Me? No darling, I drive a Maserati."

"A Maserati?"

"Yes, a Maserati; and Alex drives an Aston. The cars are en route as we speak."

He just laughed and shook his head.

"You have cars on the way and you're buying more cars?"

"Sweetie, Alex and I are busy. As soon as the holidays are over its work, work, work. We need big, big, and bigger. Flying constantly, all that luggage, trips to the airport..."

"The airport?"

"Darling, you're repeating everything I say. Are you drunk?"

Her smile was disarming.

"We have to be ready at a moment's notice to fly off to God knows where. Really, sometimes I think it's just a game to Fiona. We'll each need an assistant, then there's a cook. Surely you don't think I buy groceries, or do housework."

"Of course not, darling. We leave that sort of thing to the staff," he said, mimicking her.

She laughed. "Now you're getting it."

He amused her. She had never met anyone like him.

Dusty thought Chad Mullins' teeth were going to fall out when he and Andrea walked into the MelFrank showroom. Chad, who prided himself on his cool demeanor, scrambled to his feet and tripped on the door jamb as he hurried from his cubicle.

"Hey man, thought you were on call today. You tryin' for employee of the month or something?"

Lame, Dusty thought.

"Where's Mel or Frank?" Andrea wanted to know.

"Melinda's the Mel," Dusty said, "and Frank, her dad, is in Atlanta."

"So, who do we talk to?"

"At your service," Chad said.

They turned and looked at him.

"That's right, baby. They're all out on the lot. Now what can I help you and this pretty little lady with?"

"You it is, then," Andrea said. "I need to lease some vehicles."

"Then, by all means, please step into my office."

He stepped aside, allowing them to pass. Dusty dropped into one of the two chairs facing the desk. He knew he had to play it just right. Chad had been trying to cause trouble for him since day one at MelFrank.

They grew up together and had been friends before Dusty started attending the private school. There was resentment there, but what could he do about it? Chad viewed him as some kind of "golden boy" and pitted himself in competition with Dusty.

"I'd like to take care of this as quickly as possible," Andrea said sitting in the other chair. She crossed her legs, leaning toward Dusty.

Chad watched her as she spoke. She was perfect from head to toe. Perfect hair, perfect make up on a perfect face, perfect clothes, unbelievably long, perfect legs...*those legs, damn!* He knew exactly who she was. Anybody with a TV knew who she was; there was no forgetting those A&A jeans ads. *Smokin'!* But what was she doing in Sea View *and* with Marler?

Good old Marler, Chad thought, *he got all the breaks; went to the fancy school for free, living in a fancy house for free and most likely fucking someone else's fancy girlfriend for free.* God, he hated him. He turned his attention back to the girl. He was getting a boner. *Focus!*

"I do not intend to discuss price," she continued. "Money is not a problem. I simply want to make my selections and have the vehicles delivered to my home."

"Sure, we can do that. Would you like to step out into the showroom, have a look around?"

She was already bored. "Not really." She looked at Dusty. "You know what's out there, don't you darling?" She gazed into his eyes. "I'm only interested in the pretty ones."

"The pretty ones," he said slowly. "There's a tricked out Tahoe, blacked out windows, nice rims, leather, the works..."

"Excellent. We need two, no three of those."

"Three?" Dusty asked.

"The assistants, remember? What else?"

"The silver Limited Edition Escalade..."

"Does it come in black?"

He nodded.

"Perfect, two of those and one of the really big ones."

Dusty was beginning to sweat. "The Suburban?"

She smiled. "Yes."

Was *she* drunk? "Andrea, that's three Tahoes, two Escalades and a Suburban."

Chad Mullins could not believe his luck. Six top-of-the-line SUVs. Cha-Ching!

"Listen to you, big man," Andrea said pinching his cheeks. "You're worried. I like it."

He prayed he wasn't turning red. Not in front of Chad Mullins.

"I know what I'm doing," she cooed. "There's plenty of money, darling." Her hand touched his thigh.

Chad saw everything. The way she leaned toward him, the way she talked to him, like they were the only two in the room. Melinda would be home soon. He would have to pay her a welcome home visit.

Andrea turned back to face Brad, or Chad, or whatever his name was. She was done. She stood. His eyes followed her body up to her face. She gave him a tight smile.

"Have the paperwork sent over to South Isle. I'm sure you have the address."

Chad leapt to his feet. "South Isle, that's you...?" he stammered. "I mean, so *you* built the house on South Isle?"

She didn't give the salesman another thought.

"Are you ready, Dusty?"

He was already standing.

Δ

Back in the car, Andrea instructed the driver to drive around town. She wanted to jump Dusty and thought it best they not be alone at the moment.

"Let's drive through your old neighborhood, so I can see where you grew up," she said.

"There's really not much to see."

"Sure there is." Her eyes twinkled. "You never really know a person until you've seen where they come from." Her mother had said that.

Dusty was in this area of town all the time, but today was different. He smiled as they passed the Rusty Anchor. He pointed it out to Andrea. How many times had he heard his mother complain about dragging his father out of there night after night?

"Left at the next light," Dusty instructed the driver.

As they crept onto Crane Street, the limo was indeed an odd sight to see. The kids were in school, but he could see them with his mind's eye, running behind the big car, chasing what they could not possibly know.

"There's my old house," Dusty said, leaning forward.

His mother was loading a van with Walter's help, most likely a tasting for some upcoming Thanksgiving feast. The catering business was growing by leaps and bounds. He was truly proud of everything she had accomplished, and all on her own.

"Should we stop?"

"No, she's on her way out and probably running late, if I know my Mom."

He did know her. He also knew Caroline Marler never ran late. She did, however, take the time to point out the slowly passing limo to Walt.

"Let's head back to the house. I could use a swim."

She smiled at him and he felt the rush of color in his cheeks.

"Driver, take us back to South Isle." She turned to Dusty. "Maybe some more champagne...?"

"I shouldn't have had what I already had. There's still a chance I'll get called in."

"Oh, don't be silly, you're never going back there."

It was being laid at his feet. Alex was coming home and things would change. He would soon be living in a world where anything and everything could be his—everything except of course, Andrea.

Besides, what would he do with Melinda? She was coming home in less than two weeks and this, whatever *this* was, that he shared with Andrea, would cease to be. Who was he kidding? It was done as soon as Alex arrived. Alex was the key to everything.

"Dusty?"

"A swim does sound nice," he said.

The driver dropped them off behind the house and Andrea went straight for the pool, undressing as she went. First the strappy sandals, and Hermes scarf, then a brief stop to shed the leggings. She looked over her shoulder,

"Could you find us something to drink?" she asked before raising her arms and letting the wind take the silk shirt from her. She was nude again. This goddess, fallen to earth. It was like a dream or was it a fantasy? Once inside he caught sight of his reflection in the mirror behind the bar.

"What exactly do you think is going on here?" he asked himself out loud.

He stared at himself for a long time, lost in his own pale green eyes, looking for something. There was nothing. He had no will of his own.

"Hey, what's taking so long?" Her voice, though a distant echo, seemed close. She must have gone under the glass partition. Yes, he could hear water splashing, she was in the solarium. His mind filled with lustful thoughts; he could think of nothing but having her.

He opened the fridge, quickly found a bottle with the same label as the one they had at lunch, grabbed two champagne flutes and headed for the pool and whatever fate awaited him. She was treading water near the shallow end with her head back and hip hop music was coming from hidden speakers.

"What did you bring us?" she asked.

"Dom," he said scanning the bottle.

"Perfect." She made her way to the edge where he stood. He poured a glass and handed it to her, watching her drink. "Now put that bottle down and do a sexy strip tease for me."

He laughed. She took another sip then, did a sweeping motion with her hand, indicating she was waiting.

"You're serious?"

"This time is *our* time and it's quickly running out. Let's have some harmless fun while we still can."

Being an object of desire did appeal to him, to dance for a woman the way women danced for men, to turn on and be turned on.

"Oh my God, this is Nasty Mama," Andrea squealed. "I love this song."

Dusty took the queue. He started moving his hips from side to side to the beat. He knew the song. It was called "Take It Slow," and that's exactly what he intended to do.

CHAPTER 35

ROENSTEIN RESIDENCE — SEA VIEW, GA

Julia tried Dusty's cell again. The call went straight to voicemail. What the hell was going on? She knew he was on call at five. She could understand if he, by some odd chance, had plans she knew nothing about, but not answering her calls was totally out of character. She sipped her Disaronno on ice. *Delish...*

Maybe she would swing by MelFrank to make sure things were okay. She stood up. Her leg hurt, but she was fine, for now. She had eaten half of a sandwich and taken a bite out of the other half. For a moment she thought of finishing it like a good little girl but gave up with a grimace. The bread had already turned crusty. How long had it been sitting there? She needed a cigarette. *Where the hell was Dusty?* She peered into her brother's telescope. Nothing was going on over on South Isle; nothing that could be seen from her vantage point anyway.

CHAPTER 36

THOMPSON STREET — NEW YORK

Melinda stared blankly at her cell phone. Dusty was not working so where was he and why wasn't he taking her calls? *He'd better have lost his phone.* That's the only excuse she would think of accepting. She scrolled down to Julia's face and tapped it with her finger. She stared out her bedroom window. It was freezing in New York. She couldn't wait to get home.

"Hello?" Julia answered trying to sound distant.

"Julia?"

"Oh, it's you."

"Could you at least pretend to be nice?"

"Oh, I'm sorry. Hey Mindy Sue, what's cookin' ya'll?"

Melinda rolled her eyes. "Are you drinking already?"

"No." Julia lied. "When does your flight get in?"

"Week after next..."

"Do you need a lift from the airport?"

"No, Julia. I thought I'd take a cab from Atlanta to Sea View."

This made Julia roll her eyes. "You're not taking the commuter to the airstrip?"

"Julia, stop acting crazy. You know I'm scared to death of those little planes."

And why were they discussing her travel plans anyway?
Julia thought.

"Where's Dusty?" Melinda demanded.

"Oh, shit," Julia quipped. "Was it my day to watch him?"

"Do you know where he is or don't you?"

Julia glanced at her watch, it was four thirty. "Work...?

"I tried. He's not there."

"Well, I don't know where he is. He's *your* boyfriend."

"Sometimes I have to ask myself why I put up with you," Melinda huffed.

"Because I'm the only one who will put up with you, bitch."

"Ha ha..." She hung up.

Julia shrugged. "Tootles..."

No one will put up with me. That's what she thinks.
Melinda smiled to herself. She had met a lot of people and was making friends quickly. And adding Sue back to her name had given her an edge at the magazine. She was just as clever and efficient as the other girls, plus her sticky sweet southern charm separated her from the pack, especially in her social life.

The Yankees just loved her occasional *ya'll.* She was their modern day Scarlet and a lot of the men had made it perfectly clear that they were ready to play Rhett. She flirted shamelessly and had even gone on a couple of dates, but so far Martin (pronounced *Mar-teen*) Briceno was the frontrunner. His family was from Venezuela and he was an actor, which meant he was in the restaurant business. She smiled at the thought of him.

Her roommate, Audrey, a year older, had warned her from the beginning to stay away from actors, musicians and bartenders. And by all means avoid the bartender, slash actors. Martin was the latter.

CHAPTER 37

SOUTH ISLE — SEA VIEW, GA

Dusty was sitting on the steps in the shallow end of the pool, submerged to his chest in water. The sun had finally started to set, painting the sky a reddish, golden orange and bringing with it the cooler night air.

They were still in the solarium where they had just spent the past few hours playing Marco Polo, having water fights and dunking each other with full body contact. Needing a break and time to *deflate,* he swam to the bottom of the deep end and back, emerging to find her gone.

So he sat there and allowed his mind to wander. He was debating another dive when she returned wearing one of the now familiar, monogrammed robes. He noticed she was carrying one for him.

He was burning for her and she knew it, everything was in her hands. She gave him the robe and turned while he got out of the water.

"Are you hungry?" she asked. "We'll order in."

They had finished off two bottles of Dom and were both buzzed. He followed her through the house, watching as she twisted her hair into a knot on top of her head. He wanted to kiss the back of her neck.

"Who delivers? Can we get Chinese?"

"There's Golden Buddha," he offered.

"Golden Buddha it is. Can you be a love and order for us? I need a shower."

"Sure."

She grabbed his face in her hand the way she had at the dealership and squeezing his cheeks, kissed him on the mouth.

"Maybe I should have met you first, huh?"

She smiled and looked deep into his eyes. She had him. Now what was she to do with him? Things were progressing too quickly. The plan was to get the house in order and wait for Alex, then find Dusty. But Dusty had found her instead.

"I'll be right back. Order some veggie egg rolls for me, please?"

He wanted to say so many things, but, "Sure," was all he could manage to get out. He dialed the number and watched her as she walked out of the great room into the foyer. She shook her hair loose as she climbed the stairs.

"Golden Buddha, may I help you?"

He snapped out of it and ordered: fried wontons, Mongolian pork and an order of General Tsao's chicken, plain rice, and, of course, veggie egg rolls. Andrea was back down before the food arrived. She was once again in leggings, a black stretch tank this time with her hair pulled into a high pony tail.

"Your turn," she said.

Alone in the Blue Room bathroom, he was able to reflect on the events of the past twenty hours. She had kissed him twice. Okay, not full on kisses, but... And all the nude swimming. Was she trying to seduce him? It seemed obvious. Something was definitely going on. What was he going to do?

He showered, his dick sticking straight out in front of him the whole time. It knew what it wanted to do, but what was *he* going to do? *That* was the question. He wanted to beat off so bad, but what if?

Suddenly, his mind jumped tracks. His cell phone. Where was it? With his clothes? He knew Melinda would have called. He had not spoken to her since—oh, shit. He couldn't remember. And Julia? He grabbed a William Rast t-shirt and track pants.

The food was just arriving when he got back downstairs. She carried everything to the kitchen and he followed. After everything was laid out on the kitchen's island, Andrea reached into her cleavage and pulled out a small silver object. She twisted the top part of it, then, turned it up.

"What's that?" he asked.

"Cocaine," she answered. "This is called a bullet."

"Okay," he said slowly.

He and Julia smoked weed and he knew she snorted a little every now and then, but he never ventured further.

Andrea inhaled from the open end, repeated the twisting action and inhaled again. She twisted a third time and presented it to Dusty. He took it. Two hits, just as she had done.

"The food smells delicious," she said.

She was going to change his life and he would let her. He was drowning in Sea View. He wanted out and she was going to take him.

She grabbed an egg roll and bit into it. *Everything she did was erotic*, he thought. He could feel the effects of the cocaine now. He wanted more. He reached for the bullet.

"Do you mind?"

"Of course not, darling. Have all you want. We're going to have fun tonight."

CHAPTER 38

THOMPSON STREET — NEW YORK

Melinda took her time dressing. Though it was nearly nine and she had just showered. Today was Audrey's birthday and there was a huge party for her at a mutual friend's apartment just blocks from campus. It was supposed to be quiet, the show place. The girl's father was an antiques importer, but that wasn't why she was taking extra care with her appearance. Martin would be there. Martin Briceno. He was so charming with his Spanish accent. His dark looks were in direct contrast to hers. Perhaps that was the appeal.

She picked matching Victoria Secret lingerie, pale pink with white lace trim and tiny little bows. She stared at her reflection in the full-length mirror. Her waist was small enough, her hips and butt round enough and her breasts, with a little help from Victoria, full enough. She did wish, however, that her legs were three inches longer. *No worries,* she thought, *the right pair of platforms would take care of that.*

Dusty crossed her mind. Would she break up with him over the holiday? They were just so far apart. Shortly after arriving in New York, she made an appointment with a recommended sex therapist, and had finally been able to do the deed with Dusty without too much discomfort—but bottom line, he was just too big.

She wondered about Martin. By no means did she want a man with a small one, but she did crave that perfect fit. Both her therapist and Audrey swore that she was still tensing up, for fear that each time it might hurt, so each time, it did hurt. That was ridiculous. She thought it might hurt each time because it *did* hurt each time. She also thought both women were just obsessed with her boyfriend's big dick. *Whores!*

She carefully applied her most expensive perfume behind her knees, on her upper thighs, between her breasts and, of course, on her neck. On the way to her closet, she checked her cell phone; still no call from Dusty.

Yes, she would definitely make out with Martin tonight. If she could get him to ask her out for New Year's Eve, she would end it with Dusty over Christmas break. They were young; it was only natural that they would grow apart.

She was reaching her goals, planning for the future; but Dusty—he seemed to be standing still. How could he possibly be happy working for her father and how could he expect her to settle? He was supposed to be away at college, securing his status as an up and coming pro athlete.

If only she could go back and erase that fateful night. She sighed. The past was the past. There was nothing she or anyone else could do to change it.

CHAPTER 39

SOUTH ISLE — SEA VIEW, GA

The Chinese food had long been forgotten. Andrea ate one egg roll, Dusty sampled everything and now the bullet needed a refill. She disappeared upstairs to take care of it while Dusty nursed his third scotch. He had finally tried cocaine—*and liked it.* The stuff could definitely be trouble. Maybe he could use some trouble, he thought.

"So, are we ready for some fun?" Andrea asked returning to the kitchen, a small black bag hanging from her shoulder.

She offered the fresh stash and he gladly accepted it.

"I really like this stuff," he said.

"Yes, I can see that."

He took two hits, then, passed it back to her.

"So, what kind of fun did you have in mind?"

She unzipped the bag and produced an Olympus Evolt E520 digital camera, complete with a Zuiko zoom lens.

"I'm going to take your picture," she said.

"My picture...?"

"Yes. I spend so much time in front of the camera, but I really love photography. I photograph everything. And now, it's your turn."

The coke really had him revved up and the idea excited him. He wondered if nudity would be involved. There was a slight tingling in his groin at the thought of finally showing off for her. Was he ready for this?

"I'll pick out some things for you to wear," she said. "You can do some push-ups or whatever you guys do to pump up."

CHAPTER 40

ROENSTEIN RESIDENCE — SEA VIEW, GA

Julia peered through the telescope yet again—and still nothing, not since the delivery guy from Golden Buddha.

She reached into the pocket of her cardigan for her cell. No missed calls. It didn't make any sense. Where was Dusty? It wasn't like him not to return her calls. She could understand him ignoring Melinda, but not her. It was almost ten. Then something caught her eye.

"What the hell?"

She looked into the viewfinder. The back of the house on South Isle was lit up like a stadium.

"What is going on over there?"

Should she go check it out? No, not alone. She resumed drinking after her phone call with Melinda and had snorted a couple of Adderall. Driving was definitely out of the question. She called him again; the call went straight to voicemail. Glancing back toward the lights on South Isle, she snapped the legs of the tripod closed and hoisted the telescope up.

"Fuck it," she said, carrying the telescope to the upstairs study. Maybe if she got higher and more to the right she could get a better view. It took a while. She had to go to the third floor and the stairs slowed her a little, but she made it.

She set the telescope up and opened the corner window. *How long has it been since any of these windows were opened?* This was her step-father's study. She brought the viewfinder into focus and gasped.

"What the hell? Dusty...?"

She reached for her phone, but it wasn't in the pocket of her sweater. She must have left it on the deck. She reached for the house phone and dialed information.

"Sea View, Georgia...Shoreline Cab."

CHAPTER 41

SOUTH ISLE — SEA VIEW, GA

Andrea set the computerized lighting system to the brightest setting. Dusty walked out and immediately shielded his eyes.

"Jesus, isn't that a little bright?"

He hit the bullet a few more times, but switched from scotch to water. He was wearing dark denim jeans and a crisp, white dress shirt.

"Come here," she said. "Unbutton the shirt."

While he worked on the buttons, she opened his pants and unzipped them slightly. They were standing so close. His heart was racing.

"The lights are necessary. It's dark, remember?" She slapped his ass. "Now, lay here on the chaise."

"Like this?"

She looked through the camera lens. "Spread your legs more."

"Like this?" He smiled and pushed his hips upward.

"Exactly, like that."

Rapid fire shutter clicks.

"A few more.... Pull the shirt off your right shoulder."

More shutter clicks.

"Now lose the shirt altogether. Turn your head this way. Eyes at me.... Perfect. Now clasp your hands behind your head. You're doing great. Just a few more..."

The camera clicked away.

"Perfect. Okay, there's another change inside; linen shirt and pants."

"Cool." He started for the house.

"No underwear." She called after him.

He smiled. Inside, he undressed completely, his body tingling all over. His hand instinctively went to his penis. It was swollen, but hanging, flaccid. He wondered briefly why he wasn't getting hard, but was grateful; he knew full well the thin material of the linen slacks would be of no help.

He found the bullet, did a few more bumps, then picked up the pants and stepped into them. He pulled on the shirt and headed back outside. Andrea was waiting.

"You look terrific. Button the shirt." He did. "Now dive into the pool."

"In the clothes...?"

"Yes," she said. "In the clothes."

He shrugged and dove in. Andrea stretched out face down and waited for him to surface, which he did midway across the pool. He began treading the water, slowly moving toward her.

"Stop there," she said. "Can you touch bottom to steady yourself?"

"Yeah, I think so."

His foot found the bottom and he stood upright. Andrea busied herself focusing the camera.

"Ok now, stretch your arms straight out to the side and touch your chin to the water. Perfect."

His green eyes matched the water beautifully, thanks to the underwater lighting.

"Now swim over to the steps."

193

She got up and walked around to meet him at the shallow end of the pool. He was lounging on the steps when she got there, camera raised, shooting him as she got closer. He ran a hand through his hair, pushing it straight back.

"You do realize you can see straight through these clothes."

She lowered the camera and smiled. "That's the point. You can stand up now."

He did, the soaked linen clinging to him like a second skin. She stepped quickly, to the left and started shooting. He turned his head, following the lens with his eyes.

"You love this, don't you?" she teased.

His grin said it all. He was really into it and it was working. By the time she cut him loose tonight, he would be putty in her hands. She lowered the camera.

"You're awfully quiet," she teased. "You're not nervous are you?"

"Why, would I be nervous? It's not like you haven't been around me naked."

"Yes, but *I'm* not naked this time. Are you sure you're not embarrassed?"

"Embarrassed? Hell no...!"

Frankly, he had never felt so turned on, even without a boner.

"Honestly, I'm a little confused," he confessed.

"Confused?"

He looked down and let out a little laugh. "I feel like something should be going on down there."

"It's the coke," she said.

"Huh?"

"If you do too much too quickly, Mr. Happy might feel like playing, but..."

He squinted his eyes in thought. "You gave it to me on purpose?"

"Those things have a mind of their own. We're not shooting porn here."

"So, in a weird way, you did me a favor."

"Yes," she laughed. "Now go to the bottom of the steps and slowly walk out of the water towards me."

He did, feeling sexier by the minute, glad that he didn't have to worry about concealing his weapon for once. A current of electricity was coursing through him making his body feel more alive than ever.

"You're a natural," she said. "Ready for some nudes...?"

This was it. He knew there was a chance she might ask. *Was he ready?*

He unbuttoned the shirt and, with a little difficulty, shed the pants as well. When he looked up, she was entering the house.

"Get back in the water," she called over her shoulder.

She came back with more bottled water and the bullet. Dusty was swimming laps. He made his way to the side where she stood. She gave him the water, hit the bullet and then passed it to him.

"So, how long does this stuff last?"

"Don't worry. You'll be right as rain in the morning."

He filled each nostril.

"It's not gonna shrivel me up, is it?"

"That thing could never look small. Now stay in the water, 'til I get back. I have an idea."

This time she went into the pool house. Dusty was glad the pool was heated, since there was a definite chill in the air; no guy liked the thought of shrinkage.

Andrea returned with a bottle of baby oil and motioned for him to get out of the water. He did and she squirted the oil over his chest and back. The electricity returned. She rubbed his back, and oiled each of his arms before kneeling to do his legs. Her hands, the wind, the oil on his wet, naked body; she was making him crazy. She started at his feet and worked her way up, higher and higher until she reached his upper thighs and buttocks. Dusty closed his eyes.

His mind was racing, his whole body on fire. And then she touched him; two light strokes from a lubed up hand. He started to tremble and then his body quaked and he shivered.

"Oh, God," he whispered, gasping a little. "What was that?"

"I think you just had a little orgasm," she teased, spanking each of his ass cheeks.

"But I didn't..."

She stood. "You just learned something new about your body."

CHAPTER 42

UPPER EAST SIDE — NEW YORK

The party was in full swing. The music was great, the townhouse was amazing and Melinda was getting plenty of attention from Martin. They managed to find a semi private corner where he made his moves and she let him. After seemingly endless kisses, the two finally came up for air just as a group of partygoers erupted with whistles and catcalls.

"Go Jarrod, go Jarrod, go, go, go Jarrod..."

They looked through the crowd to see him dancing and lip-syncing to Britney Spears' "Circus," complete with hair tossing and booty popping. She had to admit, he was pretty good.

"Your friend seems to be having a good time," Martin said, caressing her cheek.

She laughed. "Jarrod always has a good time."

"Did you know that your eyes sparkle like the stars when you smile?"

Melinda lowered her lashes. *Just shut up and kiss me,* she thought.

"I just love your accent," she said.

"And I like yours. I like it very much."

He moved in, touching his forehead to hers. He was so close and smelled so good. The alcohol, the atmosphere, his words, his lips... Everything was working. The radiating warmth between her legs was quickly spreading. Melinda squeezed her thighs together. *Yes, she would give in to Martin tonight.* He seemed to have all the right moves, and this made her wildly curious.

CHAPTER 43

SOUTH ISLE — SEA VIEW, GA

Back inside the house, Andrea was busy downloading and editing the images while Dusty showered. She opened another bottle of champagne and was ready to pour when a chime sounded, indicating someone at the front gate. Puzzled, she went to the security panel. There was a young woman in the back of a cab.

"Yes?"

"Hi. I'm looking for Dustin Marler."

Andrea entered a code and the gate swung open. She was waiting at the door when the cab pulled into the circular drive.

It was that easy, like she was expected, Julia thought. What was going on and what did Dusty have to do with it? Julia was feeling a little loopy, but was enjoying this little adventure, none the less.

As soon as the front door opened and she saw her face, everything fell into place. Julia paid the fare and hurried from the back seat of the car.

"Hello," Andrea waved.

"Oh, my God, I can't believe it," she said pointing. "Sorcosi...you're Andrea Sorcosi."

Andrea met her half way down the inlaid marble stairs. "You must be Julia?"

"That's right, Julia Roenstein. I can't believe you're here. Is Alex with you?"

Andrea guided her toward the main entrance.

"He's in New York, but he'll be here soon," she replied.

Dusty was descending the staircase as they entered the rotunda. He tried to hide his panic. Thank God he was dressed and not wearing one of the house robes.

"And you," Julia shouted. "Where the hell have you been? You can't return a phone call?"

"His cell fell into the pool," Andrea explained.

"Oh. So what have you guys been up to?" Julia asked nonchalantly, looking around. "I love, love, love this place. Is there a bar?"

Good old, Julia, Dusty thought. *She was here now, and that's all that mattered.* And it was obvious she had been drinking and if he knew her like he thought he did, she was most likely overmedicated.

"It's this way," he said, escorting them into the great room.

"My, God, this is just breathtaking." Julia looked at the rounded wall with its floor to ceiling window panes. "The view is amazing."

"What could I get for you, Jules?"

She turned away from the ocean view to see Dusty smiling behind a carved, mahogany bar. She sauntered over and hopped onto a matching hand carved barstool, joining Andrea.

"This place is to die for," she said waving her arms dramatically. "I'll have the house cocktail."

"Perfect. That's what we were having," Andrea replied. "Two more glasses of Dom, please."

Dusty opened the built-in 'fridge. "There isn't any more."

Andrea smiled. "There's always more, darling. The cellar is through that door. The champagnes will be in the refrigerated section. You can't miss it. Go on, you'll find it."

He wasn't sure he wanted to leave the two of them alone together just yet, but what choice did he have. He opened the door next to the bronze-colored stainless refrigerator to find stairs leading down. An overhead light came on automatically, lighting his way to the bottom and into an elaborate wine cellar.

There were a few bottles on the wall and ahead he saw a large, glassed-in, refrigerated room. Inside, he found another refrigerator full of dark green bottles. He grabbed two, thought again, and grabbed a third. The girls were laughing when he returned.

"So, what are we talking about?" he asked, not sure he wanted to know.

They stopped, looked at him then cracked up again. He spied the bullet lying on the bar.

"You, silly," Julia said, teasing.

"Don't worry, Dusty." Andrea smiled. "Your secrets are safe."

He poured for everyone. Julia picked up a champagne glass and surveyed the situation. Her eyes darted from one to the other and back again.

"Are there secrets? You told me you guys just met and hung out this afternoon."

"We did," Andrea said. "I meant you guys. Surely you must have some dirt on him," she teased.

"Do I ever," Julia laughed. "But I'll never tell."

That was close, Dusty thought.

"Would you like another bump?" Andrea asked.

"Love, love, love one," Julia sang.

Dusty was quiet as the girls' chatter continued. He was beginning to sweat.

"So, would you like to see the house?"

Julia nodded. "Could I?"

"We hired a decorator, of course."

"So that explains the *Architectural Digest* cover look."

They went through the kitchen, by the breakfast room and up the back stairs.

Dusty poured himself a scotch and hit the bullet again. *Shit. There it was...reality. Was the entire weekend alone with her asking too much? What if Julia had not arrived unannounced?* He snorted from the bullet again. *Why had Andrea lied?*

He did another bump and stared at his reflection in the mirrored wall. He reached for the bullet again, then changed his mind. His eyes went to the windows. The moonlight danced on the ocean waves. His mind wandered to his childhood, to Alex and the first day they met. It seemed a lifetime ago. He did another bump.

"Hey, you mind sharing that thing?"

He looked up to see Julia. *They'd finished the tour already? How long had he been standing there?*

"My bad," he said grinning.

"Dusty, I was just telling Julia about our photo shoot."

"You were?"

"Well, actually, that's what lured me here," Julia said.

"Yes, she saw the lights."

Julia started to laugh that little laugh that signaled she was toasted. In a way he was glad, she wouldn't be as sharp. Still, he knew he had to be careful.

Julia giggled. "And I told her about the telescope."

Andrea smiled. "Spying on me, Dusty?"

"What? No..."

Julia was off and running. The coke had topped off her Adderall, caffeine and cigarette high.

"Oh, relax," Julia continued. "Pour me another glass of the good stuff."

Julia's hand went to her upper thigh. He did not miss the gesture and knew what it meant. He shouldn't have left her the way he did.

She sipped from her flute then held it out for a topper. "You know, this stuff is really not bad, but I prefer a sweeter taste."

"Dusty, there should be a bottle of Chambord..."

"Got it," he said.

"Oh," Julia squealed, "love, love, love."

Dusty poured.

"Just a touch—good, good, good," Julia said, taking another sip. "Perfect..."

Andrea smiled. "So, you were telling us about the telescope."

Dusty took another drink, bracing himself. Julia was cool, but he *had* been naked.

"Ahh, yes, the telescope... So anyway, I moved it to the upstairs study. I don't know why we didn't think of that before. And that's when I saw Dusty. So I called a cab immediately and presto, here I am."

"Here you are," Dusty blurted out. He was still sweating.

Who knew when he would be alone with Andrea again? It was as if he were a different person when he was around her—like he had a clean slate and anything was possible. He watched them chatting.

"By the way, I love this dress," Andrea said.

"Oh, my God, do you? I made it!"

"Seriously...? I love all this around the neckline."

Julia let out another squeal, this time catching Dusty off guard. He flinched. Julia sat her glass down and shed her sweater, something she rarely did.

"Look, it's halter-backed."

"It's fantastic. And I love the ribbons at the wrists." Andrea tried to touch one, but Julia pulled away. *Both wrists?*

"They're silly..."

"No, I think young girls will love it. An inexpensive *must-have*. But I could never wear that without a good bra."

Julia sighed. "Fortunately, I don't have that problem."

She reached for her sweater, suddenly feeling self-conscious.

Andrea stopped her. "No, don't cover the dress."

She handed the bottle of champagne to Julia and reached for the Chambord. "Come sit with me by the fire. Dusty, will you join us?"

Julia tucked herself into a corner of the plush sectional, flanked by Andrea and Dusty.

"Finally, something exciting has happened in Sea View," she said.

"Exciting?" Andrea asked.

"You're big news," Dusty said. "Well, you will be."

"Yes, you're our first celebrity resident. Tell us, is it as glamorous as it seems?"

Andrea laughed. She glanced at Dusty, and Julia could have sworn he blushed.

"Another time perhaps," she said. "I just get so bored talking about me. I'd much rather talk about this dress. So you're designing?"

"Oh, just for myself. I don't make everything but, some things."

"She's being modest," Dusty said. "She's got tons of stuff."

"Really, I'd love to see them," Andrea said. "Have you had a showing?"

"No, I never really thought about it."

"But you have to. We could do it here, in the ballroom."

"Oh no, I couldn't."

"Please say yes. I'll help. It'll be fun."

Julia was pensive for a moment. "Do you really think I could?"

"Absolutely," Andrea replied.

Dusty couldn't help smiling, watching the two girls bond. He and Julia grew close after Alex disappeared, closer still when everyone went away to college. It made him feel good that someone was taking a genuine interest in her. He got up and wandered around the room, his mind spinning.

Alex would be home within days and everything would change. Andrea would be by Alex's side and Melinda by his. And now that Julia had discovered them, the sleepovers would certainly cease.

If only...what...? If only what? Were you going to have sex with her? Cheat on Melinda? Betray Alex? He finished his drink. What was he doing? What was he thinking? The past couple of days had been crazy.

He laughed out loud. Crazy was an understatement, but he felt more alive than he had in years. She was electrifying, but she belonged to Alex.

Should he have another drink? Damn, he was really revved up. He checked his reflection. He was sweating more. He looked at the bullet and started laughing out loud again. Damn, he was fucked up. He spun around when he heard his name.

"Huh?"

"Are you okay?" Julia asked.

"I'm fine."

"This has been great," she said to her host, "but I must be going, Dusty, share a cab with me?"

"Ah, yeah..."

"Are you sure you won't stay. We have plenty of room."

"Another time..." She had to get Dusty out of there.

"Of course," Andrea said. She was trying to protect him; how sweet.

They were both quiet as the cab passed through the gates on South Isle. Julia was lost in thought. Was something good, at last, about to happen in her life? *God, how long had it been?* Once on the mainland, it was Dusty who broke the silence.

"So, I guess you're pretty stoked?"

"Apprehensive, might be a better word, but yes, I am stoked." She laid her head on Dusty's shoulder. "Andrea is so amazing and she really liked my dress."

He too, was lost in thought while she spoke quietly, wondering if he liked cocaine after all. The car rolled to a stop.

"First stop," the cabbie called.

"Hey," Julia whispered to Dusty, "I've got some good chronic."

He smiled. She paid the fare and they started up the driveway. As soon as the cab disappeared into the night, Julia produced a fat ass blunt.

"What the fuck?" Dusty asked.

"I swear, you're so white sometimes," she joked.

They stopped while she lit it, then continued to walk up the driveway, passing the blunt back and forth. It was just what he needed to take the edge off. Again, he wondered if coke was really his thing.

"So, what was it like, all by your lonesome with Ms. Sorcosi?"

"What do you mean?"

"Come on, Dusty. She's *gorgeous*... and you are a guy." She laughed at him. "And I saw your little photo session."

He panicked.

"That's right," she sang. "Through the telescope from the upstairs study. I wondered how long it took to get you out of those jeans. God, *I'd* even do her."

He choked out a little laugh.

"You didn't return my calls," she said, still singing. "I raced out of the house as soon as I saw you. Well, I showered and changed first, of course."

Her lighthearted tone signaled two things: She hadn't seen the entire photo shoot and she wasn't angry that she hadn't been able to reach him. Damn, his heart couldn't take too much more, especially after all that cocaine.

The blunt was calming him and he couldn't decide if it was a good thing or not, because all he could think about was having another bump. Maybe he did like it after all.

They made it to the front porch and sat in matching bamboo rockers, finishing off the blunt.

"This has been a crazy night," Julia said. "I can't believe Andrea Sorcosi liked *my* dress."

"It is pretty great."

"Yes... and an actual showing."

She got quiet for a moment. Dusty was calmer now, but still a little revved up, the powder still working its magic. He needed to figure out how to make his exit so he could go home and masturbate to the memories of his time with Andrea.

"Do you think I can pull it off?" she asked.

This comment snapped him back. "Pull what off?"

"Are you zoning out again? The fashion show...?"

He touched her arm. "I know you can."

They talked for another fifteen minutes or so before Dusty said good night and began the ten-minute walk to his house. Thoughts of Andrea swirled around him like the ocean breeze and with each step, he got hornier and hornier.

He couldn't wait to get home and fantasize about her and every agonizing minute he spent alone with her. By the time he opened the front gate he could feel that familiar movement against his leg. He quickened his pace up the walkway and took the steps two at a time.

"What took you so long?"

He went rigid and staggered a few feet back. She emerged from the shadows as if out of nowhere, catching him by surprise.

"Oh shit, Andrea?"

She came closer. "Did I startle you?"

He was confused, but really glad to see her. On instinct he hugged her.

"Fuck yeah—you startled me," he laughed. "What are you doing here?"

They rocked back and forth in the embrace, both laughing. Suddenly he realized he had been hugging her way too long and that there was no way she was unaware of his throbbing erection pressing against her thigh.

She smelled so good. He kissed the top of her head, then, unable to stop himself, her forehead, the tip of her nose and finally, her lips. And she kissed him back. How could something so wrong seem so right? He pulled his mouth from hers and struggled with the key. She was all over him. His neck, his face, his ear, *oh God...* Suddenly his arms were raised and his shirt was gone.

They struggled to close the door and made it into the foyer before he found himself flat on his back with Andrea straddling his hips. She sat there for a moment, grinding her heat against him, the thin fabric of her leggings almost nonexistent between them. She leaned down and kissed his mouth again. Their tongues lashed against one another and she rocked her hips, pushing down on the lump in his pants. Her mouth found his nipples and he moaned, sliding his hands to her hips, trying to hold her still.

She was driving him mad with all the squirming. She kissed him again, then went for his neck. He was going out of his mind with desire for her. She pulled away, their eyes locked and that was all it took. He held on tight as he soared over the edge.

By the second grunt, embarrassment washed over him; but by the third, it didn't matter. She mashed her mouth against his once again and he flew higher and higher. It was so hot on that cold marble floor. She licked at his neck and nibbled his ear while he struggled to regain some measure of composure, then rose up and rocked gently against him.

He took a few deep breathes and shivered from head to toe, gasping. She started to laugh softly. He released her hips and his arms dropped to his side.

"Fuck!"

She continued to laugh quietly.

"God! Andrea, I'm so sorry." He covered his face with his hands. "Fuck, fuck, fuck. What did I do?"

She placed her hands over his, prying them from his eyes. He closed them and turned his head away. He couldn't look at her. She leaned down and kissed him softly on the lips then laid her head on his chest. She could hear his heart and his breathing, but could only imagine his thoughts. At last, he spoke.

"Andrea, I don't know what to say."

"Then don't say anything"

"But..."

She placed a finger against his lips.

"Shhhh..."

She took his hand and led him silently upstairs. Once inside the bathroom they slowly undressed and turned on the shower. She tenderly soaped him from top to bottom and allowed him the same opportunity. It was both beautiful and surreal, and would be forever burned into his brain.

And when they were naked in bed and everything was still, he spoke to her.

"This cannot happen."

Her mind was whirling a mile a minute. There was something between them. She could not deny it.

"Not this way," she said absentmindedly.

He pushed up on an elbow. "This way?" he asked.

"I was supposed to come here, get the house ready and wait for Alex."

"Oh God," he groaned. "Alex."

And there it was again—reality.

He fell back, staring at the ceiling and sighed. Everything had gotten way, way out of hand. Melinda was coming home for Thanksgiving and Alex would be arriving soon. They remained silent, spooning, just being together. She held his hand in hers, nestled beneath her chin, just as she did the first night, the night she slipped Ambien into his drink. *God, help us,* she thought.

Dusty was wondering what they would do to cover their tracks. Her hair smelled so wonderful and she felt unbelievable next to him, but it couldn't last. Hell, it couldn't even *be.* He pulled her closer to him.

She never wanted him to let her go, but this could never work. How could it? Getting Alex into bed with Dusty wouldn't be a problem, but getting Dusty into bed with Alex was a completely different story.

First things first, she told herself. Alex could not know about the time she had spent with Dusty, and it was going to be tricky to make it seem like he was falling for her, when he already had. *What happened? He happened.*

Was she falling, too? Had she fallen? Was she capable of love? What she had with Alex—was it love? He was extremely loyal to her and she to him, but was it love? Her mind replayed all the events leading up to this moment. When had the game turned into something else? How could she be certain?

God knows she never felt anything for any of the men who came to see her at Sally's, but Alex was different. Surely he must love her—or was their relationship more of a partnership?

It seemed an eternity before Dusty finally fell asleep. She, of course, could not and just before the sun rose, she eased the covers back and slipped out of bed. She quickly dressed and hurried downstairs, through the kitchen and out the backdoor, through the gate and down the path that led to the beach.

There was a definitive chill in the air and the wind was high, but she didn't notice. Her mind had not stopped since the incident in the foyer. This was not supposed to happen. Andrea tried desperately to focus. She would have to do some damage control and she needed all her wits about her. By the time she made it to South Isle, she knew what she had to do.

CHAPTER 44

THE PINK PALACE — ATLANTA, GA

The Pink Palace was one of the oldest and most successful strip clubs in Atlanta. It was also the classiest.

The Palace sold fantasies and was bigger and better than ever—thanks to the shrewd business savvy of the eldest son of original owner, DaShawn L. Crawford II. The gentlemen's club had a long standing reputation of hiring the cream of the crop.

DaShawn Crawford was in his office watching the security monitors like always, so he saw her the moment she walked into the club. Who could miss the black leather boots that went all the way up to the hem of her mini chinchilla? He grabbed his ebony walking stick and by the time he made it to the main floor, the hostess was seating her in one of the plush VIP booths.

"Such a beautiful woman all alone," he said, approaching the table. "Margo, my usual set up, please." He turned his attention back to the booth.

Andrea looked at the gorgeous redhead with the creamy white skin. "Champagne, please..."

The girl scurried off. Champagne was sold only by the bottle and it was ten times the price it should be.

The owner offered his hand. "DaShawn Crawford, proprietor at-large."

"Andrea Sorcosi." She extended her hand and he kissed it. "Won't you join me, DaShawn?"

He smiled and slid into the booth beside her.

"Say, ain't you that A&A Jeans girl?" he asked.

Andrea nodded as he continued to speak.

"Yeah, you killed that French cat."

She flashed her dazzling smile. All those afternoons in Sicily spent with Josephine were instantly recalled. *A lady must never lose her composure.* The words came in a distant whisper.

"DaShawn, why speak of such ugly things? We're at the Palace. And I have a proposition for you."

This got his attention. *Like shooting fish in a barrel.* "I'll bet you do."

Another cocktail waitress arrived with DaShawn's set up.

"Patron?" he asked.

She raised a single finger. "One..."

Just then her cell phone rang. She slipped a perfectly manicured hand into a jeweled clutch then held the device to her ear.

"Sweetheart," she said sweetly. "Of course I miss you. Yes, I know it's your birthday, we talked earlier, remember?" She feared they had already been apart too long. "Yes, I'm here now...Yes, I confirmed Romeo for the party. Don't worry Sweetheart ...Yes, of course I do, darling. I love you too."

While she was on the phone the waitress returned with the champagne. *Cheap, but it would do.* Andrea nodded and smiled at the waitress who popped the cork, poured and disappeared back into the crowd.

"Yes, darling... Be careful, and I'll see you soon."

She was worried about Alex, but he was in New York and she was at the Palace. She sipped her sparkling wine. *Back to business,* she thought.

"She's stunning," Andrea said, referring to the waitress.

"I only hire the best. You could do very well here."

"DaShawn," she replied, slapping his arm, playfully. "Do I look like I need the money?"

"Touché." They did the Patron shots. "So what brings you here?"

"I'm having a party. A coming-home party and it has to be very special."

"How special?" DaShawn asked, doing another shot.

"Like I said, *very special*; I need four or five girls, young ones, for a long weekend. I'll provide lodging and transportation, of course. First class all the way, and the girls will be paid ten thousand each, for the three days."

He took a moment to answer. His cut wouldn't even cover the lawyers, should anything go wrong.

"That sounds like prostitution to me and everybody knows the Pink Palace is a legitimate business."

"Such a tasteless word," Andrea sighed. "Consider it an appearance fee. What the girls choose to do on their own is their business."

"And what exactly is in it for me?"

He was cutting to the chase. So would she. "I'm doing something for you right now."

"Are you?"

Just then, a couple of guys walked up and started taking pictures. This caught the attention of the tables nearby. *It wouldn't be long now, she thought, before the gossip mag junkies started circling, the Gossip Girl junkies started texting and the gossip column junkies started reading.*

"So, Andrea, what brings you to the infamous Pink Palace?" one of them asked.

"Nasty Mama; she loves the Palace." *Always lead in big.*

She found it amusing how perfect strangers attempted to talk to her as if they knew her. But she would play; she had called them after all.

"So, is Alex here with you?"

"He's in New York with his father, but yes he will be joining me."

"Rumor has it he's headed for rehab," the other stated. "Is that why he's coming to Georgia?"

Andrea smiled sweetly, ignoring the question. "I'm helping a friend launch a new clothing line. The Palace is the perfect backdrop."

"Any celebrities on the guest list?"

Time to send them away, she thought.

"Mama's coming, what do you think?" She trailed off, winking at DaShawn. "The infamous Pink Palace is about to become famous."

DaShawn couldn't believe his ears. *Nasty Mama was gonna perform at his club. Who was this girl?*

"What the hell just happened here?" he wanted to know.

"*I* just happened here," she said.

She liked the power of fame. Andrea Sorcosi was quickly rising through the ranks yet again, and once Alex arrived, it would be mayhem. He loved hard and he played hard but he was growing reckless. Settling back in Sea View was going to test them all. Christmas was going to be a blast, she was certain; but right after New Year's, it was back to rehab for Alex.

CHAPTER 45

THE ROYAL GRAND HOTEL — SOHO, NY

Alex sat sprawled and naked in a penthouse suite, smoking a joint. He had been partying at Random House, a hot new dance club near the village, where he met a couple named Ram and Ginger. The promise of drugs and a limo ride to and from the hotel had been enough to bait them; the money, enough to keep them.

She had been so cute, defiantly demanding a thousand dollars when Alex asked how much it would cost to watch her fuck her boyfriend. And after watching them, it was obvious to Alex why they called him Ram.

He held out as long as he could, but Andrea was not with him in New York. They had never been apart before, so after the shoot for D&G's new Men's fragrance wrapped, he let one of the lighting guys talk him into going out. Within twenty minutes of walking into the place and realizing he was getting nowhere with *the model,* the guy moved on to some Wall Street types at the bar.

Just as well, Alex thought. Ram and Ginger were much more entertaining, of that, he was certain. He had given them a standing ovation and an eight-inch salute before he flopped down on the bed in between them.

"Very impressive," he said. "Smoke...?" He passed the joint to Ram and looked at the red head. "Did you enjoy that, my dear?"

"I did," Ginger giggled. "Ram is very good."

"Back at you, babe...," Ram replied, hitting the joint.

"Why didn't you join in?" she asked.

Ram spoke, while trying not to exhale. "My baby can handle two at a time, now."

"Yeah," she said, wrapping herself around Alex. "You've got a really nice one."

Alex took the joint, hit it and passed it to Ginger. "Watching is deeper sometimes. I like to make a mental connection."

Ram started to laugh. "You've done too much X, man."

"You want a blow job?" Ginger asked.

"She's good," Ram nodded.

Alex hit the joint again, the middle was always best, before he answered.

"What I would really like is a big..." he paused for effect–Ram's heart skipped a beat as Alex blew smoke in a long steady stream–"...steak. How 'bout you Ram? Should I call room service?"

"I could eat." He hit the joint. "Baby...?"

"I don't eat red meat," Ginger cooed softly.

Ram glanced at his recently abused member and snickered.

"Since when?" he chuckled.

"Ignore him," Ginger said.

"You can order whatever you want. My father owns this hotel."

"No shit?" Ram said.

"No shit." Alex deadpanned. "You can call a few friends if you want. We'll have a party. It's my birthday and I've got lots and lots of drugs."

He got out of bed and left the bedroom.

"What do you think baby?" Ginger asked.

"Hell, yeah... Fuck Random House."

"Yeah," she said and giggled. "Damn, baby, this weed is the shit."

"Yeah," Ram laughed. "Hey, let's call Thor."

"Thor? Eewwh... He's so full of himself."

She slugged Ram in the arm, trying to keep her voice down.

"Oouww," he winced. "He'll like Thor."

"Baby, if push comes to shove, are you really gonna want to watch Thor fuckin' me? I gotta tell ya, I'd rather fuck your friend Roy and he's and asshole."

"Wait a minute. You're not fuckin' anybody."

"You were gonna let me fuck that guy."

"You don't know that."

"Baby, would you get your head outta your ass for just a minute. Now, I know the type. He's gonna get us all fucked up and we're gonna be in the buff before it's all over with. This could, you know, give us a chance to live out some of our fantasies together, that's all."

"Yeah," he said. "You're right."

"I know I'm right. Now, who do we like enough to invite to a kick ass party that we wouldn't mind havin' meaningless sex with?"

"Damn, what would I do without you baby?"

She kissed him. "Beat off more than you already do."

He passed her what was left of the joint. She shook her head, concentrating on who they should call.

"We can invite Yvonne. I *know* you want to smash her. And I wouldn't mind doin' your friend Jason. You said he's big, right baby."

"He's big enough."

"Okay, don't get defensive," she said.

"I think Thor would mess around with me."

She swatted him again. "Baby!"

"Ooouch! Cut it out. You're the one who said this was a chance to live out some fantasies. So let's live 'em."

They kissed again and she smiled. Ram was feeling free for the first time in his life.

Alex walked back in just as Ram was about to enter Ginger.

"Hey, now," he said stretching out on the bed beside them.

He slapped Ram on the ass. "Save some of that for later. I ordered dinner. Medium-rare steak okay with you big man?"

"Fine by me," Ram said, feeling himself getting sucked in. This guy wanted it all.

"...and a nice Salmon steak for the lady, with a lemon dill risotto," he added, quite pleased with himself.

This delighted Ginger. She let out a tiny squeal and kissed Alex. He kissed her back.

"I'll give you five thousand dollars for tonight and an extra twenty-five hundred, if you call the right people. I like big tits and blonde muscle heads."

Ginger gasped and kissed him again.

"Thor's a blonde muscle head," Ram volunteered.

"Then, by all means call Thor," Alex said, his interest peaked.

"Ever been with another guy Ram? That will get you another three grand."

Ram glanced at his girlfriend. Her look was encouraging. He crawled across her and kissed Alex, quickly on the lips.

"I have a certain curiosity," Ram confessed.

Alex smiled. "You can do better than that."

Ram kissed him, hard and deep. It was about control with Alex he thought, just like Ginger. Sure he was a lot smoother, because of the money, but when it came down to it, he was just spoiled and demanding—just like Ginger. And the bossier she got, the harder he fucked her. This was going to be a night to remember.

"Damn, baby, that's hot," Ginger said.

This guy had a way of making her lose all her inhibitions, even when it came to Ram. Was it because he was by far the most beautiful man she had ever been with, or because he was the richest?

Alex broke the kiss. "Okay you two, food is on the way and there's a bath waiting for Ginger. It's right through that door."

She smiled. "You think of everything."

"And what are we gonna do?" Ram asked. He was still on top of Alex.

"Well, I thought perhaps you'd join Ginger in the bath," he said laughing, "while I set up the bar and party favors before a quick shower."

Ram sniffed one of his armpits. "I guess I am a little ripe."

His face flushed red. He tried to roll over, but Alex tightened his grip and took a deep breath.

"I don't mind," he said. "But we have guests coming."

"You're a little freaky," Ram said with a sly grin.

Alex returned the grin. "I'm a lotta freaky."

Like shooting fish in a barrel.

CHAPTER 46

THE PINK PALACE — ATLANTA, GA

It took a few hours but Andrea, as always, got her way. She stalled as long as possible, but eventually decided to throw DaShawn a bone. He would receive fifteen thousand for the five girls she had handpicked for the day of Alex's arrival.

She also made arrangements to meet the girls the following day at Lennox for shopping and head-to-toe body maintenance. Before leaving the club, she asked to see each of the doormen as well and decided on six-foot-four, three hundred pound RaQuan Mitchell, better known as "Big Black." She needed security and a driver.

"So, Black, are you married?" she asked after he joined them in the booth.

"Naw," he answered. "Gotta couple of kids though."

Figures, she thought.

Andrea leaned toward him. She made him uneasy.

"Really, how old are they?"

"My girl, Miranda, is six, and RaQuan Jr. is three-and-a-half."

"How sweet... and their mother?"

"Rachel?" He let out a small chuckle. "Rachel's more bitch than mother."

Andrea decided to let him slide on that one. Maybe Rachel was a bitch, but single motherhood could do that to a girl.

"I see," she said in an even tone. "Does she work?"

"Yeah, she works, changing beds downtown at the Hilton."

"You guys live together?"

"Hell, naw. I told you, Rachel's a bitch."

"So let me get this straight," she quipped, that flawless smile on her face. "You spend what, five nights a week here sipping Cognac watching the T and A parade, while she cleans up after strangers and *your* children and she's a bitch?"

"Damn, right, she's a bitch."

"Black," Andrea said sweetly. "Seriously...?"

"Look here, little girl. You don't know nothin' 'bout nothin'."

"Sound like she got you pegged." DaShawn laughed.

"Nobody ask you, old man," Black shot back.

"You don't need to ask me shit. She still got yo' ass pegged. Now, am I right or am I right?"

"Hello?" Andrea complained. "Can we get back to the business at hand?"

"And just what business would that be?" Black asked.

"I need a bodyguard of sorts."

"You in some kinda trouble?"

Andrea sighed and said. "Trouble follows me, Black. What skills might you possess that would make a girl feel, safe?"

"I was on my way to makin' a name for myself in the UFC, when I got booted for a felony possession charge. I'm also undefeated on the underground cage circuit."

Black stared at DaShawn with flared nostrils. He bucked up and made a snorting sound.

"Oh, here we go," DaShawn mumbled.

"The position pays twenty-five hundred a week, plus room and board."

DaShawn almost choked on his tequila. *"Twenty-five hun'ard...?* Damn, e'rybody gettin' paid *but* me!"

Andrea sighed again. "DaShawn, please..."

Ordinarily DaShawn Crawford didn't take mess off nobody, but this girl wasn't just anybody. The media ate girls like her up. She could be great PR for the club on a national level.

"I gotta get back to the office," he said. "Here's my card."

Andrea placed the card in her purse. "I'll be in touch."

DaShawn headed to the back of the club.

"Make sure you take care of that bitch over there," he said passing by the bar. Yeah, he had a good feeling about this one.

"So I guess those commercials pay pretty good," Black pondered aloud.

Andrea laughed. "I made a cool five million the first year on that deal, plus a share of the profit. Nasty Mama got me for a steal. But I'm much more than the A&A Jeans thing. Do you know how much I get paid to walk a runway, RaQuan Mitchell? And I do at least forty shows a year. Then there's the Victoria Secret contract my agency is currently negotiating, and the deal I just scored with Aaric C."

"Who...?"

"Cosmetics, darling... It's a great get in the modeling world."

"Damn girl. You ballin' ain't cha...?"

"So what do you think? Want to be my bodyguard?"

"That ain't all I'd like to be."

What the hell, might as well go for broke, he thought.

Never in a million years, she thought.

"Black, think of your kids," she said. "This is a great opportunity for their future. If my boyfriend likes you, there's no telling where this could lead. He has access to important people."

He sat back, guard up, attitude in place.

"Now, we travel a lot, I don't suppose you have a passport."

"Nope."

"That's not an issue. We also party a lot. Can you handle a gun?"

"I can't carry no gun, not legally."

"We've got lawyers for that. Do you have a driver's license?"

"Yeah..."

"Consider yourself hired. You start immediately."

"Just like that?"

"Just like that."

Δ

DaShawn watched them exit the club from the monitor in his office. He tried to hold out, but in the end knew he was coming into a windfall. Hell, once word got out that Nasty Mama was gonna perform, it would be standing-room only.

He would have to speak to the fire marshal. And it wasn't going to be easy replacing Black. He didn't cause trouble; he did his job and kept his mouth shut for the most part.

Still, DaShawn couldn't complain. This was the beginning of a beautiful business relationship. Maybe he could retire sooner than later after all, while he still had a few good years left. He tried to run his club on the up and up, just like his old man taught him, but the bitches and hoes were a lot more scandalous these days.

CHAPTER 47

THE ROYAL GRAND HOTEL — NEW YORK

The party was crazy and still going at eleven the next morning when Alex kicked everyone out—everyone with the exception of Ram and Ginger. He thought he might keep them around for a while. Cab fare was distributed and the front desk was on alert to make sure all of the partiers got off safely.

His new friends had indeed chosen wisely, inviting five others, rounding up to an even eight: four boys and four girls. Ginger thought this would increase the chances of bedding down Alex. It had not; still a good time was had by all. And just as Ginger predicted, everyone ended up in a naked heap, everyone except Alex.

Instead he got fucked up and filmed the whole night, making sure to include on the spot interviews with his guests in various stages of their love making. A brilliant short, if he did say so himself.

"Okay boys and girls," he said clapping his hands. "Housekeeping is on the way to change the sheets."

He walked over to the bed and dragged their worn out asses upright.

"First we shower, then we sleep."

They did as they were told. The suite's master bath was equipped with a glassed in shower with six programmable showerheads and plenty of room for three. There was also a large sunken, garden tub. Ginger sat on a built-in marble bench while Alex shampooed her hair and Ram scrubbed himself from head to toe.

Alex watched soapy water rushing over Ram's long, lanky, tattooed frame. He was very pale, with a shock of strawberry blonde hair and sharp, angular features. Everything about him was long: long neck, long arms, long legs.

Ginger stood a petite five-foot-four, and sported a deep red and pink striped bouffant. She was also extremely pale and though tiny, had all the right curves in all the right places.

She wrapped herself in a towel, tiptoed to kiss Ram's cheek, and headed for the bed. Housekeeping had slipped quietly in and out, turned down the beds and left mint truffles on fresh pillow cases. She had never seen a more beautiful sight. The towel hit the floor and Ginger was out before her head hit the pillow.

Alex lit a cigarette, tossed the pack to Ram and sat on the side of the big Jacuzzi tub. Ram dried off, draped his towel around his shoulders and leaned nude against the vanity. He couldn't figure this guy out.

"Why didn't you join in?" he asked, lighting a cigarette of his own.

"I'm in love with someone. This is me being faithful."

"Ah, shit," Ram laughed.

"Did you and Ginger have a good time?"

Ram inhaled slowly, forming his answer carefully. "Ahh...yeah, we did." He took another drag. "And to be perfectly honest, I've always wondered if I'd dig gettin' fucked."

"Did you?"

"Best nut I ever had." He dropped his head. "Never saw that comin'; but hell, here we are."

"Here we are," Alex agreed.

"Kinda wish it had been you, though," Ram said with a wink.

Alex grinned. "Let's go to bed."

Δ

Ginger was the first to wake. When she was sure her bladder was about to burst, she forced her eyes open. *Where am I,* she wondered. Oh, yeah, the hotel...the party...oh shit, the sex...all that sex.

She sat up. Her breasts were sore. She stood and managed to walk across the suite on sea legs. She, too, wondered what this guy Alex was all about. He was rich; that was certain. She looked around at the luxurious bathroom. The tub... had she taken a bath? No, they had all showered together.

Slowly, everything became increasingly clear, starting with the initial meeting at Random House. *Who was this guy?* When she got up, the toilet flushed automatically. *Oh yeah.*

The girls at the hair salon were not going to believe this one. She caught a glimpse of her reflection. *Rode hard and put up wet.* Oh God, she thought, not in front of the rich guy.

She said his name out loud. "Alex."

It sounded good. She looked back at the sunken tub, then to the shower. She smiled at the memory of him washing her hair. Thank God, it was Sunday. She was going to need whatever was left of the day and all day Monday to recover before facing the crazed, discoed out, rainbow bright, Never Land she called work. She touched a button and the tub began to fill. This place was Heaven.

Upon re-entry into the bedroom, her petite frame wrapped in a hotel robe, she noticed that neither of the boys had stirred. My God he was beautiful. Reluctantly she had to admit her Ram paled in comparison.

Instantly her heart rose up to his defense. She did love Ram and knew he loved her too. He was her man, for almost two years now. Watching them lost in slumber, Ginger wondered what she should do. If only she had her make-up bag and something for her head and body aches. She glanced at the clock. It was 5:09 in the evening. The girls were definitely not going to believe this one.

She wandered back into the bathroom in search of something for her head and was ecstatic to find a well-stocked medicine cabinet. She wondered what else she might find and then she saw it, a shiny satin bag. Could it be...?

"Oh my God," she gasped in a whisper. "Make up. Expensive, glorious make up."

Of course, the girlfriend, she thought, or he was a drag queen; highly doubtful. That's why he only watched the sex. So nice, she thought, he *was* in love.

Ginger sat and applied the make up with ease and expertise; it was her profession after all. Just as she was applying the finishing touches, Ram walked in with Alex right behind him, both sporting morning wood. She smiled at the sight.

"Good morning, sleepy heads," she said.

Each groaned, not yet fully awake.

Ram sat on the toilet, a trick Ginger had taught him, and leaned forward slightly to control his aim. Alex went to the medicine cabinet and grabbed a bottle of pain killers.

"How'd you sleep?" he asked.

"In a drugged-out haze," she said without looking away from the mirror. "You...?"

"I try to live my life in a drugged-out haze."

"This place is amazing. I hope you don't mind that I helped myself to the war paint."

"Help yourself," he yawned. "Andrea's always leaving shit behind. She'll never miss it. The company gives it to her. She's going to be the new face of Aaric C. Cosmetics."

Ginger turned from her reflection and lowered the mascara brush.

"Who are you?" she asked.

"Alex Vandiveer."

Ginger screamed, which startled Ram. She had a very high-pitched, ear-piercing scream.

"Christ almighty, babe. Are you trying to give me a heart attack?"

"OMG! I can't believe I didn't recognize you. Baby, this is Alex Vandiveer."

"Who...?" He stood and the toilet flushed.

"His girlfriend is on the cover of this month's FHM."

"No shit."

Ginger stared at his naked reflection in disbelief. Alex took his turn at the toilet. "No shit," he said.

"Damn, man, she's fuckin' hot."

Alex grinned. "Yeah, she is."

"Wait, wait, wait," Ginger said. "This is too much. I need to process a little. I'm sitting in this fabulous bathroom in this fabulous suite in this fabulous hotel where I just witnessed Alex Vandiveer take a piss and put on makeup that belongs to Andrea Sorcosi."

She screamed again. Ram covered his ears. This was going to be a long one, followed by a series of short ones. He shook his head.

"Oh, my God, I'm dying here. Baby, he's famous."

More like infamous, Alex thought. "Hey listen, there's this party..."

Ram looked at Ginger.

"I don't have anything to wear," she said.

Alex yawned again. "I guess we'll have to go shopping."

"I don't have anything to wear either?" Ram said in a high-pitched girlie voice.

"Yes, freak, I'll buy your scrawny ass something too. Shower...?"

CHAPTER 48

HARTSFIELD-JACKSON INTERNATIONAL AIRPORT — ATLANTA, GA

Melinda hated airports and she especially hated Hartsfield-Jackson International. It was just too big. She hated waiting to deplane, with people and their bags practically pressed up against her in the aisle. She also hated the walk to the train, the long escalator (she always managed to stumble when getting off) and, of course, baggage claim.

She smiled and felt a pang of guilt when she saw Dusty waiting for her with her bags. They embraced and shared the kiss of a young couple who cared deeply for each other. A life-sized Barbie and Ken, that's what they were, perfect in every way to the travel-weary passersby.

They engaged in their usual chit-chat. He wanted to know everything about school and her job at the magazine, while she pretended to be interested in his hum-drum existence. She felt he had grown stagnant and made no bones about voicing her opinion—but it was just that, her opinion. He knew she wanted something different for him, but it was his life and as far as the future was concerned, it was anybody's guess. Suddenly Andrea filled his thoughts, but he willed the images of her away.

Dusty, carrying her bag like a perfect gentleman, held her elbow as he navigated her outside to the parking garage. He was good to her, she thought. Any girl's dream, it would seem, but maybe, especially after her time in New York and Martin, a little too vanilla. She couldn't wait to get home. She missed her own room and her own bed. The world was still a scary place sometimes and she longed for the safety and freedom of being on her own turf.

Traffic on 285 was the usual nightmare, but they easily slipped back into their comfort zones. Dusty, feeling guilty as well, was making the extra effort and it was actually paying off. He *had* missed her and he could tell she missed him, too. How could he have behaved the way he had the past couple of days? Melinda would never have done anything like that to him.

There was that business with Alex, but they were kids then. They were past that now and solid as ever. This was the woman he was going to marry.

Frank and Noreen were waiting for them when they arrived at the Johnston home. Melinda pretended to have a *tiny little headache,* cut the small talk short, kissed the top of her daddy's head and she and Dusty made their way toward her room.

He waited in Melinda's bedroom while she showered and took note of the fact that she seemed bashful somehow when she dressed. He could remember a time when he thought she was the prettiest girl he had ever seen as his mind drifted, yet again to Andrea.

Where did she disappear to? Six days had passed since he had seen her and South Isle was locked down tight. He tried to concentrate on Melinda, but it was too late. He was already on the rollercoaster and there was no end to the tracks in sight. He would have to be careful.

After Melinda's shower they were off to the Crab House for dinner with Frank and Noreen. When they arrived, Julia was waiting at the bar alongside Walter and Caroline.

Greetings were exchanged, followed by a moderately pleasant evening. Dusty always enjoyed Frank's company in a social situation. And Noreen? Well, you had to love Noreen, although Melinda didn't. And Frank enjoyed Walter's company. He liked a man who stood for something, no matter his political beliefs or religion. If he worked hard and honest, he was alright with Frank. And if he was a Georgia fan, which Walter was, hell all the better.

So, when dinner was over, the two men opted for Pilsners and cigars in the bar instead of cheesecake with the ladies. Dusty remained planted at the table. He was determined to get laid, so cheesecake with the ladies it was.

"Sweetheart, be a dear and order for us?" Caroline said.

She, Noreen and Melinda excused themselves to the ladies' room, but Melinda never made it.

"I need some air," she said, making a beeline for the patio where she secretly called Martin, who was in Upstate New York with his dorm mate.

CHAPTER 49

JOHNSTON RESIDENCE — SEA VIEW, GA

"Dustin Marler, you haven't tried any of my butternut squash. Are you feelin' alright?" Noreen asked. She always fussed over Dusty.

Caroline Marler-Roberts was at last living her life so she had not noticed that her son had barely touched his dinner. She had just inked a deal to partner with superstar chef, Edward Catrell, to open Sweet Caroline's through-out the southeast. She and Walter would have the retirement they had always dreamed about and be able to secure futures for Dusty and Walter's estranged children. She was finally happy.

"I'm fine," Dusty lied.

"You're not eating like you're fine."

"Yeah," Jimmy Ray said. "I'm out eatin' you, man."

"My boy always did eat like some kinda circus freak," Buck Daniels said and started to laugh a little too loudly.

His wife, Dee Dee squeezed his hand. He was teetering on drunk.

"Slow down," she whispered.

"We're not in high school any more Jimmy Ray," Dusty replied.

"Yes, some of us are in college," Melinda said.

Julia stared at her.

"Not everyone is cut out for *university*," Julia said making quotation marks in the air. *God, she was such a bitch.*

"Tell me about it," Reece piped up. "Chemistry is kickin' my ass."

Naomi Jackson cleared her throat. "Language..."

"I'm a man now, Mother."

"Reece Jackson, you are not so grown that I won't turn you over my knee."

"You'd better listen to your mother, son," warned Mayor Jackson.

Everyone laughed. Santana leaned toward Reece.

"Does my baby need a spanking?" she whispered.

He gave her a quick kiss.

"Ooh," Caroline sighed. "Aren't they adorable? You two make such a beautiful couple."

"We think so," Santana smiled.

Reece went rigid and she wondered if he was cheating while he was away at school? Dusty was just glad the focus was on someone other than him. He wondered for the umpteenth time where Andrea was.

After dinner Noreen, cleared the table with the help of Naomi and Caroline, in order to serve coffee and dessert. Dusty and Julia headed for the backyard deck.

"Where the fuck is Andrea?" she asked trying desperately to light a cigarette. "Fuck."

She rambled through her purse, searching for another lighter, giving him time to compose himself before answering. He had been thinking about Andrea nonstop for days, but this was the first time he heard her name out loud.

He and Julia hadn't spent a lot of time together in the previous week. Her mother was back for a short visit post-rehab, and although only long enough to pack for Palm Beach, she was there long enough to rattle Julia.

"Halle-fuckin-lujah." She finally found a working lighter. She inhaled deeply and blew the smoke skyward. Dusty took a sip of his seasonal Sam Adams while Julia stared at him, impatiently.

"Well?" she asked.

"How should I know. I haven't talked to her."

She moved to the edge of the deck and looked out over the ocean. She pulled her cardigan closed and folded her arms, hugging her torso.

"I'm so pathetic." She reached back in her purse and produced a flask. "Want some?"

He declined. She turned it up.

"It's crazy, you know. I just met her and I feel like I lost my best friend."

"I thought I was your best friend."

"Well, that'll end as soon as Alex gets here," she said.

"Come on, that's not fair."

"Life isn't fair." She took another swig from the flask. "Have you mentioned Andrea to Mindy Sue?"

"No, did you? I mean she's only here for two days and Andrea has vanished to God knows where…"

"Relax. I haven't said shit."

He *was* relieved. "Where do you think she is?" he asked.

"Who the fuck knows? She could be in fuckin' Bora Bora by now." She inhaled on her cigarette. "I'd kill for that kind of life."

As if by osmosis or black magic Lindsey Lohan's *Rumors* rang from inside Julia's handbag.

"Oh, Lindsay says I have a text."

Julia was still and would always be a diehard Lohan fan. She found the phone.

"It's her!"

"It's who?" Melinda asked joining them on the deck. "You'd better not be smoking, Dustin Marler."

He didn't smoke and could not understand why she ever felt the need to give him ultimatums on the subject.

Julia ignored her, reading the text. "Oh my God..!"

"Just because Julia's okay with killing herself," Melinda rattled on, "doesn't mean..."

Julia cut her off. "Everything isn't about you Mindy Sue."

"Of course it is," Melinda smiled.

She had made her own exit after dinner and enjoyed another secret conversation with Martin. Had she known he was about to have sex with his roommate's sister, she might have thought differently. She looked at Julia.

"So whose text warrants an 'Oh my God'?" she asked, not really caring.

"It's my new girlfriend. Haven't you heard; I'm a lesbian now?"

Melinda rolled her eyes. "Come on Dusty, Noreen's anxious to serve her famous Derby pie." She took his arm and with a laugh said, "Julia, you're so full of it sometimes."

Dusty removed her hand from his arm. "In a minute," he said.

Melinda didn't like it, but didn't push it.

"Don't take too long," she said. "You know I have an early flight tomorrow and I haven't even started to pack yet."

What's to pack? You've been here for two days. He smiled and nodded.

"And Jules, tell your girlfriend I look forward to meeting her." With that she went back inside.

"I thought she'd never leave," Julia said, doing her happy dance. "She'll be back tomorrow," she said barely able to contain herself, "with Alex."

She cranked her arm in the air as if pulling the handle on a slot machine and jumped up and down.

"He's back, he's back, he's back," she sang.

There it was. He tried to process. He was glad his best friend was coming home, but that also meant an end to...

"There's a welcome home party for Alex tomorrow night on South Isle."

Dusty was pretty much on autopilot for the remainder of the evening. He had hoped somehow, for a little more time alone with Andrea. *To do what?* he asked himself again and again. But his mind wouldn't let go, taking him back to that first night spent naked under the stars. And he had to pretend it never happened.

"You're awfully quiet all of a sudden," Melinda said.

"Huh. Oh, was I?"

"Yes, you were," Caroline added, "and you haven't even tasted Noreen's derby pie." She placed the back of her hand against Dusty's forehead. "Are you sure you're feelin' okay?"

He pulled away. "I'm fine. Jesus, Ma, I know when I'm sick or feverish or whatever......"

"Dusty, I'm just tryin' to help."

"Maybe I don't need your help." The instant the words passed his lips, he was sorry. "I didn't mean that. I guess I'm a little tired."

"Tired?" Melinda huffed. "Not from working, that's for sure."

Julia glared at her. "It's my fault Mrs. M.," she said. "Dusty's been helping me..."

"Helping you what?" Melinda challenged.

"The space above the garage: big boxes, heavy lifting and all that," she lied.

"The garage above the space..." Courtney Roenstein slurred. "Julie, I couldn't... have hired someone for... to do that."

Julia rolled her eyes. "Christ, Mother, isn't your glass a little empty?"

Courtney tried to focus on her wineglass. "I guess I could use a little topper."

"Allow me" Caroline said, taking Courtney by the elbow.

She felt for Julia and couldn't imagine what it must be like to have a mother in this condition. Caroline always preferred Julia, but she knew her place when it came to her son's love life. There wasn't one.

CHAPTER 50

ROENSTEIN RESIDENCE — SEA VIEW, GA

Julia and Dusty were in her bedroom and she had already changed three times.

"We need to be ready for this. Andrea said it was a party."

Dusty was anxious to say the least. Was he truly ready for Alex to come home?

"What time did she tell us to be there?" he asked.

"She didn't say. How does this look?" Julia asked visibly nervous. "I mean, we can show up anytime we want, right?" She twisted and turned, eyeing her reflection in the mirror. "I hate this dress."

"I've always liked that dress."

She spun around. "You never told me that."

"I tell you, you look nice all the time."

It was true, but she never believed him, never really cared; but tonight was different. Andrea did like the other dress. He got the feeling she had done more than just pot and shots.

"Okay, I'm ready," she said.

Their day had been spent driving to and from Atlanta, delivering Melinda to the airport, and the remainder with his mother and Walter at his childhood home. Finally, after a brief stop at his place for a quick shower and change, they ended up at Julia's—thus, the pot and shots.

There was a guard in the gatehouse as they approached the house on South Isle. Julia smiled and gave their names.

"You're new," she said, her smile widening.

The guard smiled back. "Yeah, I just started."

"What, no name tag?"

"They call me Big Black."

Her sly grin spoke volumes. "I'll just bet they do. I'm Julia. Coming to the party later?"

"I don't think that's part of the job description."

"Pity," she said, as she drove through the open gates.

"I can't believe you," Dusty teased.

"What?"

"You were so hitting on that guy."

"Who wouldn't? That my friend is a prime piece of Grade A beefcake."

The fountain was lit, as was the house itself. It was such a grandiose sight.

"I could die here," Julia said. She parked her Saab Turbo up front behind a black sports car.

"The cars have arrived," Dusty said, getting out.

Julia didn't hear him. She was already running toward the steps. She rang the doorbell and by the time the heavy door swung open, Dusty was by her side.

"Oh, hi." *Who is this?* "I'm Julia."

"Ginger. Nice to meet you. Please, won't you come in."

They stepped inside.

"This is Dusty," Julia said.

"Hello."

"Hi, Ginger."

It was so quiet.

"Where is everyone?" Dusty asked.

241

"Ram and I are hanging out in that amazing kitchen," Ginger said. "I mean, this entire place is crazy. You've been here before, right? I know; it's like brand new, isn't it?"

Dusty glanced at Julia, who shrugged. They followed her through a large room with an unbelievable amount of seating.

Who needs this many sofas, he thought, not having seen this part of the mansion.

"It's the Salon," Julia whispered. "Kind of a before-and after-dinner hangout. The formal dining room is on the other side of that wall."

Had he received the grand tour instead of Ambien that first night, he would have known that. There was an impeccably dressed near albino lurking about the kitchen. The black suit and turtleneck sweater made his face and hands seem whiter.

"This is Julia and Dusty, Babe," Ginger announced.

"Hey, what's up?" he asked, hand extended. "I'm Ram."

They shook hands, each noticing the tattoos peaking from inside the dinner jacket sleeve. Ginger had an ear-to-ear grin plastered on her face.

"Would you guys like a drink?"

"Oh, God yes," Julia said shedding her coat. She tossed it over the back of one of the chrome barstools. "Do you have any white wine?"

"I'll check," Ram said.

"I'll show you where it is," Dusty offered, feeling territorial. "Let's move into the great room."

The girls wandered over to the pit group in front of the fireplace, while Dusty showed Ram the wine room. Julia began to fidget with her dress.

"I don't know what I was saying—of course, there's white wine in this house," she said.

She was nervous too, Ginger thought.

"You know, we just met Andrea a few hours ago in the Green Room at the airport in Atlanta. She's upstairs changing."

Who was this girl and why was she here?

"You look great," Julia said.

"Oh, thanks. Alex took us shopping."

"I'm afraid I'm underdressed."

"No, I love that dress. You live at the beach. Besides, it's very Hamptons in the spring." *Oops...it was winter.*

Just take a breath, Ginger told herself. *You meet new people all the time.* She tried again.

"Designer...?"

"That would be me," Julia said.

"Shut up! You made that? It's to die for." Ginger said in rapid succession.

She's like the energizer bunny. Julia was beginning to wonder when that tell-tale sniffle gave it away.

"I gotta tell ya' Julia—this is all kinda crazy. I mean the way these two must live. Who knew we were going to board the company jet and fly to the Dirty South when Alex invited us to a party?" She giggled and let out a little snort.

Wow, Julia thought, *she's really going.*

"So, anyway, we flew into Atlanta, met up with Andrea and Black, boarded a private helicopter, and here we are."

"Ah, yes, Black," Julia said.

Ginger leaned in and whispered, "He's their bodyguard."

"That's our Alex—private planes and bodyguards." Julia said. *Where was that wine?*

"I'm sorry. I know I'm rambling, but stuff like this just doesn't happen to me and my Rammy. We're ordinary people livin' ordinary lives, you know? Minding our own business and keepin' to ourselves one minute, then bang, we meet this guy at Random House the other night and we're hoppin' on private aircraft and wearing real designer clothes the next. Not the knock-offs they sell in China Town."

"Here we are ladies," Ram called out as he and Dusty re-entered the room. "Babe, he's got a glassed-in wine cellar. I brought you some fuckin' Dom Perignon."

"OMG, babe, I was just telling Julia here how we met the duke and duchess."

"A fuckin' trip is what that was," Ram said.

Julia eyed the tall pale one. He was definitely not from New York. She guessed the Midwest. He was so *Children of the Corn*.

"Ram," Dusty said.

"Oh, yeah," he reached into the inside pocket of his jacket. "Here you go, Julia." He handed her a small silver vial.

Ginger let out a tiny squeal and clapped her hands. "Yeaaa, the bullet..."

"Would you like....?" Julia asked, offering her first dibs.

"Oh, no go ahead. Alex is kind of crazy with the drugs. We can't keep up."

"But we're working on it," Ram chimed in.

"He's just plain crazy if you ask me," said a velvety voice from behind.

They turned to see Andrea breezing into the room. Dusty's heart leapt then plummeted. Alex walked in right behind her, picked up speed as he crossed the room and tackled Dusty. They both crashed to the floor and into the back of the leather sectional.

Ram flinched. "What the fuck?"

Alex kissed Dusty on the forehead, "Great to see you, *old friend.*"

"You too; now would you get off me so I can kick your ass."

Andrea shook her head. "Apparently someone needs to," she sighed. "You're going to have to change now. Those Gucci trousers could not have survived that."

Alex helped Dusty to his feet. "I missed you," he said embracing him.

The moment was overwhelming. He had waited for Alex's return for so long, but things were different now.

"Come upstairs with me," Alex said. "I'll tell you all about our adventures and things for you to look forward to."

Alex smiled and in an instant everything was okay again. It was *Alex*, his friend, his brother.

Andrea glanced at her Blackberry. The food had arrived and the van carrying the girls from the Pink Palace was fifteen minutes away, right on schedule. She grabbed a bottle of water from the edge of the bar and headed for the foyer.

"Ginger, could you help please? Black just buzzed me. The caterers are coming through the gates as we speak."

Ginger was glad to assist. Anything in this world was a breeze.

"Meet them at the side entrance off the kitchen," Andrea said. "All the food goes into the dining room and I want the deserts set up here, I think, by the bar." She glanced at Ginger who smiled. "Don't just stand there, off you go. I'll check on things upstairs."

"Of course," Ginger stammered. "No problem."

The Blackberry chimed again; the deejay was on the island. Andrea stopped and turned with a sigh, noting the headlights aimed at the north wing.

"Ram...?"

He hustled into the foyer, ready to do her bidding.

"The deejay went the wrong way," said Andrea. "The ballroom is on the opposite end of the house, through the game room, the far rear corner. Meet him in the kitchen and redirect him to the entrance there. Show him where the equipment goes, it's easy to spot."

"Got it," he said.

"By the time you're done with Romeo," she added climbing the stairs, "the girls from the Pink Palace should be here. So, be a love and listen for the doorbell."

"I'm on it."

"Julia," she called continuing up the stairs.

Julia appeared and charged up the stairs. The two girls embraced.

"Sweetie, I've missed you."

Julia was relieved. "You just disappeared"

"Listen, about that..."

On the way up Andrea explained that Alex could not know they had already met and that she would fill her in at a more appropriate time.

"This is far too complicated to get into—especially tonight," she said as they reached the landing. "Tonight's about the party."

The gallery leading to their private living quarters had the desired effect. Julia faltered; her eyes wide and unblinking. It was impossible to take it all in on a single pass.

Laughter was coming from the master bedroom when they reached the apartment. They entered to find Dusty lying on the bed, propped on an elbow. The bed he had shared with Andrea. Alex was pantsless, doing lines.

"Are we interrupting anything?" Andrea asked.

Dusty stood. "Just catching up," he said.

Julia shielded her eyes. "Why are you naked?"

"I ruined my trousers. You were right about that one, my love," he said to Andrea. "The Gucci's are history."

He moved into the closet.

"Andrea Sorcosi," she said, extending her hand to Dusty.

Puzzled, he took it, a bolt of electricity running through him when they touched.

"Dustin Marler," he replied, hoping he didn't sound too formal.

"Everybody calls him Dusty," Julia chimed in. Alex disappeared into the closet.

"I feel like I know you guys already," Andrea said to Dusty. "Alex speaks of you often. That cable knit looks fantastic on you." She mouthed the words, "I'll explain later."

"Oh, yeah, thanks," Dusty replied. "You know Alex, he has to change; I have to change."

"Wear those leather pants you stole from Kazuyuki," Andrea called to Alex.

He reappeared, trousers in hand. "I didn't *steal* them." He stepped into the one-of-a-kinds, tucked himself in and buttoned the fly. "I simply borrowed them without permission."

He draped an arm over Dusty's shoulders.

"Besides, that shot of me leaving Koko in London wearing these made her year."

"Oh, so I guess you did her a favor," Andrea said, giving him a kiss.

"You guys are so cute," Julia gushed. "Aren't they cute Dusty?"

He didn't respond; his mind was on the night of the photo shoot.

"The food is being set up downstairs and the guests will be here any minute," said Andrea. "I have surprises for everyone."

"I love surprises," Alex lied. "Don't you *love* surprises Dusty?"

"Sure, I guess." He looked at Andrea. "Who doesn't?"

Alex swatted him twice on the chest. "It's confirmed. We all love surprises."

"Are you okay, darling?" Andrea asked.

"Fan-fucking-tastic, my love. Why wouldn't I be?"

"Just don't overdo. It's going to be a long night. The girls have arrived and you know Veronique and *the cupids* are ..."

Alex whispered softly to Dusty, "Here it comes, wait for it, wait..."

"...coming down from New York. I mean, really darling..."

In a stern voice, Alex said. "...you've got to slow down," just as she did.

Andrea placed her hands firmly on her hips.

"This isn't funny," she said, scolding him. "We don't need you going down *that* road again."

"She's always worrying about me."

"Isn't that a good thing?" Julia asked.

"Alright," Alex said. "I promise not to O.D. again. Scouts honor."

"You were never a scout," Dusty said, thinking it was a joke.

"O.D. as in overdose...?" Julia asked.

"It was just the one time," Alex said in his own defense.

They weren't buying it.

Alex huffed. "Okay, twice."

"My, God," Julia gasped.

"It was a long time ago."

Andrea saw the looks of concern on their faces.

"And it was an accident," she added. "It wasn't like he wanted to die. So lighten up you guys. We're having a party— remember? We can talk about all this another time."

Alex removed his arm and headed back for more lines.

"Okay, my love, I promise to be a good boy; right after a little more to straighten me out."

"Do you think....?" Dusty started only to be silenced with a wave of Andrea's hand.

"Yes, Dustin, I do think," Alex snapped. "It might even frighten you to know some of the things I think."

Who was this Jekyll and Hyde? Dusty wondered. Andrea looked at him and smiled, but there was sadness in her eyes.

"He knows what he's doing," she said.

Δ

Ram had just enough time to hit the bullet and check his reflection in the mirror in the foyer before swinging the big door open.

"Damn right!" he yelled.

The girls from the Palace entered slowly, all in short skirts or dresses with various plunging necklines.

"Hey," they said in unison.

"Welcome ladies. I'm Ram. Glad to be at your service." He bowed slightly, stepped aside and ushered them in before closing the door. "May I offer you some white wine or a glass of Dom Perignon perhaps?"

"I'm not sure," the redhead said. "Are we allowed to drink?"

"Of course, you are," Andrea said descending the staircase with Dusty, Alex and Julia all in tow.

"My God, this place," said the mocha-skinned girl with honey blonde hair.

"Ram, get the ladies whatever they'd like," Alex ordered. "As a matter of fact..." he said jumping over the railing and landing right in front of Ginger, causing her to scream. "Sorry doll face," he apologized. "Let me help the ladies get settled."

He led the girls into the great room. Everyone followed except Dusty and Andrea.

"It's going to be quite a party," she said.

"You didn't tell Alex we already know each other?"

She touched his arm. "It's easier this way, for now."

"Andrea..." He couldn't go there. "I'm glad you're back..."

"Me too," she said. It would have to be enough. "I need to check with the caterers," she lied. "You go ahead."

She watched him go before ducking into a powder room hidden in the curved wall beneath the staircase. Once inside she slipped her fingers deep into her cleavage and retrieved a small vial of cocaine. She unscrewed the cap and dipped the attached spoon into the tiny opening.

What now, she asked herself in the mirror. As if responding to her question, the Blackberry chimed. Reece and Jimmy Ray were passing through the gate. Perfect, they were the last of the dinner guests. She did a few more mini bumps and waited for them in the foyer. It was a beautiful night.

"Damn!" Jimmy Ray said when the door opened.

"You must be Jimmy Ray," Andrea said smiling.

"The one and only, sugar," he replied to the somehow familiar beauty.

Reece pushed him aside, hand extended. "Reece Jackson."

"Please come in," she said, failing to introduce herself. "You're the last to arrive." She closed the door behind them. "Follow me."

They took turns eyeing each other as well as Andrea's impressive backside on their way through a massive archway into the great room. Each had received mysterious invitations out of the blue inviting them to some anonymous shindig.

"Ah, hell to the ya'yeaaaah...!" Jimmy Ray yelled when he saw the girls.

Reece saw them too.

"Every one," Andrea announced. "This is Reece and Jimmy Ray."

"Christ," Alex said. "What are you two fuck heads doing here?"

"No way!" Jimmy Ray barked. *No wonder she looked so familiar.*

"Alex!" Reece shouted. They were genuinely shocked to see him.

"What's up bitches?" Alex countered.

They burst into laughter. Dusty's eyes followed Andrea across the room where she joined Julia. Why was she pretending not to know him? Was she doing the same with Julia?

"I love the dress, by the way," Andrea smiled sweetly.

Thank God, Julia thought.

"We need to talk," Andrea whispered. "Before the ruckus ensues."

While Jimmy Ray, Reece, Alex and Dusty got noisily acquainted with the Palace Girls over by the bar, Andrea pulled Julia, Ram and Ginger aside.

"Okay, you guys," she said. "I'm going to need your help. I'm almost certain he's going to want all of you here with us."

"What do you mean here?" Ram asked.

"I mean *living here*, with us, at least through the New Year, maybe longer."

"You're kidding, right?" Ginger said. "We have jobs and lives back in New York."

"You can work for us. My schedule will be impossible soon; I'll most definitely need an assistant. Alex needs more of a part-time assistant, part-time babysitter. Ram certainly fits the bill."

Ram looked at Ginger who for once seemed speechless.

"Wait, what are you saying, exactly?" Ginger asked.

"Alex is very private and there's no way I can manage a house this size, both of our work schedules, the parties and trips all by myself. I need a team, and the fact that he brought you two here speaks volumes. God knows he's going to be a handful; it's the holidays, so hiring strangers is out of the question. The job pays fifty thousand a year, plus benefits. You'll live here, of course, so that takes care of that."

They were all taken aback by what Andrea was saying, though she made it sound so matter of fact.

Ginger's eyes bugged out. "Fifty-thousand...?"

"Each," Andrea said.

"Plus, we'll live here?" Ginger asked.

"You can stay in the pool house."

Ginger's mind was racing. *Who were these people and what was she about to agree to? What about her clientele? A hundred thousand and no expenses...*

"Oh, I want to say yes. Am I saying yes?"

Andrea and Julia nodded encouragement.

"I think I'm saying yes." Ginger gushed. "Oh my God, this is so unbelievable."

"So what do you think, Ram? The company car is a black on black Chevy Tahoe."

He just shook his head, dumbfounded.

Ginger answered for him. "Ram is an unemployed bass player."

"Then it's settled?" Julia asked.

"How can we say no?"

"As for your apartment, I'm sure my agency can sublet. Where is it located?'

"SoHo, but..."

"Perfect, Fiona is always in need of model housing."

"I can't believe this." Ginger said again.

Julia shook her head. "Good things happen when this one's around." The three smiled, bonding.

"What's going on over here?" Alex asked, joining them in front of the fireplace.

"I was just inviting Ginger and Ram to stay through the holidays," she said with a faint smile, "if you have no objections."

"Why would I? The more the merrier," he replied, winking. "Julia will be staying, too, of course."

"Of course," Andrea said.

"Come on, Ram, we're doing shots at the bar with the girls." He glanced at Andrea, she nodded and they were off.

"Is he really that bad?" Julia asked when the guys had gone.

Andrea started across the room. "Let's show Ginger the solarium."

Δ

"OMG, would you look at this?" Ginger said. "It's so beautiful in here. Is the pool connected to the one outside?"

"Yes," Andrea answered. "The architect's idea."

Ginger clapped her hands and jumped up and down.

"This is insane," she said. "I can't believe we're gonna be living on a private island."

"That reminds me," Andrea said. "The girls will be sharing the pool house with you and Ram this weekend."

"I'm sure he'll love that," Ginger said, raising an eyebrow.

Julia pointed through the glass partition. "Don't worry, that's the pool house."

Ginger's eyes popped. "*That's* the pool house."

"There are six bedrooms on each side with a large living area in between," Andrea said. "So, you can keep him far, far away."

They all laughed at this. Ginger placed her hands on either side of her shaking head as if to keep it from falling off. She literally could not believe what she was hearing.

"So, listen, about tonight," Andrea continued, "Veronique will be arriving around ten and all hell's going to break loose. At last count, she's bringing like seventy-five of her *club kids*. The party starts right after dinner."

"Oh my God..." Ginger sighed, praying she would not faint. "This just keeps getting better and better."

She reached for Julia's cocktail and tried to get a grip on herself.

"Dinner looks incredible by the way," she said.

It was no use, she wanted to scream and she did, startling both the other girls.

Andrea smiled. "We're going to need *something* to sober those guys up." She gestured back toward the great room and the bar where she was sure the girls were doing their thing, earning their money. "Ladies, should we do a bump to celebrate?"

At Julia's suggestion, they wondered outside. Underwater lights illuminated the surface of the pool and there was a full moon in the sky. They talked about the things that young women talk about: boys, clothes and make up.

By the time the caterer found them on the terrace to announce dinner, they were already forging an alliance, which was going to make everything easier. Alex was beginning to unravel and a good support system could be useful if things turned too quickly.

Andrea rounded everyone up and led them into the main dining room. The table was set with white linens and crystal. There were dozens of white candles scattered in ordered chaos down the center and low, blood red centerpieces made entirely of roses. The wine glasses had red stems and there was a red rose motif on the napkins.

Alex and Andrea sat at either end, with him flanked by Dusty and Ram, and she by Julia and Ginger. The Palace girls split themselves between Reece and Jimmy Ray, who faced one another across the center of the giant table.

"I do love this table. The instant Camilla showed it to me I knew I had to have it." Andrea was saying, as the catering staff busied themselves opening bottles of wine and taking orders for cocktails.

"It's gorgeous," Ginger said. "And the roses are to die for."

Julia couldn't wait any longer. "Andrea, you didn't answer me earlier, about Alex. I mean, he's our friend and we love him."

Ginger sat, wide eyed.

"He has mostly good days, but there are the bad ones," Andrea began. "It was difficult to come back here, but he knew he had to. He also knows that he *will* have to grow up someday. His father demands it. And since he knows he can't run away, he's just running."

She was holding court, playing the role. Sometimes, at moments like this, Ana Maria would take a quick step into the light, just to be amazed at how far she had come, but Andrea always made sure she wasn't around more than a few seconds, only long enough for a peek.

"What happened to him?" Julia asked.

"When he left here he was really hurting, that whole Melinda thing... Anyway, just as he was to leave New York, fate intervened and we met. We stayed with his Aunt Josephine and his grandmother in Sicily for a while... it was quite lovely, really... an ancient villa, with the most amazing gardens and view of the mountains.

"We took car trips through the countryside on weekends, shopped in open air markets and indulged ourselves at meal time, but Alex was so sad.

"Once I started working, we moved to Rome and life started. We traveled and partied and saw the sights. It was all so romantic and glamorous," she said in a faraway tone, "and then that awful thing with Jean Paul..."

"Oh my God," Ginger said, "I read about that; such a horrible tragedy."

What did you say to someone about killing someone else, even if it was self-defense?

"Suffice it to say, it was a dark time for the both of us."

The girls from the Pink Palace erupted in laughter, drawing everyone's attention. Jimmy Ray was doing his version of the Harlem shake.

"Oh, God," Dusty said.

Ram laughed. "He moves pretty good for a big dude."

"Jimmy Raaaaaay!" Alex yelled, then Reece and Dusty, shouted, "Iiiyooup!" simultaneously.

Julia frowned. "This is not good."

The servers entered with the first course.

"Just in time," Andrea said.

They feasted on cracked peppercorn encrusted smoked salmon with capers, red onion and wasabi butter, on sesame garlic toast points, grilled portabella mushroom salads with roasted red pepper and hearts of palm tossed in a goat cheese vinaigrette.

The first two courses were paired with a crisp perfectly chilled sauvignon blanc, while the third course–braised racks of petite lamb with rosemary pepper jelly, grilled asparagus and vodka, mashed potatoes–was served with a hearty cabernet.

At 9:30 sharp the table was cleared. Andrea stood and signaled for Ram, who was instructed to check in with Romeo, while she ventured into the great room to inspect the dessert station.

She was pleased to find fresh strawberries, mango, red apple and pineapple for the milk chocolate fountain, ricotta cheese cakes with cherry and brown sugar topping, assorted fruit tarts, a torte and a decorative ice cream cart with five flavors of homemade ice creams and every imaginable topping. There was also a hot tea and cider station complete with flavored honeys, liqueurs and rock candy stir sticks.

She went to a drawer behind the bar and retrieved a baggie of cocaine, which she promptly emptied into a silver dish and placed on a large mirrored tray, with all the necessary paraphernalia. She also pulled a bottle of zanies and some X from the same drawer and put them in matching crystal salt dishes, along with a bag of pre-rolled chronic.

After placing the tray next to the dessert display, she looked around the expensive room in the expensive house with all the expensive drugs and wondered yet again how she had gotten there.

Back in the dining room, everyone was getting along. There were lots of laughs and stories from the past, washed down with endless amounts of wine; ten additional bottles had been uncorked and placed on the long table before the catering crew cleaned up and left.

Julia and a few of the girls were hovering around Alex and Dusty who were still seated. Jimmy Ray and Reece were also sitting, a girl on each of their laps.

It was going to be a fun night, Andrea thought. "Shall we move back to the great room? There's a chocolate fountain and a big pile of cocaine."

The girls from the Palace perked up immediately.

"Yes, girl," said KiKi, jumping up from Jimmy Ray's lap.

Jimmy Ray stood and attempted to adjust his erection. "Holla...," he said, raising the roof.

Shae and KiKi escorted him, while Reece offered an arm each to Honey and Ebonie. Lola chatted up Ginger as they followed.

Alex, Dusty and Julia remained at the table. She was next to him now and gladly accepted his wine glass when he offered, her empty one still at the other end of table.

"Why didn't you let any of us know you weren't coming back?" Julia was not going to let this go.

"But I did come back."

"After three fucking years...!"

"Whoa, easy tiger," Alex teased. "I'm back now, isn't that enough?"

"For now, I guess, but you just don't do that to your friends—especially your best friend."

"Ah, it's Dusty, is it?" Alex turned up one of the remaining bottles. It was empty. He grabbed another, also empty. "Fuck, if she's gonna get all heavy, I need a drink."

"I'm sorry, you're right," Julia said. "This is a party. We can talk later."

Alex glanced at Dusty.

"What is it with the female species?" he asked. "They always want to talk."

"Why don't we join the others," Dusty suggested.

"Ram!" Alex yelled when he saw him enter the dining room. "Is there any of this shitty cabernet left? I can't be expected to walk from one room to the next without a drink. Check the bottles!"

Midway down the table, Ram located a full bottle and delivered it.

"Now that's service."

Alex turned his attention back to Julia. "So what would you like to know?"

"For starters, why you were gone for so long?"

"Everyone grows, Julia. Sometimes apart. Who knows why?" He lit a cigarette. "I wanted to live, to see the world. I traveled, spent time with family and started a career, although my father would argue you that one. And now I'm home again."

Andrea re-entered the dining room. "We can't have a party without the guest of honor," she announced. "The deejay will be starting soon and Veronique will be arriving any minute now. The others made a pit stop in the great room."

"Okay, my love." Alex stood. "Shall we?"

They joined the rest of the group around the silver "candy tray." The sound of the deejay gearing up could be heard coming from the ballroom.

"This is some fuckin' party," Jimmy Ray said, patting Alex on the back.

"And it's only getting better," he replied. He reached into both crystal dishes and popped an unknown mix of zanies and X, before dipping a spoon into the mound of cocaine.

"Shit," Julia gasped. "What the fuck are you trying to do?"

"It's a party." He wiped at his nostrils and moved for the bar. "Shots...?"

"Hell, yeah," Reece said.

Andrea's Blackberry chimed again. Two chartered buses from the Atlanta airport, one of which carried Veronique, had arrived. Black's instructions were to direct the buses to the ballroom entrance, secure the gates and report to the deejay booth where he was to keep an eye on the crowd.

Veronique was a legendary transsexual performer from New York's underground party scene who had married well and divorced better. She was known in the transgender community as much for her outspoken politics on equal rights as her beauty, but most of all for her voice. Getting her group to South Isle had been no easy task.

"Girls," Andrea said. "Please follow Ginger to the ballroom. It's through the door on the far side of the gaming room. Just follow the bass. There's a spot for each of you and you'll find costumes in the dressing rooms, beyond the deejay cage."

She gave vague instructions just as she had done with Ram in order to test them. Ginger led the way and the Palace girls strutted to the beat toward the sound of the music, champagne flutes in raised hands.

"Wow, is there no end to this place?" Honey asked as they passed through the game room.

"No shit," Ebonie added.

Ginger continued to the far wall and pulled open the double doors. She passed through another entry hall and then she screamed. There were mirrors, projected images on the walls, cocktail tables, a bar, a stage and a dance floor with elevated platforms.

"This bitch knows how to throw a party," KiKi said.

There was an open-air stairway to the immediate left, leading to the deejay platform, and another to a loft where they found the dressing rooms. There were beautiful two piece fringed costumes covered in crystals hanging in each room tagged with the girls' names.

CHAPTER 51

SOUTH ISLE — SEA VIEW, GA

When he finally came to, Dusty found himself in the bed he had shared with Andrea and just like that first morning he could not remember exactly how it happened. He was also naked just like before, but this time Alex was lying next to him. He slowly sat up, willing the details of the party to come back to him. Ginger was right; Alex was crazy with the drugs.

"Oh, good..." he heard the velvety voice say.

He turned to see Andrea coming out of the bathroom in a white terry robe, which seemed to be the house uniform. She was toweling her hair.

"You're awake."

"Just barely," he said. "How do I always end up in this bed when I'm here?"

Her eyes dart nervously toward Alex. She responded with a faint smile and a whisper.

"Fate...?" She smiled at him. "Did you have a good time at the party?"

He chuckled. "What I can remember."

"I'll get you some water."

"You don't have to."

"I want to."

She was moving so effortlessly. He watched her disappear into the bathroom. How could she be real? She came back, still in the robe, but without the towel and sat down on the bed beside him. Her wet hair hung in big ringlets down past her shoulders. He wanted to reach out to her, to finish what they started in the foyer that night, but he couldn't and he wouldn't. She handed him the water.

"The big bottle, huh?"

"You're gonna need it," she teased. "You were a wild man last night."

He focused his blurry eyes on her. They had slept in the same bed. But all three? Surely he would remember that.

"At the party, I mean. We," she said pointing at each of them, "only slept. Well, you two passed out."

She reached out and pinched his nipple.

"Ooouuchh!"

"Grab a shower, we'll have some breakfast or should I say lunch?"

"What about Alex?"

"He usually sleeps most of the day."

She retrieved a robe from the bathroom, tossed it to him and left the room again.

Dusty put on the robe and joined her in the bathroom. She was brushing her teeth.

"And everyone else?" he asked.

"Let's see, the buses took the kids to the Inn, they're flying back to New York tonight. Jimmy Ray, Reece, and the girls are in the pool house with Ram and Ginger. Black is in the apartment over the garage, and Julia, Veronique and Vlad are somewhere in the south wing." She saluted. "All accounted for sir."

He shook his head.

She smiled again. "What is it?"

"Last night must have been the craziest night of my life."

She was sure he had never witnessed that kind of psychedelic, otherworld debauchery. She wanted desperately to reach out to him, to spare him what was sure to come.

"Veronique and the lot are an interesting group to say the least," she said.

"I still can't believe she used to be a guy."

"Brazil does do the best work, and it doesn't hurt that she was once a petite, Puerto Rican boy with amazing bone structure." She twisted her hair into a bun at the top of her head. "We'll eat in the kitchen up here."

Δ

Dusty showered and dressed in the Blue Room before meeting Andrea in the kitchen. A brisk wind was wafting through French doors, which opened to a balcony that over looked the pool. She was there, wrapped tightly in her robe.

"The wind makes me feel free," she said. "There's fruit, cereal, bagels, I think and banana bread. I brewed some coffee or I could make you a cappuccino."

"No, coffee's good. Is there juice?"

"In the fridge; we can order real food if you want."

He poured black coffee and a glass of cranberry juice. He grabbed some fruit, figuring it would fare better on his stomach. He teetered to the outside table.

"So, how do you feel?" she asked.

"Like death warmed over."

"You should never try to keep up with Alex."

This silenced both of them, each for their own reasons.

Dusty munched on melon, grapefruit and papaya while trying to pull memories from the fog with little luck. The girls in elaborate costumes dancing provocatively above an orgy-esk dance floor.

263

He had questions–about Alex, about the drugs–but sitting so close to her and looking at her beautiful face made nothing matter but her. He sipped the rich, black coffee, while trying to will the right words.

She touched his hand, her eyes saying what she did not dare to.

"Hey, what's this? I turn my back for a second and you're moving in on my girl?"

They turned to see Alex chugging from a bottle of designer water, his back to them, the refrigerator door open. He too was wearing one of the plush white robes. When he turned to face them, however, they noticed that it was untied and that he was naked underneath. He was devoid of any body hair, except a perfectly manicured strip that started below his belly button and spread into a closely cropped patch above his low hanging penis.

He leisurely poured a cup of coffee then joined them at the table on the balcony. He kissed Andrea on the forehead and Dusty on top of the head before he sat, the robe falling completely open.

"So, Dustin Marler," Alex said. "How are we this morning?"

"I feel like you look," Dusty replied.

"Then you must be feeling pretty fucking good," Alex said, a shit-eating grin on his face.

"Christ baby," Andrea said, "you just woke up."

The worried look on her face did not escape Dusty's attention.

Alex, still grinning, said, "Woke up, revved up and if you keep looking at me that way, I'll be gettin' it up."

She rolled her eyes and sighed. "I'm going for a run."

They watched as she got up and went back inside.

"She worries too much," Alex said leaning back on the hind legs of his chair.

It was nearly impossible not to see what Alex blatantly thrust into plain view.

"Jeez, could you cover that thing up?" Dusty complained.

Alex leaned forward, resting the chair on all fours, the table shielding his lower half.

"Should I use a Fleshlight?"

They both laughed at the memories.

"I haven't thought about that in years," Dusty lied.

"Funny, I think about it all the time."

Alex sipped from his coffee cup.

The comment left Dusty feeling uncomfortable. *Was Alex flirting?*

"So what shall we do tonight?" Alex asked. "I say we take a plane to Atlanta and party at the Palace."

"Sounds great, but I'm working tomorrow."

"Yeah, about that; I think you should quit."

"Just like that...?"

"Just like that." Alex stood. "More coffee...?"

Dusty followed him in and he filled each of their cups then leaned back against the counter. Andrea re-entered the kitchen dressed in running attire, her mane pulled back in a ponytail. She grabbed a bottle of water from the fridge.

"You're really going for a run, now?" Alex asked.

"I said I was going for a run, didn't I?"

"But I thought we were going to, you know," he said making blatantly obvious gestures.

To Dusty's surprise, she walked over to Alex and grabbed his junk. He felt a pang of jealousy as well as a stirring in his sweat pants.

"Is that all you ever think about?" she asked.

"It's not my fault you look like this," Alex answered.

Her hand started massaging him. "I guess there are other ways to burn calories."

"Now, you're talking." They kissed.

"Maybe *I* should go for a run," Dusty said.

"Or you could join us," Alex said.

"What happened to you after you left?"

"I grew up. Life is too damned short not to grab it by the balls," Alex said. "No pun intended."

Andrea took pity. "He's just trying to freak you out."

It was working. Dusty wasn't ready for any of this. Would he ever be?

She attempted a smile and, still holding on to Alex said, "Come on, my big man. I think you missed me."

"And did you miss me?" he wondered.

"Follow me and I'll show you how much."

They kissed again, more passionately this time.

"Dusty, Reece and Jimmy Ray must be awake by now," Andrea said.

Was he being dismissed? Did he expect to hang around and listen to them going at it? He hadn't had sex in months and the thought of a three way was turning him on. What was he thinking? He had to get out of there.

"Uh, yeah, the pool house," he stammered. "Good idea."

Alex called out as he was making his escape. "Tell them we're partying at the Palace tonight."

Dusty turned, instantly wishing he hadn't. Andrea was on her knees. Alex looked directly at him, his hips thrust forward as she made love to him with her mouth.

CHAPTER 52

SOUTH ISLE — SEA VIEW, GA

Jimmy Ray, having grown up on a farm (granted it was a thirty-two-hundred-acre farm run as efficiently as any large company), had always been an early riser, no matter how late he partied. He discovered the well-stocked kitchen and had already devoured six eggs, half a pound of bacon and four pieces of multi-grain toast. And now he was kicked back, lounging in his underwear and a wife beater, watching *MTV Cribs*. Reece walked in wearing only his boxer briefs.

"What's up bro?" Jimmy Ray asked with a smile. They had spent the night with the Palace girls.

"How can you be so cheery?" Reece wondered, going for the refrigerator.

"Man, after the night we had, I'm gonna be smiling for days to come. I can't wait to see what happens tonight."

"You got anything left?" Reece asked scanning the contents of the packed to capacity fridge. "You were like a starving man at a buffet."

"Don't hate 'cause I got skills!" Jimmy Ray chuckled.

"And strayin' hands."

"Hey, it was group sex. Don't tell me it was your first time at the rodeo."

"I've done three ways with a buddy of mine," Reece countered. "But you best believe my focus was on the chic."

"Relax! It's not like I touched your wang or anything. Just a couple of *good job* ass slaps."

Yeah, whatever, Coach, Reece thought, quickly changing the subject.

"Look at all this food," he said.

"Dude, *this* place is the shit," Jimmy Ray said. "She's got any and everything in this motherfucker."

Reece joined him on the sofa, cinnamon pastry in hand.

"Hell, this place needs to be on *Cribs,*" he said, eyeing the giant flat screen.

"No shit," Jimmy Ray agreed. "When the girls get up we're goin' skinny dippin' in that indoor pool."

He jumped up, clapped his hands twice, spun around and humped the air three times. Another of his signature moves.

"Bro, you're way too excited," Reece said.

"Yeah," Jimmy Ray replied, still dancing, "there's blow over there."

"What?"

"I told you, she's got this place hooked up!"

Jimmy Ray was in the process of repeating his dance move, when Dusty walked in.

"You dirty dog...!" Jimmy Ray whooped. "Did you guys fuck last night?"

Dusty frowned. "No, you friggin' perv." He looked at Reece. "What's up with him?"

"He's in the powder."

"Already...?"

"You know Jimmy Ray. If opportunity presents itself..."

"So where's the A Team?" Jimmy Ray wanted to know.

"Humping their brains out right about now," Dusty said, jealousy running over him.

"Damn right," Jimmy Ray hooted. "Er' body gettin' laid 'round here..."

Reece grinned. "Except Dusty that is..."

"Please don't remind me. I'm going insane."

"It can't be that bad," said Reece. "Melinda was just here."

"There was no time," Dusty complained.

"Damn, that sucks," Jimmy Ray teased. "And speakin' of suckin', the girls are still here."

"And they know their way around a dick," Reece added.

"Not necessary," Dusty said.

There was only one girl on his mind and she was currently getting banged by his best friend.

"That reminds me," he said changing the subject. "Alex wants to fly to Atlanta tonight and party at the Pink Palace."

"Hells-to-the-yizz-owh!" Jimmy Ray yelled. "I'm wakin' the girls up."

With that, he was off down one of the hallways leading to guest bedrooms.

They watched him go. Reece shook his head.

"The Pink Palace, huh...? Sounds good, what time are we leaving?"

"Not sure," said Dusty. "I guess we hang out at the pool 'til Alex comes up for air."

"It's crazy having him back."

"Yeah, pretty crazy."

"And what about Andrea smokin' fuckin' hot, Sorcosi...?"

"Yeah, she's pretty hot," Dusty said, unable to make eye contact.

"Pretty hot? Bro, what are you, blind?"

Ram and Ginger walked in, both wearing pool house robes.

"Dusty, you're alive," said Ginger. "We were a little worried."

"What exactly did I do last night?"

"Hell," Ram said, "what didn't you do?"

Dusty looked at Reece who simply nodded his head. "You were pretty fucked up."

"You got a little nuts with the X," Ginger added. "Hey babe, there's coffee."

"Thank God," Ram said. "I could drink a gallon."

Dusty dropped his head again. "Shit."

"You deserve to blow off a little steam," Reece said. "You're way too serious all the time."

Jimmy Ray bounced back in with Lola on his back.

"Stop, stop," she shrieked. "You're gonna make me puke."

The other girls followed, draggin' ass, in camisoles or tight t-shirts and brightly colored thongs.

Ram wiped the sleep from his eyes and secured his robe. "Well, well, well, good morning ladies."

Ginger rolled her eyes. "Morning girls..."

"Hey," they said almost in unison.

"Is that coffee I smell?" asked Honey.

"I just poured the last of it, but I'll be glad to make more," Ram obliged.

Ginger pushed him away. "Oh, no you don't. I'll make the coffee."

"Damn, babe, I'm just trying to be sociable."

"You were plenty social last night, thank you very much," she mumbled. Ram had also indulged in the ecstasy the night before.

"There's all kinds of food in the fridge, if you girls are hungry," Reece said.

Lola smiled, wondering if she would get another shot at that fine piece of chocolate before the weekend was over. "I could get used to this," she said.

The girls moved past Dusty into the kitchen.

Honey fluttered her eyelashes. "Good morning, Sundance."

"Yippee ki yay cowboy," Ebonie added.

The song lyric from Ride Your Man triggered something in Dusty's head and suddenly there it was; the dancers, the thumping bass. *Oh God,* he thought remembering being stripped down to his skivvies and strapped to a chair. "Oh God," he said out loud this time. And Veronique riding him like some prized pony. Dusty let out a groan.

Reece couldn't help smiling. "Comin' back to ya, is it?"

"Slowly," Dusty said. "And none of its lookin' good." Reece started to laugh. "I'll do you one better. Alex caught everything on video."

"Could this get any worse?"

"He downloaded it on You Tube."

"What!" Dusty shouted. "No, no, no."

"Inside voice please," Ginger said, massaging her temple.

Dusty made a mad dash from the kitchen, out the front door of the pool house, across the lawn and into the main house. He flew up the grand staircase, tore through the gallery and into the apartment, straight into the master bedroom.

"Please say you didn't..."

He stopped in his tracks. Not only were Alex and Andrea still having sex, but he had burst in just as Alex was bringing it home.

"Dusty!" Andrea cried out.

Alex was a skilled lover and she had already had two orgasms, but the sight of Dusty sent her over the edge again.

Alex was panting violently. "Do it. Do it!" he demanded.

Suddenly her hands gripped his throat and started to squeeze until his face turned red, then purple. *What the hell?* He watched as Alex started to convulse and seize, an animalistic groan escaping his gaping mouth. And then she released him and he collapsed on top of her, gasping for air.

Dusty stood stock still, frozen and in shock, his eyes drinking in every shudder and quake, as if in a dream.

"Oh, God I, I'm...." he stuttered and turned to leave.

Alex rolled onto his back and Andrea quickly, though barely, covered them.

"No," he coughed, breathing hard. "No, it's okay." He coughed a few more times.

"What the fuck was that?" Dusty asked. He was trying not to freak out.

Andrea tried to sound calm. "It's just a game," she said, gauging his reaction.

It could go either way. She opened the top drawer in the bedside table and reached for her cigarettes, a habit she had battled for years. They were there in case of emergencies. This qualified.

Dusty was dumbstruck. What had happened to his friend, the Alex he thought he knew?

"Come, sit," Alex said smacking the bed with his hand, loving the fact that Dusty was completely disheveled. "You stormed in, it must be important."

"Important? *Important?* Dusty thought.

He started pacing, his mind racing. Was this really Alex's fault, or his own? Nobody twisted his arm. He stopped.

"How bad is the video?"

Andrea exhaled, blowing smoke toward the ceiling. "It's not *bad*. Veronique is an artist. "Ride Your Man" is going to be a huge hit."

Alex took her cigarette and hit it hard.

"I'm backing her for a reason," Alex said. "The timing's perfect... and the bitch can actually sing."

"What's that got to do with me? Melinda's gonna kill me."

"'Ride Your Man' is her debut single. It's already getting club play in New York, Miami, and L.A.; now we release the video. The idea behind last night was to shoot live concert footage."

He coughed again and rubbed his throat.

"A little rough that time, my love," he said.

Andrea reclaimed her cigarette.

"You know you loved it," she said.

Dusty was drawn to them. He sat on the bed near Andrea's feet.

"It's just so unlike me. How did I get so fucked up?"

"You were having a good time," Alex said. "We all were. How long has it been Dance?"

Andrea lit a joint and offered it to Dusty.

"Hit this," she said. "You need to calm down."

"Since you've had a good time, I mean," Alex continued. "We got some great shit last night. Veronique is a fucking genius. She choreographed the whole thing in two minutes and those fucking Cupie dolls or whatever the fuck they're called made perfect extras."

More flashes, the meeting in the upstairs dressing area, one of the girls giving him something to relax and Veronique, performing her first single live, prancing around the stage in the flesh colored mesh body suit. Melinda was going to flip the fuck out.

"They're called Cupids, sweetheart," Andrea said. "That's why she says, *go out and spread love...?*"

"Don't you need me to sign a release form or something?" Dusty heard himself ask.

"Permission...?" Alex countered. "You're a fuckin' laugh riot. We're introducing you to the world. You should be thanking me." He ran a hand threw his hair, wet with sweat.

"You made a verbal commitment," Andrea said. "Can I have some of that, please?"

Dusty looked at her as he passed the joint. She smiled at him instantly diffusing his anger and fear. It was always going to be about her.

"At the party...? I was fucked up..." *What could he do...?*

"Dusty look, what's done is done. This is business." Alex said, sitting up. "Get over it."

The sense of helplessness Dusty felt was somehow exhilarating. Life was being laid at his feet. Was that really a bad thing?

Andrea passed the joint back. "Take this," she urged.

There was no winning with Alex. She watched intently, trying to read him. Dusty was already giving in.

"I guess I was looking for...."

"Someone to blame...?" Alex asked. "I'm happy to take the fall."

"No.... I..." He shook his head. "I can't believe I barged in like that."

"Did you learn anything?" Alex teased.

"Ignore him," Andrea said. "You're worried about what people think... People like your mother and Melinda..."

"Oh, God," Dusty sighed.

Alex swung his legs over the side of the bed. He didn't care to hear anything concerning Melinda.

"I gotta take a piss."

Dusty was silent for a moment. At last he spoke.

"What's happening?"

"Your life is changing."

She leaned in and kissed him.

Δ

In the bathroom Alex stared at his reflection. He snorted a couple of lines and then turned on the shower. "I'm going to clean up," he called out, unknowingly interrupting their lip lock. He returned to the coke and held his head back, feeling the drain.

Δ

"You have to trust me on this," Andrea said. "I told you, Alex wants you with us."

"What does that mean?"

"To have this life... Alex has plans for the three of us, and it's going to work. Just let it happen."

Dusty was totally lost to the conversation. She was naked underneath a sheet and they were alone.

"Perhaps it's time to move on," Andrea said.

"Move on?"

"She was your high school sweetheart, your first girlfriend. You deserve more."

"What are you saying?"

"You owe it to yourself."

He looked at her, at that beautiful face. "Maybe if I thought I had a chance with you."

She touched his hand but said nothing. She could not trust herself to say what she wanted to say, so she remained quiet. As did Ana Maria; she wanted to say something, too, but she was scared.

CHAPTER 53

SOUTH ISLE — SEA VIEW, GA

Julia tossed and turned restlessly in one of the guest bedrooms that overlooked the pool. She had been awake for a while and was debating whether or not to pull herself from the most comfortable bed she had ever known.

The night before had definitely been off the chain. One thing was for sure, Alex and Andrea knew how to party. And Dusty, what the hell had gotten into him? Melinda was going to flip shit.

Julia surveyed the guest room. It was so beautiful, the kind of beautiful that only massive amounts of money could buy. She wondered what everyone was up to and what the day would hold, but mostly she wondered why Black had refused to stay with her after throwing her one of the all-time best fucks to date.

The sound of voices coming from outside convinced her to get out of bed. Jimmy Ray's loud mouth was heard above all. She went to the window, looked out and saw the crew coming over from the pool house, heading toward the solarium. She decided to join them after a quick shower.

By the time she reached the entrance to the solarium, it sounded like a small-scale party was already in progress. Upon entering, she was proven right. Music was coming from speakers mounted near the frescoed ceiling and the Palace girls were frolicking topless around the pool. Even Ginger had gotten in on the act. Reece and Ram were in a breaststroke competition and Jimmy Ray was walking toward her, boner and all, wrapping a towel around his waist.

"Hey, babe," he said, giving her a wet kiss on the check. "How'd you sleep?"

"Alone."

Jimmy Ray, forever mischievous, grabbed her about the waist. "Well now, we might have to do something about that."

"Don't you wish?" she said, freeing herself from his grip.

She started back toward the great room.

"Wait, where are you going?"

He knew this game well. She would walk away, he would follow.

"To have a cocktail. Why?"

She liked toying with him. She always had. Jimmy Ray was her first and only love, but she knew she could never tame him; and Julia Roenstein could not spend her life chasing a man who wasn't worth catching.

"God, Julia, why do you have to be so dramatic all the time? I just want to talk to you."

She continued through the gaming room. "So talk."

"Don't you think this is all kinda fucked up?"

"What do you mean fucked up?"

"You don't think it's weird that Alex is back... all of a sudden? And what the fuck is up with this house?"

"Sea View is his home. And what's wrong with the house? I think it's beautiful."

They reached the great room and she walked behind the built-in bar and poured a large Bailey's Irish Cream over ice with a Tia Maria floater.

"It's on a fuckin' island," Jimmy Ray said.

He followed her behind the bar and blocked her way back out. She was caught, now what?

"Don't you think it's a bit much, even for Alex?"

"What are you getting at?"

"He could live anywhere and he comes back to Georgia? Now *that* is fucked up," he said, making quotation marks in the air.

"You look kind of fucked up yourself," Julia teased.

"Fuckin-A—it's the weekend."

They said the word fuck a lot when they were alone together. They also had a habit of fucking a lot when they were alone together. She would have to watch her step.

"So, how's school going?" she asked.

"The classes are kickin' my ass, but I'm dominating on the field."

"Are you seeing anyone?"

"Just casual dating..."

She knew in his bumbling way he was trying to protect her. Jimmy Ray Daniels was notorious for his female conquests. He was the All-American Hero, granted a slightly cruder version, but it worked in his favor. He was a big, blonde football stud with money—maybe not crazy Vandiveer money, but a catch for any girl who could put up with Jethro on steroids.

"In other words you're screwing your way across campus," she teased.

"Hey, you wanna go for a swim?" he asked, changing the subject.

"Sure, why not," she said, but did not move.

She was playing with him and he was enjoying it. Everything was a game with Julia, but it was okay with him. He loved her, even though he knew she would never come to him. He was perfectly aware that he hadn't grown up yet.

"I heard we're all going to the Pink Palace tonight," he said.

"Great," Julia responded, dripping with sarcasm. "I get to sit around bored while all you guys stock your spank banks."

"Oh, you know you'll have a good time."

"Whatever."

"Whatever," he said, mocking her. As he did so, he put a pinky out and a hand on his hip.

It made her laugh. "Why is it that we could never make it J.R.?"

He hung his head. "I guess I'm just an asshole."

She wanted to kiss him, but she wanted to slap him more. She did neither.

CHAPTER 54

SOUTH ISLE — SEA VIEW, GA

Alex walked back into the bedroom, a towel draped low around his waist, his wet hair dripping water onto perfectly waxed, killer abs.

"So what should we do for the next couple of hours?"

He toyed sporadically with the towel, adjusting it as if it were about to fall, exposing quick flashes of himself.

Andrea knew the signs well. "I think you should eat something."

"I thought I just did." He grinned, still fiddling with the towel.

"Turn your head please," she said to Dusty, as if he had never seen her naked.

"I, ah, think I'll head back to the pool house," Dusty said.

"You don't have to leave," Alex said. He smiled at Andrea, "Really, darling? You're playing the modesty card?"

She stood quickly and slipped into a robe. Alex focused on Dusty, placing an arm around his shoulders. "We always swim in the nude," he whispered. "So have no fear, my friend. You will soon see all the glories of the newest *It Girl* up close and personal."

Alex slapped Dusty's chest twice when he said "it girl," winding him slightly. Dusty's mind was plagued with images of Andrea, mainly of her squirming on top of him.

"There won't be time for a swim," she said, obviously annoyed. "Dusty, could you send Julia and Ginger up for me? And keep an eye on Alex."

"Yeah, sure," he said, not sure what he was agreeing to. "You're not coming with?"

"Darling," she said sweetly, "the Paparazzi."

"Dreaded bastards!" Alex snapped, ushering Dusty from the bedroom. "You know, Dusty, it's a tricky thing, this love-hate relationship that we must forge. We pretend that we hate them when in fact, we could not be who we are without them. It's always an event, going out with us, always a spectacle. You'll see."

"And no drinking, Dusty," she called after them. "I need you to drive one of the SUVs to the airstrip."

Δ

Andrea finished blow-drying her hair and switched on her flatiron. She would be super sleek tonight with severe bangs—an updated version of Betty Page with a hint of Dita Von Tease. *Yes, the leather Chanel gloves,* she thought, picking up her Blackberry. She dialed Veronique.

Veronique and Vlad were in the South Wing. She was seated in front of a centuries-old European dressing table in a silk robe, applying eyeliner. She put the pencil down and gazed out the window at the circular drive with the gorgeous tiered fountain and the Atlantic just beyond. She breathed in deeply lost in thought.

To say becoming a woman had been a lifelong dream would be a gross understatement. For her, life had depended upon it. As early as she could remember, she had always thought of herself as a girl. By fourteen, she was out on the street, by fifteen, performing on the drag circuit, and by sixteen she was having her first breast job.

That was half a dozen surgeries ago. Veronique smiled at her perfect face. The nose had been tweaked, the brow bone shaven, but the eyes, lips and cheekbones were all hers. The last eight years had been her best years. Getting kicked out of her parents' house had resulted in her being born again and ultimately transforming into who she was meant to be.

Vlad returned to bed after his shower. He was smoking a clove cigarette while watching her.

"You were born beautiful," he said.

Veronique smiled and turned her attention back to her ritual.

He tried again. "You don't need all that nonsense."

So lovely to have a dressing table in the bedroom she thought, lost in the grand illusion of her make-believe life.

The sound of her cell vibrating against the veined marble turned her attention from the mirror. By the time she answered, her gaze was again fixed on her own reflection.

"Hello darling," she said to Andrea in her perfectly pitched voice, thanks to years of hormone treatments, well worth every penny, and countless hours of vocal coaching. "Of course. I'm finishing my face as we speak. I just need to get dressed."

She signaled to Vlad, who got out of bed and walked across the room, a naked Nordic god in the flesh. She had met him through friends of her ex-husband during their brief marriage. He was a spoiled trust-fund baby who felt unjustly privileged, resulting in his desire to feel *unworthy*.

"Something for Ginger...?" She stood and slipped out of her dressing gown, pointing to the laces of her corset. *Tonight, he would get spanked.* "I have a vintage, shredded Valentino that is to die for...I'll see you in a bit."

Δ

Just as she ended her call with Veronique, there was a soft knock on the master bedroom door. Julia and Ginger, no doubt. She padded quickly across the giant Persian rug and let them in.

"Okay, girls we have a big night ahead of us. I've alerted the media so we must look our best. Julia, help yourself to anything in my closet except the black leather Dolce. Ginger, Veronique is bringing something for you."

"Andrea, I gotta tell ya, I feel like I've died and gone to heaven," Ginger said.

"Think nothing of it. I'll need you to shower first so you can book the flight, call the Four Seasons and pack for Dusty. Club wear, day wear, everything..."

"I thought we were flying up and back," Ginger said.

"That's the plan, but with Alex one can never be sure. The shower is right through there."

Ginger thanked her and was off. Julia and Andrea were at last alone together. They walked into the master closet.

"Wasn't last night a scream?" she asked, switching on lights and pulling out drawers.

Julia got right to the point. "What's with all the pretense?"

"Let's go dark tonight," Andrea replied with a smile. "You know, smoky eyes and deep red lips. Give the photographers something to work with."

So, they would keep pretending.

"Photographers...?"

"Well, I know we're not in New York or God, forbid, L.A., but there is a scene in Atlanta and they know Alex will be there. I had Ginger call TMZ and the local entertainment magazines with anonymous tips."

"Oh God, you're serious?"

"Yes, that's how this works." While they were speaking Andrea slipped into black lace panties and push up bra. Julia's mouth dropped open when the robe hit the floor.

"Too much...?" Andrea asked, seeing the look on Julia's face.

"You look incredible."

"They cost enough," Andrea said absent-mindedly. It was a lie, but she had her reasons.

A rush of relief swept over Julia. *She did have a flaw.* "They're fake...?"

"Of course, sweetie... I was a C cup, but the D gives me an edge. Modeling is very competitive."

"Oh my God, and all this time I thought you were...." Julia stopped herself.

Andrea moved in front of one of the full-length mirrors. "What, perfect? Far from it..." She loosened the straps a bit. "That's better. What would you like to wear?"

"Those tits," Julia laughed. She loved this girl.

"You should get some."

Julia's smile faded.

"What? I'm serious. If you want them, you should have them. I can arrange everything."

She was both embarrassed and a little put out by the conversation. Julia had never shared her desire for breast augmentation with anyone. She and Jimmy Ray had joked about it often, but he was the one who always brought it up, not her.

"I don't even know how to respond to that."

"To what...?" Veronique asked sweeping into the walk in.

"Nique," Andrea said. "You brought the dress."

"Anything for you, darling..."

They air kissed and Andrea took the dress.

"Now what is the topic of conversation?"

"Implants," Andrea said, pointing to her breasts.

Ginger re-entered the bedroom wrapped in a towel and gasped.

"Those aren't real?"

She showered quickly so she wouldn't miss anything and apparently, she had returned just in time.

"Girl you had a good doctor. You can't even tell."

"There's no scaring if you go through the armpit." Andrea said passing Ginger the Valentino.

"Oh, Veronique, I don't know what to say. It's gorgeous," Ginger gushed.

"That old thing, please; think nothing of it."

"So, Julia," Ginger asked, "Are you thinking about getting a boob job?"

"Of course you should," Veronique said, wondering why Andrea was lying. If there was one thing she knew, it was plastic surgery.

"I don't know. I just feel like everybody will start staring at me or something."

"That's the point," Ginger giggled.

"I'm going to Fortaleza to do the Maxium shoot in a couple of weeks," Andrea said. "We could make it a girl's trip. Veronique, are you free?"

"For Brazil? Always, honey." She turned her back to the mirror and looked over her shoulder. "I think I need to go a size up on the booty."

Ginger's expression was hopeful.

"Of course you're going, too, silly," Andrea smiled. "Alex will pay for everything. He's been an absolute ass lately. Julia, what do you think?

"I suppose....," she stammered. "I can't believe we're having this convo..."

"You're going to love them sweetie," Ginger said. "I've been fighting the boys off since I was thirteen when these things popped out."

Veronique laughed. "I couldn't live without mine."

Andrea looked at Julia. "You'll be ready in time for the showing."

"Oh God, the showing... How long will I be out of commission?"

"Don't worry," Andrea said. "We can hire a dozen little elves to do the sewing. It will all work out."

"Show," Veronique said. "What show?"

"Julia's going to debut her clothing line—aren't you, darling?"

What is happening here? Julia wondered. "It would appear so." Whose life was she suddenly living?

"Fabulous!" Veronique clasped her hands. "Can I be a model?"

"That's brilliant," Andrea said. "We can tie everything in together. 'Nique, when's the shoot for your second video. Julia does this super chic thing with Edwardian ruffles."

"Oh, I could wear your clothes," Veronique agreed. "*Come to Me Lover* is very rrromantic," she said rolling the *r*.

"You know I kind of want my nose done too." Julia said out of the blue. It just slipped out.

"A two for one," Veronique squealed.

The four young women rambled on and on while they dressed, swapping make up tips and talking about the boys, giggling the way girls do. They also helped themselves to a few tiny bumps, to put them in the mood.

"Let's have a drink," Veronique suggested.

"Fantastic idea," Julia agreed.

"None for me yet," Ginger said, stepping into what was easily the most expensive garment she had ever worn.

She checked her reflection, the dress was perfect, the jewelry borrowed from Andrea just the right touch.

She smiled then hurried from the room. She had to charter a plane, make hotel reservations and pack. No matter what anybody said, she thought, money made a difference. The luxurious red velvet clung to her body, hugging her every curve as she strolled through the gallery feeling more together than she ever had. Ram was going to shit bricks.

CHAPTER 55

SOUTH ISLE — SEA VIEW, GA

"God, I barely recognize myself," Julia said.

Veronique was turning to and fro, checking every angle in the mirror. "Isn't it amazing how great clothes can make a girl feel?" she asked.

Andrea blotted her lips, and noted that she was showing way too much cleavage after all. *Perfect.*

"Okay, ladies, with Alex it could be a day or a week. So we'd better pack some shit.

Dusty and Alex were entering the bedroom when the girls walked through.

"Be still my beating heart," Alex said with outstretched arms.

"Don't touch me," Andrea said, raising a hand to stop him. "You're all wet."

"Julia, you look fantastic," Dusty said.

She twirled for him. "Do you think so?"

Veronique put her hands on her hips. "What am I, chopped liver?"

"You all look great," Dusty said. He felt his cheeks flush. *Fuck!*

Veronique gave a coy smile. "Sundance, you're going to make my video ssssizzle," she said, narrowing her eyes seductively. "And it's going to launch both our careers."

Alex nodded and smiled. Dusty smiled, too, but didn't know what to say.

"Oooooh, Andrea he's so cute when he's nervous," Veronique said.

Andrea nodded. "Absolutely... Where are the others?" she wanted to know.

"They all went back to the pool house to get ready," Dusty replied.

She smiled at him and his heart skipped. Alex took note. The girls continued out into the apartment.

"Don't bullshit around you two," Andrea said over her shoulder. "We're leaving in one hour."

Alex saluted. "Yes, ma'am." He stripped the towel away. "Come on Dusty, time to hit the showers."

The implication was clear. *It was a big enough shower,* Dusty thought, no different from any public shower and God knows he had spent a lot of naked time with his friend as a teen, though it was usually Alex who was naked. He followed. *No big deal.* Alex turned on the water, then went to the vanity and retrieved his stash.

"A bump, Dusty?"

The question brought him back to the present. Alex was sniffing, checking his nostrils.

"Sure, why not."

He was about to board a private plane and fly hundreds of miles away to party for the night. Alex busied himself preparing the pure, white powder and then stepped into the shower. Dusty took his turn and checked his nose in the mirror. He glanced at his friend standing under the rush of water from multiple jets. *It's just a shower,* he told himself.

Alex, Jimmy Ray and the Palace girls had all ended up completely naked during the little swim party; but Dusty and Reece opted to keep their trunks on—unlike Jimmy Ray who proudly sported his arousal.

He took one last look at his reflection, snorted another line and suddenly felt as if he were living someone else's life. The old Dusty was losing hold and a new creature was emerging. He was so tired of doing the right thing. He hooked his thumbs in the waistband of his trunks and with a what-the-hell shrug, shoved them down. This was a different world. The coke was doing its thing and he felt great.

"Hey, don't hog all the hot water," he said playfully pushing Alex aside.

"Oh, you wanna play rough," Alex said, assuming a boxer's stance. He thumbed his nose.

"Ohhh, no," Dusty replied, bracing himself. "I was kidding."

He and Alex played their own games. The rough and tumble horseplay of young men clinging to the days of boyhood. Alex bobbed, weaved and threw a right hook. Dusty blocked and countered, wincing when Alex made contact with an open hand slap to the shoulder. Dusty tried reasoning once again.

"Okay, seriously, this is not the time or place..."

Alex, always one to push the envelope, laughed and swung again.

Dusty ducked then made his move, locking him in a full on bear hug.

"Come on," he said, "cut it out. Someone could get hurt." They were both wet and slippery, and the groin-to-groin contact difficult to ignore.

"Maybe that someone will be you," Alex countered with a few not so playful kidney punches."

Dusty had had enough. He tightened his grip and reared back, lifting Alex off the tile floor and squeezed the air out of him.

"Jesus, Alex, give it a rest, will ya?"

"Okay," Alex gasped.

Dusty squeezed harder, the cocaine making him more aggressive than usual. He applied more pressure and bounced.

"Uncle, Uncle," Alex pleaded.

"You had enough?"

"Yes," Alex choked.

It was too much. The drugs, alcohol and Dusty's dominance flipped the switch. Alex's cock started to pulse against Dusty's abdomen as he lowered him back to the shower floor and suddenly their lips met. The kiss lasted but a few milliseconds, still long enough for Alex's tongue to dart into his unsuspecting mouth.

Dusty pulled back, releasing his hold. "Fuck, man. What'd you do that for?"

"It was just a kiss."

Just a kiss? That was the problem. His eyes dropped.

"You've got wood?"

Alex laughed and moved back under the water spray.

"What'd you expect with all that grinding?"

"Hey, I didn't mean it like that and you know it."

"Gotta blame someone," Alex said matter-of-factly. "So, how's Melinda?" Playtime was officially over.

"Exactly the same," Dusty answered.

Alex finished up and skirted past his pal, landing another shoulder punch. "Tag! You're it," he said.

"Man, you're impossible. I should kick your fuckin' ass."

Alex reached for a towel and returned to the stash on the vanity. "You'd better hurry the fuck up, or Andrea's gonna kick *both* our asses."

He walked into the massive closet.

"Let's see," he said. "How about Armani and A&A Jeans?" he called to Dusty when he heard the shower stop.

Getting no response, he walked back into the bathroom to find Dusty standing naked, dripping wet over the powder. Alex smacked his bare ass.

"Jesus, take a minute to dry off first. Do you know how much that shit costs?"

He pushed Dusty aside. Of course, he didn't care about the money, but he did enjoy tormenting his friend. The first time Dusty choked him was going to be cosmic. *Sweet agony*.

Alex cut six more large lines on the marble vanity top, all the while watching Dusty's reflection in the mirror, as he dried himself.

Dusty watched Alex watching him. He wrapped the towel and saddled up beside his pal for two of the lines. He loved the shit already.

"So, what was up with that kiss?"

Alex held his gaze through the mirror. He did two lines before he answered.

"I love you, Dusty. Don't you know that?" He did a third line.

"You mean in a brotherly kind of way, right?'

"In a human being kind of a way," Alex said, going for the fourth line.

"Damn, why you gotta be so greedy?" Dusty asked.

Alex turned and walked back into the closet. "There's always more."

They did dress in Armani–black shirt for Alex, chocolate brown for Dusty–and leather stitched A&A Jeans with suede pocket flaps. Dusty's pair was tighter than he would normally wear, since they belonged to Alex. "Don't I have these same jeans in my closet?" he asked.

"Those are perfect," Alex said. "You will definitely end up in the press showing all that. Very 'Stud of the Month.'"

Dusty grinned. He liked his new self. "Are there really going to be photographers there?"

"Seriously, you're asking me that? Andrea is the 'It Girl' of the moment."

"What does that mean, exactly?"

"Her star is on the rise," he said, cutting more lines. "She's done *GQ* and *FHM* with good numbers and she's about to do *Maxium*'s Hot 100, and she's a shoe-in for the cover. That's a wide demographic and her agency is pushing for a *Sports Illustrated Cover*, which, is going to launch her into the stratosphere."

"She's doing *Sports Illustrated?*"

"Fiona works wonders."

Dusty shook his head. "Man, did you ever think growing up that you'd end up living like this?"

"The money makes everything possible, Dusty."

They heard the front door of the apartment slam.

"Yo! Where the fuck are you guys!?" Jimmy Ray yelled.

"In here," Alex called back.

"Andrea sent me and Ram up here to change."

"And I can see why," Alex said, giving them the once over. He grabbed a black suit. "Here, this should work for you, Ram. Jimmy Ray, you're gonna have to check Dusty's closet."

Jimmy Ray gave his friend a sideways glance.

"Dusty's closet...?" he asked.

"Come on, it's in the Blue Room," Dusty said.

"Well, la-de-fuckin-da." Jimmy Ray said.

CHAPTER 56

THOMPSON STREET — NEW YORK

Melinda Sue Johnston was too wrapped up in her own drama to wonder too much about what was going on in Sea View. Her boss was being a royal pain in the ass, and it was incredibly cold in New York. If it weren't for the fact that Martin was keeping her warm on a regular basis, she might have considered returning to Georgia. She was contemplating giving him what he had worked so diligently toward since that first make out session at Audrey's birthday party. He was with her now, hanging out, watching her while she busied herself getting ready for their date.

"What are you looking at?" she asked.

"A vision," he smiled.

So damned charming. She wasn't stupid by any means and it had only taken her a few weeks to figure out that he was full of shit and himself.

Still, he was so unbelievably handsome and she longed for painless sex. There had been rumors circulating about him and his roommate's sister, but she didn't care. They were not an item, nor did she believe there was anything real between them. So he was a cheater. Wasn't she becoming the same thing? Besides, this was what college was all about—exploring options and spreading one's wings.

"Maybe you're just having a stroke," she teased.

"Why would you say such a thing?"

It was bordering on comical, his too thick accent, and hot-blooded Latin ways. Upon further investigation, she learned that there were and had been a plethora of girls and women in and out of Martin's bed and now, it was her turn.

Melinda simply giggled at his comment, which made him wonder. She could see the wheels turning inside his pretty head. Not many said no to Martin and it shook his confidence. She wondered how long he would chase her, how long he would wait, how long she herself could wait.

"So, where are you taking me tonight?"

"A party uptown," Martin said. "My friends have a loft and I hear the view is spectacular."

"And this view?" she asked, placing a hand on her hip and one behind her head.

He got up and crossed the room. "Breathtaking," he said, pulling her into his arms.

She allowed him to run his hands over her body. He nuzzled her neck, but she stopped him when he tried to kiss her.

"Ah, ah, ahhh, my make-up," she said, pushing him away. "You can mess it up later," she whispered, reeling him back in.

CHAPTER 57

SOUTH ISLE — SEA VIEW, GA

Everyone was waiting in the great room when Alex and Dusty walked in. The Palace girls were all sitting in the pit, sipping Dom and doing lines. Ram, Jimmy Ray and Reece were discussing the NFC championship, placing bets on the possibility of the Jets going the distance and Farb finally snagging that ever-elusive Super Bowl ring. Andrea stood at the bar with Julia and Veronique, watching. Alex walked straight over and poured himself a large scotch.

"Dusty?"

He shook his head no. "I'm driving."

"I think you can handle one," Andrea said, joining them.

Dusty smiled. "Okay, then, sure."

Alex poured for him. "My, my, my, she's got you jumping through hoops already, does she?" He slid the glass across the bar. "Careful, when she sets it on fire."

"Ha, ha," Andrea said, dialing her cell. "Black...?"

"The SUVs are packed and waiting," he replied.

"Thank you, darling," she said.

She ended the connection. "Well then, everyone, shall we?" she checked her diamond-encrusted Cartier wristwatch. "If weather permits, we should arrive at the Palace within the hour."

All nine girls piled into the Suburban, Julia claiming shotgun, while the guys followed in the tricked out Tahoe with Dusty in the driver's seat.

"So, Coco," Veronique began.

"It's KiKi."

"Whatever," she continued with a dismissive wave. "How's the money at the Palace?"

"Some nights are better than others, but four shifts a week can easily bring in two grand."

Veronique's eyebrow raised. "With or without sexual favors?" she asked.

Ebonie responded to this. "That's another fifteen hundred, if you work it just right."

"Okaayyy," KiKi said, giving a fist bump.

"It just depends," Lola added. "If there's a convention in town, or someone from the music industry drops in, an athlete..."

"Girl, remember that time I pulled five Gs in a week?" Ebonie bragged.

KiKi shook her head. "I *still* don't want to know what you had to do for that."

"Nothin' the rest of you bitches ain't done. I just do it better."

This sparked an argument.

"Damn," Ginger said, ignoring the quarreling strippers. "I'm in the wrong profession."

"What do you do, sweetie?" Veronique asked.

"Before last night I was a hair burner."

"Ooooh, girl, can you hook a sister up? I can feel my roots growing as we speak."

"Sorry, darling," Andrea cut in, "she's my new assistant."

"Hmph, touch you, girl," Veronique said, checking her nails.

"Which reminds me, Ginger, did you set up the video conference with Camilla about decorating South Isle for the holidays."

"Yes," she replied, reaching into her Coach shoulder bag for her leather-bound day planner. "And we're already getting footage of last night from the Cupids."

Andrea smiled. "Most excellent."

"Do you go all out with the décor?" Veronique asked.

"Go big or go home," Andrea laughed. Then as an afterthought she said. "Alex loves Christmas. I just hope we survive it."

Δ

"So, Vlad," Jimmy Ray called from the back of the Suburban. "What's it like to fuck a trannie?"

"Ignore him," Reece said. "He's got no home training."

"No, it is okay, I don't mind. He's only curious?"

"The fuck I am!" Jimmy Ray was obviously already pretty buzzed.

"Then why'd you ask?" Reece countered.

"I just wondered what his deal was, that's all."

"Sounds like curiosity to me," Ram laughed.

They all laughed, but it did not bother Jimmy Ray. He enjoyed a good ribbing almost as much as he liked giving one.

"Okay, I'm curious, so shoot me"

Vlad smiled and nudged Reece. "It's the same as a real woman, but better. The doctor built her extra snug, you know?"

This was of definite interest to Jimmy Ray. "Shit, can they do that?"

"Of course, yes. They can turn a man into a woman, so why not—whatever the patient wants. They are geniuses.

And I must tell you, because she was born male, she is extra aggressive in bed."

Jimmy Ray wanted to ask so many things. "So, did you guys ever do it before she got snipped or what?"

"Jeez, Jimmy Ray," Ram said, "you just met the guy."

"Or what...?" Vlad laughed. *This one truly was curious.*

"You don't have to answer that," Reece said.

"I don't mind," he said. "This is legitimate question. You're out and about; tossing back a few...We all know that she's fine, then bam who's on first? Right, Jimmy Ray?"

They all laughed.

"The answer is no. I did not know Veronique before her surgeries. I was not that fortunate."

"Fortunate..." Jimmy Ray said.

"Yes, I am the man for her in public, but she is the man for me in private. You want to know my deal, as you say; I am a submissive. We use a variety of wearable tools, of course. But there's nothing like the real thing, yes."

"Oh snap," Reece said, unable to contain his laughter.

Ram laughed as did Dusty and Alex.

Jimmy Ray sat back. "Damn, Vlad. You're a wild motherfucker." He had not expected the Russian to be so forth coming but was glad he was.

Vlad felt humiliated. It was delicious.

Now Ram had questions. "Do your folks know?"

"There must be a reason for me to lose my inheritance. So, yes, I think they know. But you would have to ask them yourself, since they refuse to speak to me."

Now Reece was curious. "You turned your back on your family for her?"

"It is they who turned on me. In my country, my father is a very important and powerful man. The family would not stand for such a scandal."

Jimmy Ray was astounded. "You walked away from the money?"

"You Americans are such capitalists. It's not always about the money. Veronique is willing to do whatever it takes to please me and I am *more* than willing to do the same in return. This, my friend, is true love."

Alex hit the bullet then placed it under Dusty's nose.

"Pretty freaky shit, huh?" he whispered.

"Whatever floats your boat, I guess," Dusty answered, after snorting the cocaine.

Δ

There was a Gulf Stream fueled and ready when they careened into the small airport. The Suburban and Tahoe pulled into parking spaces and everyone except for Black piled out.

"When do you want me here to pick you up?" he asked.

"Pick us up? You're coming with us silly," Andrea replied.

"Oh, I thought..."

"We're not paying you to think," Alex said, walking around to the driver's side of the Suburban.

The bodyguard glared at Alex, but Andrea silenced him with a look before he spoke.

She turned to Alex. "Sweetheart, please assist our guests in boarding."

"As you wish, Madame," Alex said with a bow.

He winked at Black and turned toward the aircraft.

"Follow me everyone!"

Black got out of the vehicle. "You think I'm going to put up with that, shit?"

Andrea, at five-foot-ten, stood eye level with him, thanks to six-inch platform pumps.

"Yes, quite frankly," she said. "And I expect you to do it with respect."

She was not afraid of him. Andrea Sorcosi was not afraid of anyone.

He stepped toward her. "You're kiddin' me, right?"

She didn't budge an inch.

"Hey, is everything okay?" Julia asked. She hung back while the others headed for the plane.

"I was just explaining to Black the relationship between employer and employee."

"I don't take shit from nobody, especially some rich ass punk."

Julia gasped, but Andrea stood strong. "It's like that, is it?"

"Yeah, it's like that."

"Fine, you're fired."

"What?"

"Julia, did I stutter?"

Black's nostrils flared. "Look here girl; you don't know who you're fuckin' with."

"Neither do you," Andrea said slowly.

Julia felt an approaching panic attack. "Come on you guys, this is supposed to be fun."

"Hey, what's the hold up?" Jimmy Ray yelled from the top of the boarding stairs.

Black rethought things, took a step back.

"Listen, I..."

"No, you listen," Andrea interrupted. "You don't know dick about me and the only thing you need to know about Alex is that his money can change the lives of your children."

"I take care of my kids," he fumed.

"Really...? Let's see...you're not married to their mother, you don't live with them and before you met me, you spent most of your nights in a strip joint." She laughed, "Yeah, you're doing a bang up job. Now suck it up. We have a party to get to."

Black followed. *She had balls; that was for sure.*

CHAPTER 58

THE PINK PALACE — ATLANTA

It seemed as if the jet had just reached the proper altitude when they started their decent into Peachtree Dekalb Airport. There was a ginormous stretch Hummer waiting on the tarmac when they landed, and in less than a half an hour, they were entering the Pink Palace through an array of blinding camera flashes.

As their group walked past the velvet ropes, Andrea purposely lagged behind. She grabbed Dusty's hand and signaled for Veronique and Julia to position themselves on either side. Turning her body toward Dusty, she placed a hand on his rock hard chest and struck a seductive pose, which had the photographers clamoring for the best shot of the foursome.

"What the hell?" Julia half giggled. "This is crazy."

Dusty, caught off guard, looked from Andrea to the cameras and back again. It lasted less than a minute before Black led them past the doormen and into the club. Alex handed over his Platinum American Express card to the floor hostess, who in turn made sure everyone in his party got a purple wristband.

"What the hell was that?" Dusty asked.

"Fame," Veronique offered.

"Is it always like that?" he wanted to know.

"New York is worse, L.A., insane."

"I wanna go back out there," Julia said.

Andrea laughed at this. "Don't worry. They'll be waiting for us when we leave."

"They're just gonna stand out there the rest of the night?"

"You're in the presence of royalty, my dear," Veronique responded. "And scandal."

Alex joined them.

"Speak of the devil."

"There you are." Alex placed his arm around Andrea's waist, pulling her to him. "What kept you?"

"Posing for the paparazzi, baby," Veronique said.

"So, how was your first time, Dusty?"

"The guys from *TMZ* are here," Andrea said.

Black was standing nearby, taking in the whole scene. They caused quite a commotion entering the Palace, which seemed unusually crowded.

Alex sneered at him. "What are you looking at? Take everyone up to VIP; I'm sure you know where it is."

Andrea glanced his way and he silently rounded up the others. Alex smiled at her.

"I see your little talk worked," he said.

Andrea cocked her head. "You saw that?"

"I see everything when it comes to you, my love. Make sure he stays in line. Dusty, you're not driving tonight. Let's have a drink."

Andrea watched the two walk toward the main bar instead of the reserved VIP area, causing heads to turn. There were more girls in the crowd tonight than one would normally find in a gentleman's club and her always on point gay-dar suggested a quarter of the men were not there for the talent. Word had definitely gotten out that the very handsome, very rich and very bad Alex Vandiveer was in town to party.

"Christ, he can be such an asshole at times," Andrea said, a smile on her face. She, too, loved his badness.

"You want me to cut that bitch?" Veronique asked.

Andrea laughed. "I'll keep you posted."

Julia laughed, too. The girls mounted the stairs leading to the balconies reserved for special guests of the Palace, aware that they too were commanding a lot of attention. It was all new to Julia, but Andrea and Veronique relished the envious stares. Not only was Andrea a stunningly beautiful model, linked to one of the country's wealthiest young bachelors, but she was also notoriously known for getting away with murder—or so said the tabloids.

The Pink Palace was a converted movie theater from the twenties, complete with a sweeping circular balcony. The seats, long since removed, had been replaced with leather banquets, cozy couches and cocktail tables. Freestanding arches, with elaborate velvet draperies separated, or joined, a dozen VIP sections, four of which had been reserved for Alex and his group.

They were located dead center, giving them a perfect view of the main stage and everything else going on below. Two would have been more than sufficient for a group of sixteen, but in order to seclude themselves from the other partiers, the sections on either side were to remain empty.

A dimly lit hallway ran the length of the balcony along the back wall and each private section had its own entrance.

DaShawn, approaching from the opposite end of the hall, followed them in. It was, after all, his club so he could do as he pleased.

"Well, well, well, Ms. Sorcosi," he said, an ear-to-ear grin splitting his face. "You have returned."

"As promised," Andrea smiled. They exchanged an air kiss. "The Pink Palace will be known nationally by nightfall tomorrow. This is Julia and Veronique."

He nodded and tipped his hat. "DaShawn Crawford; at your service," he said.

"Julia's the designer I was telling you about."

"I'm looking forward to your fashion show."

"We all are," Veronique added.

"Is everything set with Nasty Mama?" DaShawn asked.

"Of course, darling," Andrea replied.

A series of squeals turned their attention toward Jimmy Ray dancing on a table, surrounded by the Palace girls.

"I see you brought my girls back."

"Technically, they're still mine." Andrea said. "The weekend isn't over."

"Where's that billionaire boyfriend of yours?"

"He's not a billionaire yet." She smiled. "Though it is inevitable..." *If he lives long enough,* she thought. "He's at the main bar."

Jimmy Ray was inciting more squealing. Julia rolled her eyes. "He'll be naked before midnight."

Δ

A small crowd was forming around Alex at the bar; cell phones hovered in raised hands, videos streaming. He and Dusty were downing shots and nursing tall scotch and waters, the water, being Dusty's idea. The cocaine was fulfilling its purpose: Dusty felt as if he were on top of the world. Someone bumped him and groped his ass. He turned to see a guy and a girl smiling sweetly and realized it could have been either one.

Dusty nodded. "Hey."

"Hey, yourself," the obviously gay guy replied.

"Aren't you Alex Vandiveer?" the girl asked.

Alex flashed a wicked smile. "In the flesh..."

"OMG, I told you," said gay boy. "Is Andrea with you?"

"As a matter of fact, she is."

"You know Andrea?" Dusty inquired.

"Of course he doesn't," Alex laughed, "but he would like to, right...?"

"I'm Clint. And this is my friend Daisy."

"Pleased to meet you," she beamed.

"And I you," Alex said. "This is Dusty." There were smiles and nods. "Clint, would you and Daisy like to join our party?"

Clint responded with an enthusiastic "Hell to the yes," finger snaps included, while Daisy seemed to be doing her best bobble-head impression.

Alex turned to the growing crowd of onlookers and started pointing, choosing others to crash the party. He chose thirteen in all, four guys, four girls and five gay boys, leading them like the pied piper to the balcony.

DaShawn was watching. He looked at Andrea.

"Your party is doubling in size," he stated, his mental cash register going haywire.

"Indeed," Andrea remarked. "We're going to need at least a case of champagne, two or three handles of your best vodka, your oldest scotch and Jack Daniels for Jimmy Ray."

DaShawn simply smiled, snapped his fingers and made his exit, waitresses in tow. The bitch held true. She was on her way to a five-thousand-dollar tab and the night had just started. By the time the case of Cordon Negro was gone, the party was in full swing. KiKi and the girls made sure that no other dancers were allowed in. This way if any money was to be made on private dances, it would be made by them.

One of the cocktail servers also made sure the guests brought up earlier from the main floor were tagged with purple wristbands to ensure no unauthorized party crashers. They worked their scantily clad asses off, knowing full well the gratuity would more than justify their efforts.

As Julia predicted, Jimmy Ray was indeed naked before midnight, offering a table dance to any female who requested one. Ram, not to be outdone, joined in. The Palace girls were thrilled to see males stripping for a change and offered up the dollars as well.

Everything was going great until one of the drunk gay boys groped Dusty one too many times. Although he did not appreciate the unwanted attention, it was Alex who threw the first punch, clocking the guy square in the jaw and knocking him back into a cocktail table. The mess created was the least of worries. Two other gays and someone who turned out to be a power dyke lunged at Alex, causing a full-scale brawl to break out. Veronique and Ginger screamed and quickly scrambled for safety with the Palace girls, while Jimmy Ray and Ram, both still naked, dove from their respective tables right into the thick of things. Black instantly sprang into action, pulling Alex away from the chaos, but it was Andrea, who put an end to the unruliness with a single shot fired into the air from her platinum dipped, nine millimeter handgun.

Just as the falling plaster settled, DaShawn and three security guards, hands on holstered pistols, pushed their way past fleeing guests to see just what the hell was going on. They arrived to see three of the Palace girls emerging from under a table and Vlad, Ram and Jimmy Ray crouching behind a banquet, while Reece and Black detained two of the instigators in chokeholds. Julia was attempting to ice the small cut over Alex's left eye, but it was Andrea, cool as a cucumber, standing calmly by a visibly shaken Dusty, who caught DaShawn's eye.

She calmly sipped from her glass of champagne. By her calculations, he must have been nearby when he heard the gun go off, but did he know who fired.

"What the fuck is going on in here?" he demanded. "I open my place to you and this is the way you thank me. The cops are on the way. So somebody better start talking."

He directed his tirade straight at Andrea, who silently finished her Cordon Negro.

Reece spoke up. "This guy started the whole thing."

"Fuck you, man."

He tightened his grip. DaShawn turned to Black.

"It's true, Shawn." Black said. "He was pawing at the blonde kid—this one, too."

He looked at Jimmy Ray, who was now standing, his hands cupped over his genitals. "Is it any fuckin' wonder?"

"Not the naked one," Black said. "Him." He tilted his head toward Dusty, keeping a firm grip on the asswipe.

"Get 'em outta here," DaShawn bellowed to security. He then turned his focus to Andrea. "Who brought the gun in? Cops are a little touchy about concealed weapons in a public place. So, there will be questions."

"Then I suggest you escort us out quickly before they get here. I'm underage."

"What?"

"Are there any cameras in here, if so....?"

"Not in VIP," he snapped. This bitch had some fuckin' nerve. This could jeopardize his liquor license. He didn't like it, but what else could he do?

Andrea looked at Alex who at last stepped in. "Listen DaShawn, you've got my card; we ran up a good tab. I'll pick up the damages and throw in say... twenty-five grand for you. How's that...?"

"There's a side exit."

Everyone in the initial group, with the exception of the Palace girls, quickly followed, allowing Jimmy Ray and Ram only enough time to struggle into their borrowed designer pants.

Once they were all safely inside the stretch Hummer, Jimmy Ray and Ram finished dressing. "Damn, what a night!" Jimmy Ray whooped.

"You best thank your lucky stars you got your naked asses out of there alive, honey," Veronique laughed. So did Ram and Vlad.

Ginger flashed a warning look at her man. "I don't know what you're laughing at."

"Ease up, babe, it was all in fun."

"Fun...? Did you miss the gunfire? We could've been killed."

"Relax," Alex said. "Andrea is an excellent marksman."

Ginger gasped. "That was you?"

"Girrrl, no...!" Veronique cried. "Are you trying to kill somebody else?"

"Quite the opposite," Andrea stated in a flat tone.

"Those fuckers had it coming," Vlad said. "Dusty is an innocent and they were taking advantage of...."

"An innocent...?" He was fed up. "What the fuck is that?

"Dusty," Veronique tried, "I'm sure Vlad didn't mean..."

"Yeah, I think he did mean it. So I'm not from New York and I don't have a bunch of weirdo gay friends. I'm not some fucking kid that has to be protected either. I could have handled those guys myself and I didn't need any help."

"Okay, okay," Alex said. "Calm down. Here, do another bump."

"Do you think he really needs that?" Andrea asked.

Dusty grabbed the bullet. "It's exactly what I need. My life! My choice...!"

"He's right," Ram added. "Dusty is just as much of an adult as the rest of us."

"You said it, brother," Jimmy Ray slurred.

Reece, ever the voice of reason intervened. "Whoa, whoa, whoa...! Everyone just chill the fuck out. All and all it's been a great night, even if it did end with a bang, literally. We're all friends here."

"And none of us went to jail," Julia added. "Now, let's all take a collective, deep breath."

"Amen, sista," Veronique said. "The night's still young and so am I. What say we head over to Back Street?"

Vlad shook his head. "No. The thought of Charlie Brown's Cabaret has me bored already. I say we go to Club Anytime *or*," he paused, "... dare I suggest The Clairmont Lounge."

"You *would* wanna go there," Veronique said, popping her neck.

"What's at the Clairmont Lounge?" Dusty asked, intrigued by Veronique's tone.

"Pimps and Hoes," she answered with a dramatic sigh.

"Then the Clairmont it is, baby...." Dusty said with a hoot.

"That's the spirit," Alex laughed.

"Yeah, bitch!" Jimmy Ray yelped.

CHAPTER 59

UPPER EAST SIDE — NEW YORK

The uptown brownstone, elegantly furnished with a beautiful crystal chandelier in the entry hall and an extensive early American art collection, was everything Martin had promised. Over the years, Martin had been lucky enough to meet a vast array of people from all walks of life— although he would gladly argue that luck had nothing to do with it, claiming it was his charisma that allowed him easy access into the lives of New York's elite.

He was blindly unaware that he was the topic of frivolous conversations among the socialites he thought he was bedding. In reality, they were simply passing him around.

The party, if you could call it that, was very low key, more like an opportunity to network. It seemed that every conversation had to do with pending law cases, corrupt politicians or Wall Street, all of which bored Melinda to illness.

The wives, mistresses and what she was sure were paid companions simply nodded and smiled during the designated cocktail hour (which lasted for three hours), complete with passed sushi, sashimi and assorted meat canopies. When she was absolutely certain, she would scream it was over.

"My God, that was boring," she complained as Martin hailed a cab.

"Those people are very important," he said, holding the door. Once inside he asked, "Should we go somewhere for a nightcap?"

"I would rather head back to my place. Audrey will be out most of the night, so we can be alone."

"Whatever you'd like," he said but *it's about fucking time* is what he thought. He slipped his arm around her shoulders and wondered how much longer he would go out with her before he dumped her. Melinda's mind was on a similar track. She was tired of being the good girl and simply wanted to satisfy her curiosity. She had only been with Dusty and as much as she hated to admit it, as ridiculous as it sounded even to her, his dick was just too big.

Word had it that Martin was a skilled lover, but half way in, she prayed for it to end. Although his erect penis was the perfect size, he was rough and lacked the tenderness she had grown to expect. This might be what the jaded middle-aged women of New York wanted but it sure as hell was not going to work for Melinda.

She showered as soon as he left and thought of Dusty. How could she have done this to him, or to herself? Melinda scrubbed every bit of Martin away, both physically and mentally, deciding never to see him again. She did not cry, however, but stood bravely under the shower spray, the hot water cleansing her body and mind. Melinda Sue Johnston was finally growing up.

CHAPTER 60

CLAIRMONT LOUNGE — ATLANTA

The Clairmont Lounge was literally the basement of the old Clairmont Hotel, which now served as a halfway house, slash shelter, slash soup kitchen, located on Ponce de Leon, just northeast of downtown Atlanta. Gone was the grandeur of its heyday. Its elegant clientele had been replaced by a combination of the homeless, crackheads and crackwhores. Because of the low ceilings and virtually no central airflow, many of the partiers were outside taking advantage of the cool November night.

The stretch Hummer captured everyone's attention as the driver maneuvered it carefully through the packed parking lot. Romeo recognized Andrea the instant she stepped out of the sleek, shiny vehicle.

"Andy, baby," he said, making his way toward them.

"Darling, what a surprise?" They kissed cheeks. "Are you spinning tonight?"

"Normally, Sunday's only, but I might make a guest appearance just for you"

"Romeo, Romeo, where the fuck art thou, Romeo?"

"Van Dee, what is up?" He grabbed Alex's hand and the two shoulder-bumped. "Jesus, what a motley crew.

Come, let's go forth. But I must warn you, there is no VIP at the Lounge."

The place was jammed packed and hip-hop blared from the deejay booth. Romeo led the way, pushing past the uptowners and downtowners alike. All eyes were on them as they crowded into a small area opposite the bar where a one-legged stripper balanced herself atop the beer slicked surface by holding onto the ceiling.

"Lulu," Romeo yelled over the thumping bass. "These are friends of mine, so be on your best behavior."

Lulu pushed her tits up and flashed her biggest, somewhat toothless smile. Jimmy Ray leaned close to Reece and Vlad. "Fuck, Toto, we are not in Kansas anymore."

"What could I get you, bitches?" Lulu asked in a low graveling voice.

"Something self-contained," Reece said. There was no way in hell this place passed health inspection.

Veronique saddled up next to Andrea. "Darling, isn't there a stocked bar in the limo?"

"My thoughts exactly," Andrea said. "Romeo, could you help us back outside? Black, keep an eye on the boys, would you?" She signaled for Julia and Ginger to follow them back outside.

"What the fuck is this place?" Julia asked once they were back outside in the fresh air.

"It's not that bad, once you get used to it," Romeo said. "But next time ladies, dress down. You never know who's in need of a rock."

"Don't worry, honey," Ginger quipped. "Andrea's packing heat."

The girls all laughed.

"Where's the Hummer?" Veronique asked.

"Probably around front," Romeo replied. "Only place for a beast that size."

They walked around the corner of the building to find not only the waiting Hummer, but a few clever photographers as well, who quickly charged, cameras raised and flashing.

"What the hell?" Romeo blurted.

"Christ, they found us," Andrea said. "Best faces ladies."

As they snapped pictures, the photographers hurled questions about the gunshot and speedy back-alley exit. Thank God, Romeo was there to ward them off while the girls climbed into the stretch.

"What was that all about?" he asked.

"There was an *incident* at the Palace," Andrea answered.

"An incident...?"

"More like a riot," Julia replied.

Romeo was intrigued. "You carrying' a weapon sweetheart?"

"Could we please talk about something else?" Andrea asked, silencing Julia and Ginger.

"No matter," Veronique said. "It will all be in the morning edition. Cocaine, anyone...?

CHAPTER 61

THOMPSON STREET — NEW YORK

Melinda was awakened by the sound of Audrey quietly stumbling in. Funny thing about drunk people trying to be quiet—it never worked. Apparently, someone was with her judging from the not so hushed whispers and slamming of kitchen cabinet doors. Ice clinked into glasses and music erupted.

When she heard a crash followed by a thud, Melinda decided to investigate. She was wearing flannel pajamas so there was no need to cover up. Still, she cracked her bedroom door and peeked to see who was about. It was Hilary. Audrey was getting up from the floor and placing a chair upright.

"Hey Hil," Melinda said.

"Oh, hey," Hilary managed between hiccups.

"Did we wake you?" Audrey asked like a busted teenager. "I tol' Hilary to keep it down."

"Bitch, *you* the one, fell on the floor."

"No, I wasn't sleeping," Melinda lied.

"Want a drink?" Audrey asked, expecting her prudish roomy to decline.

"Sure, why not," Melinda answered, helping herself to a glass of Chardonnay.

Hilary glanced at Audrey through half opened eyes. Something was up.

"Did'n you go out with Marteeen tonight?" she asked innocently.

"Tha's right, tha's right," Audrey slurred. "How'd it, was it...I mean, did jou have fun?"

"It was dreadful," Melinda replied, sipping from her wine glass.

"What was dreadful?" Hilary demanded.

"Hilary," Audrey said. "Don' be so nosey. Did jou finally give him some?"

"Yes, if you must know."

"Oh, my God. Tell us everything. He's good, huh?"

"Hardly," Melinda scoffed.

"What? I thought he was great in bed," Hilary said.

"Hilary, shhhh. Shut up, shhhh." Audrey scooted her chair closer to Melinda. "Details, details."

"Well, the party was boring," she started.

"Who cares 'bout the party? It's Martin, di he curl your toes?"

"He curled mine," Hilary giggled between hiccups.

"God no," Melinda huffed. "And quite frankly I don't know what all the fuss is about."

"Are you kiddin'?"

"Maybe he had an off night," said Hilary

"Or maybe you girls don't mind being treated like a two-dollar whore."

Audrey and Hilary burst into laughter.

"She, *hic,...* serious?" Hilary wanted to know.

"What? Ms. Priss, here? Yeah, she serious."

"I am not a priss," Melinda complained.

Audrey rolled her eyes. "Yeah, hon, you kinda are."

Yeah, well you're a bitch.

"Hilary, do you think I'm a Priss."

"More like persnic*tiny,*" Hilary replied.

"You mean persnickety," Audrey corrected. They both howled with laughter.

Yeah, and you're a bitch, too.

"Who cares any way," Melinda said. "I have a gorgeous boyfriend who loves me." She pushed back from the table and grabbed her glass of wine. "I'm going to bed."

"Wait, wait, wait...," Audrey said, trying to compose herself. "We want to hear about Marteeen."

She was the only one in their circle who hadn't slept with him. After all, never sleep with bartenders who are wannabe actors *was* her rule.

"Fuck her," Hilary hissed. "But I'm glad she brought up her boyfriend. Check out the link Jarrod sent me today."

"Broadway Jarrod, no thank you. I'd rather not see any grossed out fag shit," Audrey said.

Hilary moved to the desktop located in the corner of the living area of the tiny apartment. "Don' worry, you're gonna love this."

Melinda retrieved her cell phone from her handbag after locking her bedroom door behind her. She dialed Dusty's number even though it was nearly two in the morning. It was cold in her bedroom. It was always cold. Melinda looked around the tiny room, longing for the spaciousness of home. She hated New York. The connection went through, but the voice on the other end was the last she expected.

"Alex?"

"Yeah, long time no chit chat."

She was silent, stunned. As if reading her mind, he said, "If you're calling for Dusty, I think he's getting a lap dance." She hung up the phone, dazed. This couldn't be. Where was Dusty and why was he with Alex? She gulped her wine and returned to the kitchen for more. Hilary and Audrey were glued so intently to the computer screen that neither noticed her.

"Fuck, he is hot," Audrey was saying The two nearly jumped out of their skins when Melinda screamed, "What the hell is that?"

"Jesus H. Christ, you scare the crap..."

Melinda couldn't hear their babbling. She shoved Audrey aside to see if she was really seeing what she thought she was seeing. OMG!!! It was a YouTube video of Dusty on stage at what appeared to be a strip club, tied to a chair, blind folded and wearing only his boxer briefs.

"Tell me this is some kind of a joke." Melinda heard herself say.

"No sweetie, it's no joke," Audrey said.

"How did you find this?"

"Jarrod sent me a link," Hilary replied.

"Oh, God," Melinda whispered, the air sucked out of her. She watched in horror as he and four other blind folded guys were given the royal treatment by gyrating, half-naked girls. Dusty, front and center was obviously the love interest for someone she'd never heard of.

"Who the hell is Veronique?" she demanded.

She did not like the answer.

CHAPTER 62

CLAIRMONT LOUNGE — ATLANTA

Alex hadn't lied entirely. The Palace girls, having received a text from him about their whereabouts, were taking turns sandwiching Dusty on the crowded dance floor. He never got word of the phone call, but then again, Alex didn't tell anybody much of anything for the rest of the night. By the time Andrea and the cocaine clutch made it back from the Hummer, he was being propped up between Reece and Vlad. His half opened eyes were rolled back, showing only the whites and his head bobbed back and forth as if his neck were rubber.

Andrea immediately called the driver with instructions to get as close to the entrance as possible; but they basically had to carry Alex out, shielding him from the cameras.

"Christ," Andrea said, once inside the Hummer.

"What's he on?" Dusty asked, still out of breath from the dance-athon with the Palace Girls.

"Anyone's guess," Andrea sighed. "I need a fucking cigarette."

Veronique, noting Andrea's stress, took over as mother hen. She gentle patted his face. "Alex? Come on honey. Talk to me, baby. Alex...?" The others look on as panic began to creep.

"Had you going, didn't I?" he slurred.

"Son of a bitch!" Jimmy Ray exploded. "He's fuckin' with us." He had genuinely been scared.

His eyes had not opened, however. "Quiet, I'm sleeping," he mumbled, before fading to black.

"He's fine," Veronique cooed. "Just taking a little nap, aren't you, baby?" She looked at Andrea who sat staring out the window. "Anybody know what he was doing tonight?"

"Nothing," Ram said, looking at Andrea. "He'd already had a lot of coke, so I was watching him, like you ask us to. And he ordered water." Then, as an after-thought, he added. "Oh and he did pour a little vodka in it."

"Vodka? What vodka?"

"He had it in a tiny flask. It was such a small amount; I didn't think...."

"He doesn't drink vodka," Andrea said.

"I saw him getting something from Ebonie at the Palace," Julia said.

"What was it?"

"She said it was aspirin, that he had a headache."

"No tellin' with that bitch," Black stated.

He had barely spoken to anyone the entire night, and then it was only after he was spoken to. They all looked at him. As a rule, he stayed out of other people's business, but the look on Andrea's face told him this was serious.

"Ebonie's a downer chic," Black said. "She likes to numb herself for the tricks. If he got something from her, it was probably oxies."

"Fuck," Andrea said. The night had just gotten longer. "We're almost at the Four Season's and those assholes are following us. His father is going to flip shit if the media gets wind of this. We need to get Alex inside as quickly as possible."

Vlad offered a solution: "Why don't we just take cameras?"

"Because, darling," Veronique said, "That leads to charges and jail time."

"My father can take care of any legal ramifications," Reece offered, the alcohol doing the talking. "He is the fucking mayor."

"I couldn't ask you to do that," Andrea said.

"Yes, you could," Jimmy Ray replied. "Reece never gets in trouble. His daddy owes him a freebie."

"Shut up, Jimmy Ray," Julia said.

"He's right," Reece agreed.

"I'm in," championed Ram.

"Lord, they think it's the Wild, Wild West." Veronique said, half under her breath.

"Me too," said Black. He wasn't crazy about Alex, but a good fight would make his night. "You're sure about your daddy helpin' us out, right?"

"Absolutely," Reece said, hoping he was.

Black nodded and cracked his knuckles. "It's been a while since I've had any fun. What's the game plan?"

Vlad grinned. "To smash heads and cameras."

Julia and Ginger sat in stunned silence.

Dusty tried to be the voice of reason. "This is crazy. There has to be another way."

"He's your friend, correct?" Vlad asked.

"Yes, but..."

"Then this is the way,"

They were right. Dusty sighed, "Shit, count me in."

"No," Andrea said. She needed him with her. "Someone has to help us get him inside."

The Hummer slowed to a stop at the hotel's entrance.

"Okay, boys," Veronique said, living for the drama, "it's show time."

And what a show it was. The instant the Hummer came to a halt, Black, Jimmy Ray, Reece, Vlad and Ram leapt from the vehicle and terrorized the photographers, actually slamming six cameras to the impeccably paved, brick-inlaid, half-moon driveway.

And even the ones who got away were unable to snap any shots of Dusty carrying Alex's dead weight. Julia and Andrea, each with a leg, teetered on their platform heels through the exquisitely elegant lobby toward the express elevator to the penthouse. Their presence did not go unnoticed by the front desk clerk.

"Is he okay?" the clerk shouted.

"He's fine, honey," Veronique responded holding the elevator door.

Julia dropped Alex's leg once the ride upward began.

"What are you doing to me?" he groaned in a twisted voice.

Veronique whipped her hair back. "What are we doing to you, honey? The question is what are you doing to us?"

"Do you think we should call a doctor?" Ginger asked.

"Not yet," Julia said. "I've seen my mother like this too many times to remember and, sadly, she didn't die once." She grabbed his foot again.

Veronique giggled quietly, while Ginger looked on. Andrea remained silent and Dusty watched her. She was still so young, they all were. It was too soon in their lives for something like this, especially for Andrea. He wanted to reach out to her.

Alex groaned and mumbled again. By the time they reached their floor and Alex was safe in bed, it was nearly three in the morning. Andrea closed the door to the penthouse suite and turned slowly, rubbing her neck.

"You must be exhausted," Dusty said.

She looked at him, thinking of how good he was. "I am."

"Sit down, let me massage your neck." Anything to touch her.

"That sounds nice," she whispered. "And my feet... I've got to get out of these shoes. She placed a hand on his chest, the way she had when they entered the Pink Palace. When she stepped out of the first shoe, she dropped five inches quickly and fell against him. It had been a long night. He looked at her and she looked at him for what seemed an eternity.

As she fooled with the ankle strap of the second shoe, her knee did a little bump and grind against his groin, all the while their eyes remained locked. When the shoe hit the floor, he pulled her tightly into his arms and mashed his mouth against hers for the longest, most agonizing kiss of his life. Then it began. She could hear Alex heaving. She rushed for the bathroom waste container, a ritual she had grown accustomed to.

"Could you get some cold towels please?" she asked Dusty. "And help me undress him."

Dusty did what she asked then watched silently as Andrea lovingly dabbed Alex's face and upper body with the cool towels. After about twenty minutes, he stirred.

"Where is everyone?" Alex asked.

"We're back at the hotel, sweetheart. They're all in their rooms."

"Okay, okay," he said, lying back only to shoot up again. "Where's Dusty?" He seemed frightened.

"I'm right here, Alex."

"Don't leave me," he said before passing out again.

Andrea rubbed his back tenderly. "He doesn't really sleep anymore," she said softly. "He just medicates."

"What happened to him?" Dusty asked.

She had never said the words out loud, but finally someone else would know the truth.

"Alex killed Jean Paul," she said in barely a whisper.

"What?"

She stood and led Dusty back into the living area of the suite.

"It was an accident, but his father must never find out. Baron is trying to control Alex, to force him to live in New York. So I took the blame."

Dusty's mouth dropped open. "For killing someone...?"

"None of that matters," she said. "It was an accident. Jean Paul was such an asshole. I'm not saying he deserved to die but..."

"And now he can't forgive himself," Dusty said.

Things were falling into place. He knew his friend.

"Something like that, but it's much more complicated. He's angry at his mother for leaving him and he hates his father for never being there. He feels all alone."

"He's got you." Dusty said. His words hung heavy in the air.

"And you," she whispered. "He would rather die than live with his father. Baron wants to create some kind of clone of himself and Alex is no *Mini Me*."

That was for sure, thought Dusty. "You can't force Alex to do anything," he said. He ran his hands through his hair. "God, what a night."

"I'm so tired."

"I know," he said, wishing he could take her away from it all.

"You're going to have to sleep with us, you know," she said. "He's already asked for you once. It's going to be like that for the rest of the night."

Is that how it keeps happening, he wondered, *the waking up in bed with them...*the not wanting to be alone? He thought about Melinda, but just for a fleeting moment. It was already too late. Plus, there was something between him and Andrea; there was no question.

He had always hoped his friend would come home but he must have known things wouldn't be easy. Hadn't he expected chaos?

"I doubt we'll be going home tomorrow," she said. He'll be depressed and won't want to get up."

"Wait, because he'll want to sleep in, we're stuck twiddling our thumbs?"

"Not exactly," she said, her tone soothing. "There's still a million things to do for Julia's show, and you... well, you'll have to babysit. Vlad and Veronique will be flying out late afternoon and the girls will all be taxied home."

Even now, after the night they had, she was so enchanting. They were standing very close to one another.

"That just leaves Ram and Ginger," he said.

"We can't live without our assistants, silly. You don't think *I'm* going to make all those travel arrangements, do you?"

"You are so spoiled."

"Yeah, well, I wasn't always, but that was then. We're rich now."

"You and Alex are rich," he whispered.

"*We* are rich."

There was a murmur from the bedroom. "Andrea...?"

She responded immediately, moving quickly to Alex's side. "I'm here darling."

The rest of the night and most of the morning was cold towels and extra blankets. He was hot, he was cold; he was sick and dehydrated.

CHAPTER 63

FOUR SEASONS HOTEL — ATLANTA

Dusty slept some but doubted Andrea had at all. He heard her on the phone at eight giving Ginger instructions on who was going where and what cars were to be waiting. *"Julia and I are going to do some shopping. You have to come with... Fab, smooches."*

Then she was back to bed for another attempt at rest, and around ten a.m. all fell quiet. The next time his eyes opened it was mid-afternoon and she was up and already dressed.

"You're amazing," he said in a hoarse whisper. "What time is it?"

"Two oh nine," she said, hooking an earring.

Well, he wasn't going to make his five o'clock shift.

"I need to call my job," he said.

"Ginger already did."

He grinned. "Funny," he said. He knew he wasn't still sleeping.

She grabbed a scarf and wrapped it loosely around her neck.

"No, really, she did," Andrea said.

"Ginger, called in for me?"

"Sweetie, you're never going to have to work again. Well, not the way you think. Alex already has credit cards and bank accounts set up for you. And I have an idea for the next A&A Jeans campaign that's hotter than anything Marc Jacobs has *ever* done."

She might as well have been speaking a foreign language. She gave him a quick kiss on the forehead. "Don't worry; everything's going to be alright. You'll see."

But was it? She had to wonder. They were caught up in the worst kind of triangle.

"Julia and I are going shopping," she said.

Her eyes darted toward Alex.

"Make sure he eats today. Just call room service. Oh, and Ginger packed things for you. They're tagged and in the closet."

Then she was gone. Just like that. He sat there for a moment, looking around the room. The bed was so comfortable; still he pulled himself from it. The night before had been a rough one and he felt the after effects.

He walked naked to the other side of the bed to check Alex. Out like a light, but breathing steadily. So he went to the fancy bathroom to get ready for whatever the day held. *What a crazy fucking weekend!* He thought of Julia. She had to know. *Did she know?* She could only suspect. *So, he was sharing a suite with them.* Yeah, that's not weird.

He wondered if he could actually have a three-way with Alex. Dusty had always thought of sex as something between two people, but if there was anyone he could do that with, it would be Alex. Growing up together, they had shared everything. But could they share Andrea?

After he dressed he ordered a couple of club sandwiches with potato salad. When he finished the call, it dawned on him that he did not know where his phone was. *Shit, Melinda must have called.* He quickly looked around the room. *No, why would it be here.* Then it hit him. He had given it to Alex at the Clairmont Lounge.

What a fuckin' trip that place was. He went into the bedroom searching for Alex's clothes and noticed him stirring.

"Are you awake?" Dusty asked in a hushed tone.

"The question is am I alive? And dreadfully, the answer is yes."

Dusty smiled. "What are we going to do with you man?"

"Right now you can help me to the bathroom."

"You're kidding, right?"

"No, I'm fucking hurtin'." He started to cough and dry heave, causing his body to convulse.

"Jesus, are you okay?"

"No!" Alex snapped. "I just said I was fuckin' hurtin'."

Dusty hurried to his side, alarmed.

Alex made a feeble attempt at laughter. "I overdid it a little—that's all."

Dusty helped his friend to his feet. "God, I thought Andrea was spoiled, but I've never had to help her out of bed."

"But you'd like to, wouldn't you?" Alex said.

"All those drugs are making you paranoid."

Δ

After lunch at Twist, the girls piled back into the waiting Town Car, courtesy of the Four Seasons, and with Black at the wheel, they headed to Kay's Fabrics on Cheshire Bridge Road.

"The hotel concierge said the building was nothing to look at but the fabrics are the best in the city," Ginger reported, falling quickly into her role as Andrea Sorcosi's assistant. It was like a game to Ginger. As soon as she mentioned Andrea's name, everything fell into place.

Julia was wearing a perma-grin when the car pulled into the parking lot. In fact, she had been wearing it all afternoon.

"I can't believe this is really happening to me," she said.

"Julia, aren't you the one who said good things happened around this one?" Ginger asked pointing at Andrea.

"I did say that, didn't I?"

Selecting the fabrics was both exciting and overwhelming. Julia wanted to create a no-nonsense collection that screamed both extravagance and classic simplicity, with an understated sexuality in sensuous textures and luxurious fabrics.

And Kay's was just the place. The building itself was a bit off-putting but inside they found everything from exquisite Italian silks to luxurious Egyptian cottons. After the address for delivery was given and a credit card swiped, it was back to Black and the waiting car.

"Ladies, our work is done," Andrea said once they were settled in the back of the Town Car. "It's almost seven. We can just make it to Lennox for a little power shopping. There's a Saks *and* a Bloomingdales."

"I love Bloomingdales," Ginger said.

"Perfect, because we're shopping for you."

By the time they made it back to the hotel, it was just past nine. Alex, Dusty and Ram were all watching football highlights when Andrea entered the suite. Alex was smoking, nervously.

"Christ Almighty," he blurted before she even had a chance to put down her shopping bags. "I didn't think you were ever coming back."

"Did somebody miss me?" Andrea replied innocently. She knew damned well what he meant. She had hidden the drugs.

"I missed you," Ram said, with his nerdy laugh, then regretted it. "Ahh... Where's Ginger?"

He amused Andrea, then again most men did. "She's probably on her way up as we speak. I asked her to stop at the desk for today's papers. Are you guys hungry?"

"I could eat," Dusty said.

"Me too," Ram agreed.

Alex groaned. "Okay, I guess I'm out numbered, but if we're going out babe, you gotta help me here."

Suddenly feeling anxious, Ram stood. "I'll go see if I can locate Ginger."

"We'll meet you guys downstairs for dinner in twenty minutes," Andrea said.

Ram nodded and left the hotel suite.

She turned to Alex. Smiling, she said, "If Dusty says you were a good boy while mommy was out, I suppose a treat is in order."

Dusty threw him a bone. "He was a very good boy."

"I even showered and brushed my teeth *and* my hair."

She was laughing now. He could always make her laugh. He was her savior, her knight, though the armor was cracked, and the halo tarnished. She went into the bathroom and opened her makeup case. There was a hidden compartment behind the mirror. She called him and he hurried in.

On her way out, she said, "The reservation is for ten o'clock. They're staying open late for us."

Twenty-five minutes later they stepped off the express elevator and strolled into the nearly deserted fine dining establishment. Their hostess, server and remaining kitchen staff had already received generous tips, so they were warmly welcomed.

Dinner was both delicious and uneventful, to everyone's relief. Alex was well-behaved and kept his drinking to a minimum. He even ordered *and* finished a filet of sole with vegetable medley. He did it for her. He would do anything for Andrea.

When dinner was over and the three of them were alone together, however, Alex threw down the gauntlet.

"So, what are we to do, the three of us?" he asked.

Andrea felt her heart skip. Alex busied himself pouring a drink.

"A nightcap, anyone?" he asked, pointing the bottle at each of them.

"It's late..." Andrea began.

"We're drinking!" he shouted. He gulped at his scotch and grimaced. "I mean, it is pretty obvious how you feel about each other. So why not talk about it? Hell, a blind man could see it," he laughed. "But I'm not willing to give her up." He poured another shot. "And she would *never* leave me. Right, my love?"

Her eyes welled up. "No," she said. It was barely a whispered.

"What exactly are you saying?" Dusty asked, not sure to which one.

"Andrea," Alex said as if reading his mind, "is saying *she will never leave me* and I'm saying *I* will never allow it." He paused. "But I am willing to share."

This was it; the moment of truth. Hadn't she expected this? They had shared a cornucopia of woman but on those rare occasions when they brought another man into their bed the guy was always a replica of Dusty. She decided to wait Alex out.

He continued. "Dusty you're my best friend and I love you. I want you to be happy. I love Andrea, too." He hesitated before voicing his fear. "But, perhaps, not the way she deserves to be. I'm too needy, too self-involved, if you will." He poured shots for each of them. "Maybe she needs someone a little more stable. Maybe we both do."

Dusty downed his scotch.

"So, I'm willing to compromise," Alex said. He raised a finger in the air and gulped the remaining liquor from his glass.

"Hold all thoughts," he said. "...'til I've had time to drain the lizard."

He headed for the bedroom knowing Andrea would take the ball and run with it. They had played this game before, but never with stakes this high. This time she loved the other guy. Alex had no idea how things would play out, but he intended to enjoy the ride—even if it took them all straight to hell.

"This is ridiculous," Dusty said.

She went to him and touched his hand. "Is it?"

"We're already sleeping in the same bed. What more does he want?"

She grabbed his arms. "Don't you love him?"

"Not like that." He couldn't look at her. *Why was she doing this?*

"He needs you..."

"Andrea, I'm in love with *you*." It was out. Had he spoken too soon?

"Then do this for me."

She knew she was asking a hell of a lot, but was it too much?

"I can't promise you anything."

"I'm not asking you to."

"Now, that's the spirit," Alex said bounding back into the room. He startled both of them. The pee break had been all about the powder. "Don't just stand there, man, kiss her."

Her big brown eyes were brimming with tears and once he looked, it was over and he *did* kiss her, like his life depended on it. And didn't it?

"Okay, okay, enough," Alex protested. "I've cut lines for us," he said, feeling every bit the son of darkness in this deal with the devil.

Dusty wasn't kidding himself; it was only a matter of time before someone got burned. The kiss alone was enough to set him on fire. They joined Alex, snorting four lines each.

"You can have the bed 'til two," Alex said lighting a cigarette, "then I'm coming in."

He grabbed his drink and headed for the other bedroom, glancing at his Louis Vuitton wristwatch. "You would have done it behind my back anyway."

The statement cut Dusty like a knife, just as Alex intended. He walked away feeling confident; *no one ever said no to Vandiveer money.* He closed the door behind him.

"Well...?" Andrea asked.

"This is madness. What about Melinda?" It was a knee jerk response.

"Melinda?"

He was terrified of what he was about to do. "She *is* my girlfriend."

"Alex just dropped this on us and you're worried about Melinda?" Andrea sighed and took a deep breath. She attempted a smile.

"Look," she said, struggling to remain calm. "We can't fight this. The question has never been if, but when." She looked at him, pleading with her eyes. "Nothing can stop whatever this is that's happening between us. You feel it, and I feel it."

He did feel it, right in his groin.

"So, we do this the hard way or the easy way." Who was she kidding, there was no easy way.

He had done just enough cocaine to rev him up, but not enough to stop the growing stiffness in his pants.

"Let's go to bed," he said, sweeping her up in his arms.

They took full advantage of the time allotted and she was everything he dreamed she would be. Alex was an aggressive lover in a domineering fetish kind of a way, while Dusty was aggressive in the *I'd better take good care of her in case this is my only shot* kind of a way. He touched her deeper than any man had before, but when she looked into his eyes, fear engulfed her. They said he would not live without her.

Dusty, never being able to go full throttle with Melinda, felt in so many ways like he was making love for the first time. He had never felt so high, so alive—until reality came knocking. Alex, right on time, entered, naked, carrying a room service tray.

"Look, everyone, I have mango juice and fruit tarts." Alex said, entering the bedroom.

There was also jam, chocolate croissants and whipped cream.

Dusty propped himself against the headboard, watching. His friend could still be that sweet, shy kid, but no one could feel sorry for Alex Vandiveer. No matter how he played it, he was always in control.

"You always loved my mom's fruit tarts," he said with a sniff and a weak smile.

"You remembered the croissants," Andrea said sweetly.

Alex looked lovingly at her. "They're your favorite."

Her heart ached. How could they ever betray him?

"We'll just put the tray right here on the bed," he said, placing the silver tray near the foot. "And I'm sitting next to Dusty, *my* friend."

The guilt Dusty felt was overwhelming. He tried to keep it light. "What about my favorite?" he teased.

Alex looked at him and frowned. "Wha...? You just fucked my girlfriend. What do you want from me? I give you my money; you live in my house; I buy your clothes *and* feed you. Let's not talk about how much you eat...." He was laughing. He had obviously been indulging in the blow.

Dusty sipped the mango juice, instantly tasting the raspberry rum. He and Alex had lived on it the summer he turned sixteen. They shared a lot of history. *Could this actually work?*

Dusty took a spoon full of whipped crème and smeared it on Alex's cheek, then licked it off seductively. His tongue grazed the corner of Alex's mouth, instantly defusing the tension, and Andrea laughed. Alex was magnetic. Still, if and when the time ever came, could Dusty go through with it, whatever *it* turned out to be?

"You guys wanna watch a movie or something?" Alex asked. "I've got a little more coke."

"Don't you always," Dusty said, slugging Alex's shoulder.

"Oh, you want a repeat of the shower, do you?" he asked, preparing for battle.

"Oh, God," Dusty laughed in protest. "Please no."

"What'd I miss?" Andrea wanted to know.

"Your new boyfriend here," Alex confessed, "hit on me in the shower a few days back. Dreadful, the whole thing, really. I just want to put it all behind me."

Andrea laughed.

"No, you lie," Dusty said, defending himself. "You were flirting with me."

"Alex flirts with everybody." Andrea giggled.

"Only the pretty people," he quipped. He kissed Dusty's check and smiled with his eyes closed.

"So, what are we watching?" Andrea asked.

Alex grabbed the remote. "Let me check pay-per-view."

"We should have popcorn," Andrea said. "I think I spied some in the kitchen."

"And weed," Dusty added.

Andrea jumped up and grabbed a robe. "Don't start without me."

"What about *The Mexican,* with Brad and Julia?" Alex called after her.

"I love that movie," she said tying the belt. "Brad is so funny."

"Yeah, sounds good," Dusty said.

"Are you sure?" Alex asked rapidly fluttering his eyelashes. "Because I only want you to be happy."

"Shut the fuck up," Dusty laughed, pushing him away.

Alex pounced, trying to tickle him, but as always, Dusty was the stronger and ended up pinning his friend, tickling him with no mercy. Alex had been pulling the same stunt for years—and it always worked.

"Stop, stop, stop!" Alex pleaded. "I'm gonna piss myself

Dusty had heard these same words dozens of times during their youth. Even in his sleep, after Alex disappeared, Dusty heard him begging for mercy. And he always waited for the final *stop, stop, please stop,* before he did.

But this time, as Dusty watched his closest friend squirming hopelessly beneath him, he realized Alex's actions were not that innocent. The unmistakable throbbing beneath him spelled it all out. Their laughter subsided as the moment grew serious.

Alex smiled. "I've always loved you."

Dusty rolled back to his side of the bed. "I know."

He stared at the ceiling.

"It just gets twisted sometimes," Alex whispered.

Andrea bounced back into the room. "Everything about you is twisted. Did you start the movie yet? Brad is so funny in this one."

The boys rolled their eyes. Dusty draped his arm over Alex's shoulder and pulled him in for a hug.

"Come here, you," he said.

Alex breathed deep, his friend's musky odor was intoxicating.

"Popcorn?" Andrea asked. "It's organic caramel..."

They ate the sticky sweet treat, took a powder break and made it through to the end of the movie before they slept, content as children on a sleepover playdate—if children drank, smoked weed and did cocaine on said playdate.

To Be Continued...

White Sands

A DIFFERENT KIND OF FRIENDSHIP

Coming Soon

Made in the USA
Charleston, SC
26 March 2016